DEATH OF A DOCTOR

A SAM JENKINS MYSTERY

WAYNE ZURL

For Bazzie, as always

CHAPTER ONE

January 2012

I was sitting at my desk in the back office writing a diplomatically phrased report of my investigation on a candidate for deputy sheriff. Effectively, I'd be ruining the young man's life and the chances of him ever getting a job at any police agency in Tennessee or elsewhere. I felt bad because he was a cop's kid. But he was also a thief who, over several years, systematically glommed almost fifty thousand bucks' worth of resalable equipment from the phone company who employed him. That's life. He cast his fate. I only learned about his kleptomania through good investigative techniques and informed the appropriate people.

The door to the outer office opened and closed with a bang. Moments later, a pair of high heels click-clicked across the tile floor and became increasingly louder until they stopped at the threshold of my office door.

For a woman pushing fifty, she had a face years younger with loads of character. Her blonde hair ended an inch from her shoulders, creating the perfect frame for the aforementioned face. Unless she was a very careful shopper, the lavender dress under her pearl gray topcoat must have cost as much as a good late model used car and accentuated a figure any twenty-year-old woman would have been proud of. She hadn't yet spoken, but her smile and a pair of sparkling hazel eyes lit up an otherwise dreary winter day.

"Hello, darlin'. You doin' all right t'day?" Her soft Smoky Mountain accent made Scarlett O'Hara sound like an alcoholic bag lady with smoker's cough.

I smiled back, projecting undying but platonic affection for my current employer. "Whaddaya say, Blondie? Since when does the county sheriff make a personal call to pick up the report I'm writing?"

"It's not about that, Sammy. I've got another job for ya."

"I'm not finished with this one. Don't I get a day off?"

"Like you always said, Sugar, 'Crime never sleeps.'"

"You're a tough boss."

"I learned from the best."

"Flattery will get you everywhere."

She winked. "I know that."

"So, what have you got for me...or us?"

"I've asked Lieutenant Joiner to oversee an administrative task force to review CID's open or exceptionally cleared cases from the last five years. With Ryan Leary's thumb on everything for so long, I don't trust very much. I need you and John to take a look at something for me."

Exceptionally cleared cases are those that required a formal investigation but were closed without an arrest being made. The circumstances surrounding those cases could vary. Recently defrocked Chief Deputy Ryan Leary, currently doing hard time in one of the Federal government's country club slammers, left a scar on the Blount County Sheriff's Office that only time and short memories would erase. Bettye Lambert, the new interim Sheriff and my former administrative sergeant at Prospect PD, didn't have an easy job restoring public confidence in her department.

"Besides D.L. Joiner, who's on your task force?"

"Bo Stallins is helping him coordinate things, and I got approval to hire four retired detectives who used to work for the National Accreditation Commission."

"You don't think Bo was one of the detectives who sloughed off or falsified cases, do you?"

"No. That's why I asked him to work with D.L. on this."

"Umm, Kemosabe, Bo heap good man. What you want from me?"

She sat in my guest chair and crossed one lovely leg over another, right over left. "First, I want you to stop the Injun act. Then I'd like you and John to re-investigate a shooting death written off as an accident. It's not that old, and the insurance company's investigator seems to think it looks more like a suicide."

I raised my eyebrows. "And suicide negates the death benefit?"

"Yes, it would."

"Who did the initial investigation?"

"Leo Turner."

"One of Ryan Leary's handpicked henchmen."

"He was."

"And since he's been disgraced and forced to retire, you're assuming he'll tell you to go jump rope rather than offer assistance."

She shrugged. "Be my guess."

"Well then, I guess the elite team of Jenkins and Gallagher, private cops, had better dust off our official Special Investigator badges once again."

"Sounds like a plan."

"If this gets complicated, how about picking up Terri Donnellson's paycheck, too?"

"If you need her. But keep the hours to a minimum, please."

"Pfui. You can't get a good investigation if we go home every day at five o'clock."

She made a production out of sighing. What an actress. "Oh, all right."

I smiled. "Since you're in such an agreeable mood, how about a raise? We've been giving you almost sixty years of investigative experience at bargain basement rates."

"Darlin', have you started usin' hallucinogens since you left Prospect PD?"

———

Six months earlier, June 20th to be exact, a Doctor Paul D'Amato died from a .38 Special to the right temple. An estimated three days elapsed before his sister, Angela, found him slumped over the dining room table in his Maryville home. A target revolver and cleaning kit lay on the table along with a pool of congealed blood. Angela called 9-1-1.

After a deputy and his road supervisor responded to the house, they called the duty detective—Leo Turner—to conduct an investigation. Leo, in turn, called a police surgeon for a death pronouncement.

A police surgeon is not a medical examiner—not a forensic pathologist. He simply states for the record that a person is in fact dead when a family physician doesn't wish to sign the certificate and state the probable cause of death. It's not a difficult call when there's a hole in the victim's head that allowed a pint or more of blood to escape. At that point, it's up to the attending detective to take the investigation further.

In New York, where John Gallagher and I worked for many years, any unattended death under those circumstances would have been considered reason for an autopsy—the law said so. The medical examiner would be charged with conducting a post mortem examination, and the detective would begin an investigation to determine if the deceased might have committed suicide, been murdered, or was just unlucky and accidentally killed himself.

In Tennessee, an autopsy isn't mandatory. It's the detective's call, in this case Leo Turner's call. In this case, and without further ado, Leo summarily ruled the shooting accidental. Easy peasy. No more troublesome work. No more bother. And as it turns out, D'Amato's sister Angela Scarano would not only inherit the doctor's home and his estate, but a half million dollar insurance policy where she had been named beneficiary after her brother's second divorce three years earlier.

Since an investigator for Lone Star Mutual Insurance questioned Turner's opinion, I thought interviewing this investigator while John Gallagher ran a complete background check on the victim was a reasonable way to begin. Getting to know a little about her before we met was only prudent.

———

Janetta Galloway, our office manager, accountant, secretary and all-around assistant, buzzed my phone. "Boss, I've got a Ms. Barnett from Lone Star Insurance to see you."

"Don't call me boss. It'll make John feel bad."

"She says she's a little early. May I send her back now?"

"Does she seem friendly?"

"No sir, there is nothing else on your calendar."

"Are we having the same conversation? By the way, what's she look like?"

"Very good, sir. I'll tell her."

"Jeez."

I didn't hear the pitter-patter of high heels from this female visitor. In less than thirty seconds, a middle-aged brunette wearing a black pantsuit, dark gray button-down shirt and soft-soled loafers stepped up to my desk.

"Hello, I'm Velma Barnett."

She was medium height—five-five, five-six or so—with a pair of broad shoulders. The snug suit jacket showed that her waist may have thickened with the years, but she didn't look fat. The lines on her face and her dark suspicious eyes told me her career of investigating arsons for the Dallas Fire Department and more recently assorted and questionable insurance claims for Lone Star Mutual held more stressful moments than not. But after meeting Velma, no one would stretch their imagination to think that she wasn't at one time woman of the month for *Soldier of Fortune* magazine. She might have appeared in the centerfold biting the head off a cobra.

I stood and offered her a professionally courteous smile and a hand to shake. "Hi, I'm Sam Jenkins. We've been retained by the Sheriff to re-investigate the death of Paul D'Amato."

Velma's handshake showed me that she didn't want anyone to confuse her with a sissy. I pointed to the guest chair in front of my desk.

"Please sit."

She did and got right down to business.

"Good idea to take it out of house," she said, "since the first investigation was bullshit."

I raised my eyebrows. "I've been told you think so."

"I don't think. I know so. That was no accidental discharge."

"I haven't gotten that far into it yet. Tell me why you say that."

"Easy. The dick who caught the case didn't do jack squat. No neighborhood canvas. No background on the deceased. No forensics. No work at all. He just kissed it off. And in doing so stuck my company with a half million dollar pay off."

"What recently happened to Leo Turner is public record, so I don't feel like I'm telling you tales out of school when I say he wasn't the best detective Blount County ever had. He's recently been forced to retire for questionable conduct."

Velma nodded. "I know. I checked him out."

"He put himself into quite a jackpot."

"He did. And I also know it was you who cleaned up that entire mess—and got screwed for your troubles. I checked on you, too."

Turner, Leary and a third detective were caught in a cover-up of a brutality case, and Leary's problems went much further onto the dark side.

"I'm flattered. I guess."

"Don't be. I wouldn't be worth my salary if I didn't do a complete job. I didn't want to waste my time if you were just another hack like Leo Turner. I ran your partner, Gallagher, too. You're both clean far as I'm concerned."

"Wow. Can I get a discount on an insurance policy now?"

She frowned.

I smiled again. "Just kidding."

She didn't smile. "Sure."

"Besides knowing what Turner didn't do," I said, "have you learned anything about D'Amato that would suggest suicide or even murder?"

"Not as much as you can do. Your shield gives you more horsepower than me. But I did find out that the S&W model 14-4 that killed him was manufactured in 1974. I checked records with Texas where he's lived most of his life as well as Tennessee where he's been for the past three years. I also checked with the Feds to see if the gun had been registered to him and when he got it. I figure if I can establish long-term gun ownership then it's less likely he had a fatal accident. Not proof of anything, but when we're building a case, it could add to the preponderance of evidence. So far, I can't trace that gun to him, but something is still in the works."

I shrugged. "I don't know what the handgun laws are like in Texas, but in Tennessee more used guns are sold off paper than go through established firearms dealers. So, there may not be a paper trail. Did you get BATF to give you the name of the first dealer to receive the gun from Smith & Wesson?"

I didn't think Texas was too restrictive when it came to shootin' irons. You could probably buy one legally on any street corner.

"I've still got a few connections with them—guys I knew from investigating explosions. The best I got was the distributor and the first retail dealer who's now out of business. ATF is checking for the 4473 sales form, but they have to do it manually for something back that far. We're talking 1975 in Mississippi."

"Good luck with that."

"I know. A dozen idiots could have had hands on that gun since then."

"How about other registered handguns? Did anyone at the TBI or whomever in Texas does records checks to satisfy the Brady Bill show anything for D'Amato?"

"Couldn't find anything."

"We'll be sure to ask the people we interview if he was a known gun owner."

"Good."

"Have you talked with anyone who thought he may have been distraught?"

"Not yet."

"We'll do that, too. Was he a boozer? Womanizer? Terminally ill? Still in love with his ex-wife and didn't want to live without her? Any other form of social miscreant who'd get so tired of himself that he couldn't stand looking in the mirror for another day?"

"His sister thought he was the next best thing to sliced bread."

"She would, wouldn't she?"

"For a half mil, I'd say Charlie Manson was a choir boy."

Good point.

"Did they send you all the way from Dallas just for this? The Sheriff would have entertained a complaint from your company by phone or letter. She's got a pretty modern department. We could have had this talk by video conference."

"I'm not going back to Texas just yet."

"Oh?"

"I'm working this case."

Not exactly what I wanted to hear. "Are you assuming we're not competent enough to reach a truthful conclusion?"

"I didn't say that. Are you trying to get rid of me?"

"I don't want to start tripping over you or watch you zig when we zag and see this investigation get loused up. If you want to stick around and wait for news from us, I can't stop you, but I don't usually work with an outside partner."

"You're right about one thing. You can't stop me."

I can't stand tough guys trying to intimidate me and wanted to make my position perfectly clear. "But if you interfere with our official business, I'm sure I could find a uniformed cop who'd love to write up an arrest for what we call obstructing governmental administration. We've got this one. Let us do the job."

"I'd prefer you didn't threaten me."

"And I prefer you and your company not assume we'll pursue this matter with tunnel vision. I wasn't put on Earth to save you money. If this was a covered-up suicide, I'll let you know. But if I uncover a homicide, you're still on the hook for the half million."

She thought for a long moment. "I'm not asking for more than that. But how about we do it this way...?"

CHAPTER TWO

Velma wanted us to give her office space to spread out and do what she called working the case. I had planned on utilizing Terri Donnellson, a good cop from Prospect PD, as our part-time assistant. What we'd come to refer to as *Terri's desk* was the only place Velma could get comfortable and not be in the way. And that wasn't going to happen. So, I arranged for Bettye Lambert to give our visiting insurance investigator a desk or table somewhere in the Justice Center.

John was still busy with his background investigation. I thought speaking to the two uniformed cops who answered the call from D'Amato's sister might provide me with most of the basic information.

———

A good rule to follow when you're interviewing someone you suspect of wrongdoing is never ask questions to which you don't already know the answers. Leo Turner may have been guilty of taking a bribe to write off Paul D'Amato's suicide as an accident or just being a lazy detective with lousy ethics. The bribe—if there was one—would have come from D'Amato's sister. So, who might provide answers, or at least opinions, to questions about the day Angela discovered the doctor's body? Only two people who might give me honest answers—the cops who answered the call. Specifically, they were Deputy Varnell Woodruff and his road supervisor, Sergeant Hadley Runyan. Unfortunately, I didn't know either one. I had seen Runyan around the Justice Center, but never had dealings with him. I decided to begin with the sergeant, hoping a supervisor might not build his *blue wall* too high that I couldn't collect some good information before speaking with Turner.

I learned that Hadley Runyan had been employed by the Sheriff's office for eighteen years, nine of them as a sergeant. In a department with a basic retention problem because of low pay for the rank and file, sticking around as a patrol cop for nine of those years was unusual. Perhaps Hadley possessed a love for police work or his department or both. I was hoping he'd tell me the truth about an incident where a co-worker might have crossed the honesty line or just sloughed off an investigation that should have been carried a lot farther.

Runyan was working days. I told the dispatcher to give him a 10-12 to room 201 in the Justice Center. Any cop would immediately know that meant to report to the Sheriff's personal second floor office. *Forthwith* was implied.

It took the sergeant less than fifteen minutes to show up in Bettye's outer office. When he checked in with her secretary, Cynthia Wilkins, I told him the reason for his summons. With that out of the way, we adjourned to the Sheriff's conference room. My job status has its perks. Bettye gives me run of the facility when I need it, and using rooms like this makes the workers think I have all kinds of hidden power.

I liked thinking of Bettye as the new sheriff in town. Only

six months ago, she was the desk sergeant at Prospect PD, and I was the chief. After the Ryan Leary extravaganza, things figuratively went south for me, and after my five-year contract expired, I got canned with few blessings from the local politicians. But before leaving office, I called in a massive favor and arranged for Bettye to be named interim sheriff. She took office immediately after the incumbent made a hasty retreat to pursue a career elsewhere in politics—before the local press corps embarrassed the hell out of him or the Feds charged him with malfeasance.

In any event, I felt happy for Bettye, and although I wasn't crazy about being a private detective, I liked working cases for the Sheriff as one of her two special investigators.

———

I tossed a yellow legal-size, lined pad on a tabletop that was big enough to have been used as a car ferry across the Little Tennessee River. Runyan, who appeared friendly enough, took a seat to my right.

"You want coffee or some other appropriate seasonal beverage?" I asked.

"Uh-uh, I'm good."

"Okay, let's get started. You remember much about the shooting death of a Doctor Paul D'Amato from Maryville?"

Runyan frowned. He was a big man in his mid- to late-forties, about six-two or three with his last day under two-hundred-and-forty pounds sometime during the Carter administration. He had a ruddy Irish complexion and an old-fashioned little boy's haircut—short on the sides and dark on top, slicked down with pomade or quick drying epoxy before he combed it. All of a sudden, he didn't look happy to see me.

"You workin' for Internal Affairs, sir?"

I chuckled. "Sarge, I'm the last guy you'll ever catch in a rat squad—even for the current sheriff."

That got a crooked smile from him. "Rat Squad? That's what they say on TV."

"I can assure you, I've been saying that since long before the current crop of TV cop shows were even a twinkle in a producer's eye. I don't get my kicks working over other cops. I just work directly for the Sheriff."

"You're talking about an old case, sir. Why bring it up again?"

"It's past time for the insurance company to either pay up or controvert our detective's conclusion. They're trying to save a half million dollars and chose the latter. And you don't have to call me *sir*."

"Okay, whattaya need ta know?"

I shrugged. "Everything you know. Let's start at the beginning. How'd you get there?"

"Simple. The patrol officer who got the assignment called me. They gotta have a supervisor present with a DOA like that."

I nodded. "I know. What happened when you got there? What did you see?"

"Woodruff, the deputy who got the call, he was there with the dead guy's sister. She made the 9-1-1 call. I can't remember her name. I got it in my memo book if ya need it."

I shook my head. "I've got it here somewhere."

"Well, anyways, they were waitin' for me in the livin' room. The body, it was in the dinin' room."

"Tell me about the body. What did you notice?"

He didn't need time to think. "Man was slumped over the table. Bullet hole in the side o' his head. Dried blood on the table. Gun and cleanin' kit on the table, too. Big dent in the wood top where the gun hit the table. Musta been the hammer or sight, one, makin' it after it fell from his hand."

"How many shells were in the gun? How many fired?"

"Didn't touch it. Not my job. Left it for the detective."

"Did you call CID?"

"Varnell did."

"Varnell Woodruff?"

"Uh-huh."

"He call the police surgeon?"

"Leo Turner did."

"So Turner got there first?"

"Yes, sir."

"Did he call a crime scene unit?"

"Not while I was there."

"When did the doctor arrive?"

"I had already left. I understand it took 'im almost an hour."

"What was Turner doing while you waited for the doctor to arrive?"

"Talkin' ta the sister. Looked around a little. Not much. Mostly talkin'."

"Did he ask you or Woodruff to do a neighborhood canvas? You know, talk to people? See if anyone saw or heard anything? Anyone know the victim? Standard stuff."

Runyan raised his eyebrows. "He didn't ask."

"And you left before the doctor arrived?"

"I did. Needed ta get back on the road. Was nothin' more for me ta do there."

"Did you speak to Woodruff after he left the scene?"

"Saw him back here before goin' end o' watch."

"You questioned him about the incident?"

"I did."

"In detail?"

"Pretty much."

"Why was that? Turner had taken over the case."

"Just routine. Just interested, I guess."

"What did he say about what the doctor did?"

He shrugged. "Pronounced him dead. About it."

"Any discussion about signing a death certificate?"

"Like what?"

"Under the circumstances, did the doctor want to? I understand he didn't know the victim."

"I wasn't there then."

"But you questioned Deputy Woodruff."

That brought a long moment of silence.

"I've got a death certificate here, Sarge." I slid the document from the case folder. "He signed off, but doesn't it strike you as odd? I mean the doctor only saw a bullet wound. How did he know that was the only contributing factor?"

"I'm no doctor, sir."

I raised my eyebrows. "But you've been a cop for more than eighteen years. How many DOAs have you handled?"

He shrugged again.

"I'm guessing quite a few," I said. "Would you automatically assume the man accidentally shot himself? You looked over the scene."

He gave an almost imperceptible shake of his head.

"Did Turner do a Harrison test for the presence of gunshot residue on the man's hands?"

"I didn't see that."

"Did Turner fingerprint the victim and voucher the pistol to check for a print comparison?"

The eyebrows went up again. "Not while I was there."

Runyan began to fidget, blink and look generally uncomfortable.

"Did Woodruff mention any of this?"

"Not to me."

"If Turner didn't call Crime Scene, did he take any pictures himself?"

"Not while I was there."

"You said he looked around. Where did he go?"

"Jest the dinin' room."

"It's a two-story house. Upstairs? Bedrooms? Closets? Just the dining room?"

"That's all I saw. I left pretty early. Woodruff can tell ya' better."

"Uh-huh. Did Woodruff say that Turner encouraged the doctor to sign the death certificate?"

"Sorta."

"Sorta?"

"Varnell said he, Leo that is, kinda like suggested it was an easy call—an obvious accident."

"What did the doctor say to that?"

"Turner kinda took him aside ta talk more. He didn't hear."

"What you're saying is hearsay from a conversation with Woodruff. Now I need your expert opinion."

He reluctantly nodded.

I asked a repeat question. "Would you have assumed that it was an accident, Sarge?"

Another long pause then he lowered his eyes and shook his head. "Probably not."

"Neither would I."

"You're puttin' me in a bad position here, sir."

"Thanks to Leo Turner, we're all in a bad spot. Now we've got to do the right thing."

"Uh-huh."

Sergeant Runyan made me feel about as popular as a Burger King in Mumbai.

———

Paul D'Amato's death certificate, signed by a Dr. J. Newley Bascomb, was vague and non-committal. The only established fact being the victim was no longer living. It read, 'Gunshot wound, approximately .38 caliber, to the lower right temple area. Revolver of that caliber lying next to victim. Unknown if any other factor contributed to victim's demise. The *No* box following the question of whether the attending physician had prior knowledge of the victim contained a rather large X.

An hour after I finished speaking with Sergeant Runyan, Deputy Varnell Woodruff showed up at the Justice Center. He had been off duty and dressed as if he'd just been out hunting turkeys. I was surprised I could find him standing in Bettye's outer office, he being dressed from head to foot in Real Tree camo. Once he spoke, I followed the sound and shook his hand. We too adjourned to the big conference room where I explained the reason for me calling him in. He sat but didn't remove his cap.

Thanks to his road supervisor, I had a secondhand account of what Woodruff had reported after working a potential crime scene. I wanted to see if his answers to my questions jelled with what he supposedly told Sergeant Runyan.

"You want coffee or something else to drink?" I asked.

"No, but mind if I smoke?"

I did mind. "We don't have an ash tray, and you know the rules about smoking in public buildings."

So far, I wasn't encouraged.

He spent a protracted time wiggling into the swivel chair. Maybe he wanted to blend into the surroundings and disappear on me.

"Am I gettin' paid for comin' in on my day off?" he asked.

I nodded. "Sure. The Sheriff said you get a minimum of two hours. If we go longer, you get the actual hours at time and a half."

"Good. I was kinda busy. Could use the money, too."

I raised a hand, palm up. "Can't we all? Well, let's get down to business. Tell me about the call you handled at Dr. D'Amato's home."

"You want me to talk against Leo Turner."

It wasn't a question. If I had been in New York, I believe Woodruff would have shown up with his PBA delegate and a lawyer. In Tennessee, he sounded like a real union man, just without a union.

I smiled and shook my head. "Not really. I want to get an idea why he didn't think it necessary to do further investigation on the man's death."

"Why don't ya ask him?"

After only five minutes, I was already sick to death of that guy.

"Maybe I did. And now it's your turn."

Varnell chose to remain silent.

"Is there any reason why you'd rather not discuss this?" I asked.

"I'm not the type who wants ta second-guess another cop. And b'sides, I don't remember that much."

"That's why God gave cops memo books."

"Ain't got it on me. You didn't ask me to bring it."

I shook my head another time. "Where were you born, Varnell?"

"Me?"

"Yeah, you."

"What's that got ta do with anythin'?"

"Indulge me."

He sneered before answering. "Right here."

"In the Justice Center?"

He gave me a look. "Murr-vull."

"Oh, good. I was beginning to think you came from outer

space. Come on, my friend, let's cut the crap. I'm not from Internal Affairs, but if you continue to break my balls, I'll turn you over to them. So, how about it? I'm just looking for a few truthful answers. Let's start over."

He thought for a moment and then nodded.

I looked at my notes. "You got a 9-1-1 call at 10:39 a.m. You started heading toward Paul D'Amato's home in a subdivision off Old Tuckaleechee Pike. What happened next?"

He took me through much the same story as I already heard from Hadley Runyan.

"So, you were still there up until the time Leo Turner cut you loose? Runyan went back on the road, and you and Leo hung around until the mortuary people removed the body?"

"Nope. We was waitin' for the police surgeon, and the funeral home people was takin' their time, so Leo told me I could go back in service."

"And during all the time you were present, you never heard Leo call crime scene or the ME. He never took photos, never rolled or dusted for prints himself and never swabbed the victim's hands for GSR."

"Nope, but—"

I held up a hand to stop him. "And it says here you were the only one who recorded the serial number of the revolver."

"I guess. Don't know if he did or not."

"No one vouchered the gun into property?"

"Accordin' ta Turner, no reason to."

"Uh-huh. Hard to believe he'd leave a handgun with blood all over it for the next-of-kin to deal with. Did you or anyone else look through the house for other gun paraphernalia? More ammo? A target shooter's box? Other guns? A belt and holster. Anything that might make you think D'Amato was familiar with firearms?"

"I didn't search nuthin'."

"And as far as you know, neither did Leo?"

"I didn't see him. Don't know what he did after I left. Like I said, you gotta ask him."

"Were you one-hundred-percent sure this was an accident?"

He hesitated, blinked rapidly and the right index finger he'd been tapping on the tabletop stopped abruptly.

"Me?"

"Yeah, Varnell, you. You've been a cop almost fourteen years. You've handled cases like this before. Did you form an opinion, or did you want to know more before you walked away?"

"I ain't no detective."

"Right, and I'm wondering if you're the right man to be driving a sector car if you have no instincts for police work. Would you rather be a jail guard?"

"You threatenin' ta change my job?"

"Based on our conversation here, if I was your boss, I'd start thinking about firing your ass. And I could do that because you deputies have no union, no bargaining unit and no tenure guarantees."

"Do whot?"

"What's more important to you, Sport? Keeping your current assignment or sticking up for Leo Turner, a guy who's already been given the sack for illegal conduct?"

"He mighta got him a raw deal there."

I smiled at his naiveté. "Bullshit, Varnell. Leo got a sweetheart deal for rolling over on Ryan Leary. Everything was proven. Turner and his buddy, Artie Bonnet, skated on some serious jail time because they told the truth about their accomplice. They all were bad cops. They beat people, they lied, and Leary was a lot worse."

I let that sink in for a moment.

"Guys like Leary, Turner and Bonnet make us all look bad,"

I said. "The public now smells a nasty stink every time a Blount County cop walks by, thanks to those three."

He hung his head. "I guess."

"Yeah. You guess, but I *know*. So, what's it gonna be? Play ball with me or, after I speak to the Sheriff, spend forty hours a week babysitting the scumbags in lockdown?"

He sighed, and his shoulders dropped three inches. "If it was me, I woulda done more forensics on the guy. Nuthin' I saw told me that was definitely an accident."

———

No matter how homespun folks from the foothills of the Great Smoky Mountains think they are, I've yet to find a general practitioner who still makes house calls in a horse and buggy. Dr. J. Newley Bascomb wouldn't even leave his office on business, driving his year-old, horribly expensive Range Rover. But he did grudgingly grant me a few minutes of time during his day of tending to the sick, lame and lazy of Blount County.

His office occupied a large suite of rooms in a professional building in the city of Alcoa. I arrived at the mini-hospital by three p.m. and ended up walking a quarter mile because the parking lot, so crowded it resembled the New York police impound yard, was damn near full capacity.

It was unusually cold for January. The dampness and wind made it feel even worse. A fully overcast sky, the mottled gray color of a dead squirrel, kept any warmth the sun might offer way above my head. I was not a comfortable special investigator.

The sprawling, one-story medical center consisted of a warren of offices and hallways. If I worked there, it would take me a month just to find the men's room. But soon enough I arrived at my destination and spoke to a young blonde receptionist wearing a diamond-like stud in her nose. With all the emotion of someone suffering from anhedonia, she assured me the doctor would be with me shortly.

Twenty minutes later, a middle-aged nurse, in sage green scrubs and looking rather world-weary, opened the door to the inner offices. "Mr. Jenkins?"

I stood and smiled for her. Sam Jenkins, ever the ambassador of friendliness. "Hi. Busy today?"

She shook her head, not in disagreement, but in what I took to indicate near exhaustion. "You wouldn't believe. The temperatures drop drastically, and these people still refuse to wear an adequate coat. Then they all get colds and think we have a magic medicine for 'em. You'd think after being sick once or twice, they'd learn."

I continued to smile, although she couldn't see me, as we walked down a long hallway, and I thought, 'Too much information.'

"The doctor only has a few minutes before the next patient, but he's in his office waitin' for ya."

Goody.

At the end of that long corridor, the woman knocked twice, and without waiting for an invitation to enter, opened the door and ushered me in.

J. Newley was a smooth-looking article in his mid-sixties, trim, and healthy-looking all around, with thinning gray hair and a close cropped Van Dyke on the lower regions of his face. He looked something like Tennessee's version of the Dos Equis man. He stood, faked a smile and extended a hand over a desktop at least three feet wide.

"Nice to meet you, Investigator Jenkins. How can I help?"

I gave him a brief rundown of what the insurance company initiated and what the Sheriff asked me to do. Less than halfway through my dissertation, the doctor's impassive expression turned to a concerned frown. Had I been able to read his thoughts, I'd bet two words would have been captioned: 'Oh, shit.'

He sat in his oversized swivel chair and me in a comfortable guest seat. The doctor took a deep breath and exhaled—what people caught in an embarrassing situation might do.

"I knew that one would come back and bite someone in the ass," he reluctantly said.

"So far, Doctor, I don't see this case as one of Leo Turner's best investigations."

He nodded slowly for a few seconds. "I followed that Ryan Leary business in the papers and on TV. I wasn't surprised that Detective Turner ended up in such a terrible mess."

"I don't want to influence your statements, but as far as I'm concerned, Leo Turner has been playing it fast and loose for a long time. Too long. I can only assume he believed himself untouchable."

"Well, I don't mind telling you, I'm glad I left that death certificate noncommittal."

"A good move on your part."

He nodded, but didn't look encouraged by my comment. "Turner wanted only one outcome—death by accident. But no one—no one—had enough information to draw that conclusion."

"I agree, Doctor, one hundred percent. Did you know Paul D'Amato professionally or personally?"

He shrugged. "I knew who he was and that he was relatively new to the area. But I never had professional dealings with him. I understood he was a well-educated man—got his MD in psychiatry and a PhD in clinical psychology. I would have called him semi-retired. I think he almost exclusively took referrals from the Veteran's Administration."

"My partner is looking into his background now. Did you have occasion to speak with D'Amato's sister while you were making the pronouncement?"

"Only to offer my sympathies. I wasn't there very long."

"Do you remember specifically what Turner said to you or asked you?"

"I do. And I was on the verge of refusing to sign the death certificate. He wanted me to concur with his idea of an accidental shooting. But, as you know, I have the latitude to simply pronounce a death—lacking other medical information from a family physician. But in the case of a gunshot death, that wouldn't be pertinent. However, he should have referred the body to the Medical Examiner for autopsy."

"Did you see any good reason to suspect suicide?"

"Nothing specific, but more of a possibility than assuming it was an accident."

"How about murder?"

He paused to consider my question. "Possibly, but I'm no expert on that."

I nodded. "Did you sense any collusion between Turner and D'Amato's sister?"

"I didn't see them discuss anything."

"How did she appear?"

He took another moment to think. "Somewhat impassive. She wasn't weeping nor did it look as if she had been."

"Thanks for your time, Doctor."

CHAPTER THREE

The next morning, I met John Gallagher in our office on Home Avenue in Maryville. I made a fresh pot of coffee. He spread out the breakfast he picked up at the Hardee's, two blocks away on Calderwood Road, on the spare desk in the outer room so he, Janetta and I could discuss what he learned about Paul D'Amato.

"You know," John said, "this guy should be living in a bigger house than the one he bought. Guy's been a doctor for almost forty years. Only drives a Honda, too. It was me—"

I interrupted his editorial. "John, if you were a counterman working at the burger joint where you get your breakfast every day, you'd buy more than you could afford. Tell us about the doctor's life."

"I don't buy breakfast there *every* day."

"John!"

"Okay, gimme a chance. He was a shrink, but you probably knew that. He lived and worked in Austin, Texas since he graduated from medical school. Did time in the Army, too—three years. Got drafted as a doctor. Got to be a captain right away. That never seemed fair to me, ya know?"

"You think doctors should be PFCs?"

"No. I guess not. But still."

John is five years older than me. He continues to work because his wife spends money like a kamikaze pilot on the night before his big mission. He looks like a large version of an Irish leprechaun, reddish brown hair with less gray than me, and a tummy that took him years to cultivate.

"What do you know about his life in Texas?" I asked.

He took a bite from a sausage patty wedged between the two halves of a greasy-looking biscuit before answering. He chewed, licked something off his right thumb and continued. "Well, he was married to the first wife for nineteen years before they got divorced. No kids with that wife. Then, six years later, he marries another doctor. That lasted until three years ago. Still no kids, but another divorce. She had retired, and he didn't."

"The doctor who pronounced him dead told me D'Amato worked for the VA."

John took a long sip of coffee. "Almost. He was like a contractor. They sent him patients who needed or wanted to get their heads shrunk. He got paid for what he billed the VA at an agreed-on scale."

"I wonder just how crazy his patients were. If we had a buck for every lunatic who killed their shrink, we could go out for one hell of a lunch."

"Do you two know how callous you sound?" Janetta asked.

John was quick with an answer. "Who us?"

I offered, "We're just a little jaded with ninety-five percent of the human race. I like most dogs though."

"Oh, Lord have mercy."

"She sounds like her cousin," John said.

"Kinda looks like her, too."

"I do not know how Bettye could stand you two for, how long? Five years?"

"We're cute?" I asked.

She made a face. "Sure. That must be it."

"Anyways," John continued, "the VA guy I spoke to can't release any info on the people they sent him, but the doc had a part-time secretary assigned to him who agreed to give me the names, if she could manage it, without anyone else knowing about it and let the patients decide if they want to talk with us."

"At least that's something," I said. "We can always hit the VA a second time and see if we can get more cooperation. You get anything from his neighbors?"

"Not many neighbors out there. Everybody has five acres. Nice subdivision. Kinda upscale, but not overly flashy. Know what I mean?"

I nodded, wanting him to get on with it.

"Everybody seemed to say the same thing. This guy was very quiet. Stayed mostly to himself. Seemed kinda odd, but not in a bad way. But listen to this...I met this one guy, a retired dick sergeant from Milwaukee PD who lived diagonally across the road. He was more helpful—you'd figure that from an ex-cop, right?"

I nodded. "We would hope so."

"Anyways, this guy," John flipped through the pages of his spiral memo book, "Name's Bill Horne—with an E—said he was surprised when he first heard about the doctor buying the farm. No local cop did a neighborhood canvas. This guy sounded like he knew what he was talking about. He said if he had been asked, he would have told somebody that only a few days before the shooting, he met D'Amato at the mailboxes outside this gated community. He said the doctor invited him and his wife to a late New Year's party he wanted to have. So, Horne said he was about to decline the offer—he sounded like you, Boss, kinda anti-social. Know what I mean?" John got the stupid look on his face he gets when he tries to bust my chops.

"Yeah, John, I know what you mean—the homicidal look I get when you stretch my patience to the limit."

"See, Janetta," John said with his village idiot grin. "See how hostile he gets for no reason at all? Maybe he should go to the VA and ask for psychiatric help."

Janetta rolled her eyes and shook her head, her honey-colored blonde hair swung from side to side.

"John, if you don't wrap this up, I'll kill you and claim temporary insanity."

"Boss, you're more impatient than my wife. And that's sayin' a lot. Okay, so, this guy, Bill Horne, he says D'Amato interrupts and says, 'But you probably don't want to come. I can't blame you.'"

"Did Horne say D'Amato was usually this upbeat?"

"He thought D'Amato always looked and sounded depressed. He didn't do any socializing with him, but whenever they spoke, he thought the doctor was real gloomy. He called him Doctor Demento."

I smiled. "Sounds like something a cop would say."

"So, maybe the idea of suicide isn't too far off."

"Any idea if D'Amato was seeing a shrink himself?"

"Haven't gotten there yet. I ran outta time yesterday, but I'll track down his ex-wives today and get more into his financials with the banks and credit bureaus."

"Good. Anyone know if he had a new girlfriend or anyone outside the subdivision he socialized with?"

"Everybody seemed to know about his sister living in Louisville, up by the river or a lake, and a couple people mentioned him having a regular housekeeper. Supposedly she came in once a week or so. The ex-cop thought she might be an illegal alien. He said she looked Hispanic and never waved or acknowledged any of the neighbors. Not very friendly."

"Get a possible name for her from his checking account?"

"Oh, man, that hurts. You think you're dealing with an amateur?" He didn't allow me to comment. "Her name's Margarita Gonzalez. She has an account in the same bank as him. I got a Maryville address for her."

"Good. While you're finishing up your end, I'll track her down and then spend some time with Dr. Demento's sister."

———

From the Department of Safety's Driver's License and Motor Vehicles files, I learned that Margarita Gonzalez was thirty-three years old, lived in a very blue-collar area of Maryville and owned a Plymouth minivan that qualified for antique license plates. There was no phone number listed for her. I took a chance; it wasn't a long drive.

It took me less than fifteen minutes to find the house—a cracker box cottage that might have had two bedrooms. It had once been painted white, but the years and weather turned it to the color of a dingy car towel. With only fifteen feet between a cracked concrete sidewalk and the front door, there wasn't much lawn to cut during the growing season. Heavy frosts had killed off the grass and weeds that bordered the foundation and turned them a sickly tan. A late model but not new, white BMW 128i sat in the driveway behind the maroon '85 Plymouth minivan with sun-bleached, fake wood sides that belonged to Ms. Gonzalez.

Margarita answered the door immediately after my knock. She was short, dark and unmistakably Mestiza. She kept her hair long, pulled back tightly against her head and fastened in a ponytail. At one time she may have been considered attractive in an exotic sort of way, but the stress of hard times, scratching out an existence only an inch and a half above abject poverty showed in the lines at the corners of her eyes and mouth and the dark semi-circles under her eyes. Her current life without a husband had done nothing to keep a painful look off her face. She wore faded black sweatpants and a bright blue T-shirt with something printed on it I couldn't read beneath a well-worn green wool cardigan.

After showing her my impressive-looking badge, she invited me in where I found a short, dark-complexioned young man sitting on the sofa.

The gentleman promptly said, "Officer, what are you doing here?"

"I'm on official police business. I'll soon ask you the same question, but for now, I'll begin with who are you?"

He showed me what I assumed was his version of a personable smile, something he used while trying to get away with something.

"But I asked you first," he said.

I saw his smile and raised him a look at my dazzling white teeth. "But I'm a cop, and I'll bet you're not."

After listening to his next remark, I teetered on the brink of taking offense and getting really professionally nasty.

"Who obviously likes to throw his weight around. I'm Ms. Gonzalez's attorney. So, I'll ask again, what do you want?"

"I'm looking into the background of a man who previously employed Ms. Gonzalez—probably off the books. I'd like to ask her a few questions. That's my answer. What's yours?" He just looked at me but said nothing. "Do I need to repeat my question?"

The counselor was a good-looking little guy in his late thirties, on the verge of being dapper, but his slightly wrinkled medium gray suit looked more like he bought it in Target than one of the expensive men's shops on Kingston Pike in Knoxville. Not exactly the picture of an overly prosperous attorney. While not all well-heeled and slick lawyers are fashion plates, I coupled his cheap duds with the 1 Series Beemer, which may have been purchased used, and on its newest day wasn't something in danger of breaking anyone's bank. My best guess was that Shorty was no F. Lee Bailey.

The look on his face told me that my answer wasn't exactly what he expected. "I'll have to tell Ms. Gonzalez first and let her decide if I should keep her business with me confidential."

His smile of moments ago had faded into a look of moderate annoyance. When he said Ms. Gonzalez was one of his clients, I took that to mean Margarita had need of a lawyer for some reason other than the matter I was investigating.

The sight of a plainclothes cop and her legal mouthpiece mixing words did something to get Margarita slightly unglued. At least her strained expression conveyed that message.

Quickly and in heavily accented English, she said, "It's okay. Jou can talk with Mr. Goldbloom here and now."

"You're sure?" I asked.

"Jes. It's okay for me."

I wondered how Mr. Goldbloom would react if her welfare benefits and pay checks from people like Dr. Demento came in simultaneously. And while Margarita didn't fully understand my situation, she did give me a green light to ask away. And if Goldbloom got upset, I might be able to smooth him out with a little schmaltz.

"Mr. Goldbloom, will you be representing Ms. Gonzalez in what may become a criminal matter?"

"Uh, I'm not a criminal defense attorney, but for the time being, I'll advise her if necessary."

"Good. Would you care to tell me in what way are you representing her?"

"At the moment, no, but since Margarita has agreed to speak with you, please do continue."

Just another time when I wanted to strangle an attorney on general principles. I didn't want him to see steam escaping from my ears so I nodded to him and turned my attention to Margarita.

"Ms. Gonzalez, I understand that you once worked as a part-time housekeeper for a Dr. Paul D'Amato. Is that correct?"

She hesitated before answering. Her dark eyes shifted back and forth between Goldbloom and me.

Carefully, she said, "Jes, I did. Once. But not now. Not for a long time."

"How long is a long time?"

"Since the springtime, I think."

"When in the spring? March, April, May?"

"I think Abril." She pronounced it the Spanish way.

"April."

"Si."

"I'm sorry to tell you that Dr. D'Amato had a serious accident. Very serious."

"Serious?"

"Yes. He died."

"Died? Oh, Madre de Dios. I didn't know."

"Didn't you see anything in the newspapers? The Sheriff and the detective handling the case were also on television. Didn't see that either?"

"No, señor. How did he die? Por favor."

"That's what I'd like to talk about. Is that okay with you?"

Before Margarita could answer, Goldbloom spoke up, "Margarita, as your lawyer, I urge you to say nothing."

I shook my head in mild disgust. "Hey, Counselor, I'm asking again, just what kind of law do you practice?"

He withdrew his head about two inches and looked at me as if I just asked if he slept with his sister on a regular basis.

"Immigration and Naturalization law."

"Cool. I have nothing to do with enforcing Federal immigration or naturalization laws, so don't get your law books in a spin. And just so you know, I don't suspect her of anything terribly illegal. I want to get her opinion about D'Amato's state of mind during the last few times she saw him."

Goldbloom looked at Margarita. "Do you understand what he's said?"

"Que? No, no."

Her lawyer rapped out a few sentences in Spanish much better than mine.

Margarita nodded her understanding.

"Are you saying this doctor committed suicide?" Goldbloom asked.

"At this point, I don't know. The detective who handled the call—a while ago—thought it was an accident. The insurance company's investigator questions that. And so far, no one else involved agrees with the detective."

"How long ago did this happen?" he asked.

"Back at the end of June."

Margarita frowned. "Oh."

That date didn't sound good for Margarita.

"You're sure you stopped working for him in April?" I asked.

"I don't know. You have me confused, I think."

"How long did you work for this man, Margarita?" Goldbloom asked.

Margarita hung her head. She knew the jig was up. "One years. No, two years, maybe more, I think."

"I see," he said.

Time for Jenkins to jump in. I tried not to smirk and look as if I was gloating. "Now, I'm thinking Margarita could be in a little trouble. According to information I obtained from the doctor's bank and the Department of Public Assistance, Margarita has been collecting welfare checks simultaneously with her employment with Dr. D'Amato. Does that throw a monkey wrench into your bid for obtaining US citizenship?"

I took a moment to wink at Margarita before speaking to Goldbloom. "Why don't you and I talk about this later, Counselor—when we leave here—after I'm finished. Okay? What is your first name, by the way? Don't you think we should back up and get a little friendly? You don't want to treat me as an adversary, do you?"

"No, no, of course not. My name is Ramón, Ramón Goldbloom." He dug into the side pocket of his suit jacket and came out with a business card that he handed to me.

"Good. Now, let's see what Margarita can tell me. If my questions are in need of translation, how about a little help?"

He nodded. "Of course."

I turned my attention to Margarita Gonzalez. "How often did you clean the doctor's house?"

"When he called me. Not so much. He was not a dirty man."

"Neighbors say they saw you come once a week. Is that correct?"

She looked even more distraught after my question. "Jes, sometimes. I think maybe. Not always."

"Was Dr. D'Amato mostly happy or sad?"

"Not so happy. I don't think."

"Was he depressed or despondent?"

"Que?"

Goldbloom explained, and Margarita shot back an involved answer in rapid Spanish.

"She thinks he was a nice and polite man—a gentleman—

but he never seemed happy. She understands depression. She thinks he could have been clinically depressed."

To Margarita I said, "Did the doctor talk much when you were working in his house?"

"No, not so much talk. I clean the whole house. No time for talk."

"Ramón, explain *suicide* to her, and ask if she thinks he may have been so sad that he could have taken his own life."

He did, in enough words to negotiate a free trade agreement with Mexico.

To which Margarita gave back another long and rapid answer.

Goldbloom raised his eyebrows. "She says Dr. D'Amato was a Catholic. Suicide would have been a sin. She never saw him cry or look so depressed that she might think he was suicidal."

"Is Margarita here legally?" I asked.

"She has a green card."

"Good. She has children?"

"Two. A boy and a girl."

"A husband?"

"Gone. She's heard that he took off with a younger woman."

"I'm sorry."

"Happens all the time."

Wanting to get back to the original topic, I asked, "Margarita, did Dr. D'Amato ever have guests at his house when you came to clean?"

She thought for a moment. "Not so much, that I see. Only once, maybe. No, I think twice. Si, twice."

"Who were they?"

"Once I arrive, and a young man was there. I do not know who he was. He left soon."

"You said twice?"

"Yes. Once I was cleaning and a different man, still younger than the doctor, but more old than the first man I saw."

"What happened to him?"

"Oh, not come in. He came to the door and then walk away." Then she shot a few sentences in Spanish at her lawyer.

And he translated for me. "She says, for some reason she thought the first younger man had been there a long time. Maybe overnight. She arrived about 9:30 in the morning, and he looked...fresh as if he might have just gotten out of the shower. The second man never came into the house. The doctor took an envelope from him, gave him an envelope in return, and sent him away. That's all she remembers."

Experience has taught me that it's never all someone remembers.

"Did you see what was in the envelope the doctor took from the man?"

She shook her head. "No."

I asked yet another question. "Did the doctor ever say he may have any enemies? Enemigos? People who might want to do him harm."

Margarita looked confused once more. Ramon stepped in and translated again.

"No," she said.

I nodded. "Thanks. One last thing, Margarita. Did you ever see Dr. D'Amato with a gun—a pistola—or do you know if he owned one?"

Ramon was about to help again, but Margarita shook her head and answered. "No. I never see a gun. But I don't know what he owned."

"Thank you, Margarita. Gracias."

"De nada."

"Mr. Goldbloom, can we go now?"

"Sure. Margarita, I will call you. Soon."

"Si, Senor Goldbloom."

———

I stood on the driver's side of Ramón's Beemer. He unlocked the door, but didn't open it.

"I'm very disappointed with her," he said. "She should have told me she was working—even once a week, if it was that often. Now I have to wonder, how many other part-time jobs has she had? What other things has she done to jeopardize her petition for citizenship? These things tend to surface at the worst possible times, and I'm the one who gets embarrassed. Has she done things that could jeopardize her legal status here?"

"I was looking for information. I didn't want to talk in front of you, and I'm sorry if I put you in an awkward position, but I'm glad you could help with the translations."

"Nothing here is your fault."

"I think it is. Listen, let's discuss this...I'll buy you a cup of coffee. What I said before was true. I don't want to be your adversary. I don't want to put the kibosh on Margarita and her kids living a nice life here in beautiful downtown Maryville. Understand?"

He nodded. "Okay, but there's not many places around here to sit down, and I'd rather not drink gas station coffee."

"Mind driving to the Vienna Coffee House?"

"Not at all. How do you want to go?"

"Down Broadway, then zig-zag over to Church Avenue. We'll go in the back door from the parking lot."

"I'll follow you."

———

As we stood in front of the counter ready to order, Goldbloom said, "I'll get something to eat and skip lunch. You order, and I'll pay."

"That's not necessary. I'm asking for Margarita's help...and by extension, your help. Let me pay. I insist. The Sheriff gives me an expense account."

"If you say so. I always try to save a buck when I can. I don't mind saying that my chosen field of law doesn't pay as much as other attorneys collect."

"I understand, but then again, you can probably look at yourself in the mirror with less guilt than most criminal defense guys."

He broke a smile. "There is that."

A young counterman waited patiently for our next move.

I said, "Black coffee, please."

"Breakfast blend, hazelnut, organic Guatemalan or bold?" he asked with a less than patient expression on his face.

"Yikes, all those choices." I kept a straight face. "The boldest."

A moment later, the kid set a large steaming mug on the counter in front of me, and Ramón placed his order.

"Guatemalan, a little milk, one sugar and a cinnamon bagel with cream cheese on the side."

With all that paid for, we found a table in an otherwise unoccupied corner of the back room.

Before getting down to the business of saving my helpful witness from getting into hot water with the Welfare Department and perhaps the Immigration cops, I thought I'd soften up Margarita's legal beagle.

"Ramón and Goldbloom aren't exactly two names that go together like gefilte fish and tamales."

He laughed. "You're right. But don't forget all the Sephardic

Jews in the world…of which I'm not one. My mother was Puerto Rican, and father was a Jew from the Bronx. And if I'm not mistaken, I hear more than a little Nu Yawk in your accent."

"Guilty," I said.

We took a few minutes to talk about New York before settling down to business.

"Do you really think the ICE people might bust Margarita for working a part-time job while collecting welfare?" I asked.

"One that we know about. If you learned about it, someone else might. They just don't rubber stamp citizenship applications, you know." He spoke while adding a little *schmear* to his bagel.

"I'm a fairly ethical guy," I said, "but I have no desire to ruin her life for some piddly little administrative violation. Can I assume you can put enough pressure on her to see the light and get her to weigh the amount of money she might make working off the books as a housekeeper against the potential cushy life she can look forward to living here in the lap of Appalachian luxury?"

He set the knife on the edge of his plate with a click. "Lap of luxury? You saw where she lives. She's not bad compared to some of the *undocumented* Hispanics I represent, but still…"

"Okay. Point taken. Only trying to be a little humorous. I know she stopped working for Dr. D'Amato. I might need to talk to her again if I can find either of the men she saw at D'Amato's home. I don't want her to disappear into the hinterlands leaving me high and dry."

"Yes, but if she—"

"Stop and let me ask a few questions. I told you, I'm not about to drop a dime on her with the Feds."

He frowned and took a healthy bite of bagel.

"Confirm how long has she been on welfare."

"Public Assistance."

I rolled my eyes. "Sure. How long?"

"Almost three years."

"Is that when the husband left? I only have some sketchy information. I haven't spoken to her case worker yet."

"Long story, but that's when he started not coming home every night. Then his absences became more frequent and longer, and the money stopped coming in. And then, he was gone. She told the Public Assistance case worker all that."

I nodded. "Did she start out on assistance with two kids?"

"Yes."

"And she didn't have more children to increase her allotment?"

"No, but—"

"Yes or no will do. When we finish, you can *but* all you like."

He frowned. "Damn, you are tenacious." Then he ripped off another chunk of bagel.

"I know. It's a curse. Obviously, Margarita hasn't bought a new car lately. That van of hers belongs in The Museum of Low Class America."

He smirked and nodded.

"It doesn't look like she buys her clothes in Talbot's, and I'll bet her son doesn't wear Air Jordans."

"I know. You're right."

"Has she worked elsewhere at all during those three years?"

"Yes." He lowered his eyes and took a sip of coffee.

"And she told you and the Public Assistance people about it?"

He nodded and took another sip.

"And paid taxes?"

"Yes. The jobs were on the books."

"And her allotment was reduced accordingly?"

"It was."

I shrugged. "I don't have a problem letting her skate because of working for D'Amato. I might even be persuaded to go to bat for her if ICE ever knocks on her door."

Ramón made a noise someone might describe as a snort. "Your good intentions might be meaningless to those people. They can be like vampires. Margarita is really one of the good ones. I hope this news never gets to the Feds."

"They won't hear it from me. Look, she learned a valuable lesson today. She knows she can get caught. Scold her. Then let it go. She'll be indebted to you for life."

Goldbloom bit off another piece of bagel—a smaller one this time—and took his time chewing. "I would have figured you for being a tough cop."

"I'm only a part-time cop now."

"Yeah, right. But you're soft on damsels in distress?"

"Not all the time."

"Big deal."

"So, how about it? Gonna lighten up, give a hand with some information and figure I may call you some day and ask for a free interpreter?"

"Okay, I guess."

"Not so hard, was it?"

"I'm an officer of the court. I could get seriously jammed up over something like this if it goes too far."

"Nuts. I bought you coffee and a bagel, right?"

"Yeah. So?"

"Look at that as your retainer. I get attorney-client privilege now."

"My life has never been easy, but meeting you is not one of its high points."

"Oh, shut up. Your coffee is getting cold."

———

I left Ramón Goldbloom in the coffee shop and wasn't far from the Maryville post office where I wanted to see if *Dr. Demento* rented a box or had only gotten rural delivery. The clerks would know what kind of mail he received.

I got back on Broadway, continued through the downtown section and finally turned onto Keller Lane where the post office shared acreage with the Social Security Administration offices.

I bought a roll of *Forever* stamps at the counter and asked the clerk if I could speak with the postmaster. She wasn't too keen on that until I tinned her and claimed to be on official business.

John Riggins once told me he was pushing for fifty years of government employment. After thirty years in the Air Force, he took on a second career with the Postal Service. John stood equal to my six feet in his work shoes, but far exceeded my hundred and eighty pounds. John was only slightly wider than a cement truck. He sported a full beard and wore his hair long—with a fifty-fifty split of black and gray. It seemed that after his Air Force time, John decided to go native.

In his office, he pointed me to a metal armchair while he took a seat in a swivel affair that listed significantly to the left and sunk beneath his weight like a cheap mattress.

"What can I do for ya, Chief?" he asked.

"I'm not a chief anymore, partner, just a hired hand working for the new sheriff."

He showed me a lecherous grin. "Good lookin' woman, your boss. Wouldn't mind workin' for her m'sef—if for nuthin' more than ta get a look at her each day."

"You betcha."

"So, what can I tell ya that'll make the Sheriff happy?"

I told him enough about the Paul D'Amato incident to spark an interest and then got into specifics.

"Did he have a PO Box, or did he get home delivery or both?"

"I think he's got him a box, but lemme check."

He tapped a few lines into a computer, but I couldn't see the screen on his monitor.

"Here ya go. He gets rural delivery on Route One of the 803 zip code. And here's another. Paul A. D'Amato has a box paid up 'til 30 June this year under his name with another name o' Paul DeAntonio authorized to receive mail."

"Any idea who DeAntonio is?"

"No relationship mentioned."

"He's been dead almost six months. Is he still getting mail delivered to the box?"

"I don't see that anyone cancelled use o' the box, so, yeah, if somethin' was addressed to either person listed on our card, it would be delivered—until 30 June, that is."

"Can we ask your clerks if anyone has ever met Paul DeAntonio? I assume at some point he may have needed to pick up something that didn't fit in the box?"

"Could be," he said. "We can ask. Cain't guarantee anyone will remember, but we'll check."

He picked up a phone, tapped in a few characters and when someone answered, he asked the appropriate questions.

I nodded, willing to take anything I could get. "Can we look in the box to see if the mail has been picked up since D'Amato's death, or if there's an accumulation?"

"Not supposed to."

"I'll give you the death certificate to copy if that helps. So far I've not ruled out homicide."

His eyebrows went up at the mention of the H word. "In

that case, okay. Follah me. We've got access from the back room."

The facility in Maryville was larger than most of the little POs in small Tennessee villages, but compared to some of the New York postal centers, it was only a hole in the wall.

John Riggins didn't bother to bend over to look into the box rented by Paul D'Amato. He pointed to the location and let me do the dirty work.

D'Amato's box was the largest size available, about ten-and-a half by six inches. Although I found plenty of mail stuffed inside, it was by no means overflowing. As I pulled out what looked mostly like second class mail and larger envelopes addressed to Paul DeAntonio with only sketchy return addresses, a female postal worker, dressed in the light and dark blue uniform of the service, walked up to us.

"What did ya find out, Wanda?" John asked.

"No one here knows DeAntonio. We've all seen Dr. D'Amato when he comes to the counter, but no one knows any more than he's quiet and polite."

"Okay, thanks," John said.

"So, my search for Paul DeAntonio begins...if he exists," I said.

"Ya know," John said, "I was just thinkin'. He, the doctor that is, come in here once. I was workin' the counter, and it wasn't busy. He was the only customer. So, I kinda just made a little small talk, like nice weather, we need rain, that kinda stuff. And he says somethin' like, 'You're lucky ya don't have my job. I deal with depressin' people all day long. Sometimes I think I should take my .45 and blow my brains out ta stop the frustration and aggravation."

I looked at him in surprise. "I'm glad you remembered that one."

He looked a little sheepish. "Yeah, me too."

"Did he sound serious? I mean about the blowing his brains out?"

John shrugged. "I didn't take him serious at the time. But now that he died from a gunshot, I shoulda."

"How long ago did this happen?"

He shrugged. "Not sure. Sometime early summer maybe."

"And he said he'd use a .45? You're sure?"

He nodded vehemently. "Positive. Positive. Once before he told me he bought a gun because some o' the patients he was seein' were pretty scary guys. He said he bought the .45 because he trained with one in the Army."

"I guess I have to track down this DeAntonio and a GI .45 now."

I signed a receipt for the contents of the PO Box and promised not to lose or destroy anything in case postal inspectors wanted to see what I was going to examine.

With this much documentation to look over, I temporarily scrapped my plans to interview Angela Scarano, sister of Doctor Demento, on that day.

———

I parked my truck in front of the Jenkins & Gallagher headquarters building and braved the cold before slamming the front door and shucking my navy blue top coat.

"Hey," I said to Janetta. "What are you up to?"

"Hey, your own self. I'm doin' what you pay me for."

"Which is?"

"Makin' sure you two characters don't get audited by those evil agents of the IRS."

"Good. I tolerate Feds when I'm in control. I have no

interest sitting in front of one of their desks feeling like a defendant."

"I can imagine. What's all that stuff you're holdin'?"

"Mail from a PO Box rented by our boy Dr. D'Amato, but mostly addressed to a Paul DeAntonio."

"Who's that?"

"Beats me, but I'm gonna find out."

CHAPTER FOUR

I only opened a half dozen envelopes before I learned that Paul D'Amato was seriously into kinky sex—mostly conventional homosexual porn, but also a smattering of bondage and discipline. My first thought was that DeAntonio was simply the alias that afforded D'Amato a modicum of anonymity when receiving the actual pornography or advertisements for it.

Janetta was pouring herself a coffee just outside the doorway to my office when I made the brief statement about what only a few minutes of delving into our victim's mail provided me. She looked my way and got a glimpse of a full-page, an exceptionally graphic example of photographic smut I just pulled from an envelope and left lying on my desk.

"Holy crap!" I said, referring to the same illustration of which she could see a bit.

"What's the matter?"

She stepped briskly over to my doorway.

I held up a hand. "Don't come in here. You do *not* want to see what's in the last envelope I opened."

My warning was well meant but worked more like waving a red cape at a cranky bull.

She stepped into my room, hovered over my desk, and gasped, "Oh, Lord have mercy. Is that entire pile of mail like *that*?"

"I've only cracked the surface, but I'm guessing most of it is."

"And this man was a psychiatrist?"

I shrugged. "I've always said shrinks are crazier than their patients."

She stepped back and looked at me rather than the hard-core advertisements.

"Why's he gettin' all this filthy mail? Can't everyone just get all kinds of free pornography on the Internet?"

"You can get free legal porn, but maybe he wanted some more exotic stuff. We won't know exactly what he was into until we get hold of his computer."

"How do you...we do that?"

"That's the $64,000 question."

"I hope you can."

"Let's see if there really is a Paul DeAntonio out there," I said. "Run the name through everything we've got—Motor Vehicles, criminal history, county records, financials, you name it. I'm not sure he really exists."

"If he does...Oh, sweet Jesus, this job surely does get ya ta meet some o' the lower life forms."

"Afraid so. Now we need to get a look at Dr. Demento's computer if it still exists."

"Might be more disgustin' than his mail."

"Yeah, it might," I said. "Probably is. Now, here's something you should know. The postmaster mentioned a conversation he had with D'Amato last summer. Seems the doctor said he felt like blowing his brains out—but with a .45. Shortly thereafter, his brain and a bullet got together, but it was with a .38."

"Did he own two guns?" She asked. A reasonable question.

"We can't even find one yet. Leo Turner never found a .45, or if he did, it wasn't in any report. I hope the sister is up to giving us truthful answers."

"What would *you* do if the wrong answers might cost you a half million dollars?" she said.

———

Janetta had no luck finding a Paul DeAntonio anywhere near Blount County. One showed up in Kingsport—more than one hundred miles and a two-hour drive away—and not a good candidate to look at as Dr. D'Amato's cohort, but we would check on him anyway.

Other than that, I made appointments to meet with Angela Scarano and Leo Turner tomorrow. I just couldn't wait to experience the cooperation I anticipated getting from that pair. I also planned on speaking again with Margarita Gonzalez. Since my questions might delve into the doctor's possible bi-sexual nature or his fondness for pornography, I figured that taking a female along with me would be appropriate. So, I called Terri Donnellson at Prospect PD to get her working for us on her next days off. But Terri's Spanish wasn't quite as good as mine, so thoughts of asking Ramón Goldbloom to tag along while I further questioned his client also crossed my mind.

———

At ten to four, John Gallagher walked into the office. He dropped his folders on the spare desk and hung his topcoat on the clothes tree to the right of the front door. Janetta was sitting at her desk, and I had my head hovering over a file cabinet looking for something I couldn't find.

John said, "Cripes, it's cold as a son of a bi..." For Janetta's benefit, he cut his comparison short. "I don't remember it ever being this cold in Florida."

"Yeah, John," I said, "and Tennessee doesn't have summer three-hundred-and-forty days a year. You moving back to Boca?"

He immediately got defensive. "No, no, I'm just sayin'."

I wasn't in the mood for complaints. "Grab a coffee. You'll warm up."

He frowned at me. "What are you in such a good mood about?"

Janetta answered for me. "We've made a horrible discovery about your Dr. D'Amato. He really is demented."

"Oh, yeah? What's up?"

"Seems that he was pretty heavy into gay porn," I said.

"*Gay* porn? No kiddin'. He was married twice. Switch hitter?"

"Be my guess, but who knows? Based on some of the stuff I pulled out of his PO Box, the goats in Blount County weren't safe."

"Jeez, I got a lot of stuff on the guy today, but didn't hear anything like that."

"And we haven't hit Texas yet."

"Yeah, right."

"You want to tell us about what you learned now or wait for the morning?"

He thought about that for a moment. "Tomorrow's *Martha Luther King Day*. We won't find anyone working in a government office, and other places are closed, too. Maybe tomorrow is better."

"Works for me. You planning to celebrate the holiday?"

"Me?"

"Just kidding, John."

"Hmm. I remember the day *Martha Luther* died. That KKK guy, James Earl Jones, shot him," John said.

"And for all these years, I thought it was James Earl Ray."

"Who?"

"Doesn't matter. If you want to wait to talk about your day, we may as well lock up and go home."

"Works for me," Janetta said. "My son's driving up from Chattanooga for his day off, and I'm making him a special supper."

"Then we're outta here. What could go wrong on a beautiful frosty night like this?"

———

Thanks to the modern magic of Netflix, Kate and I were about a half hour into a British World War Two movie called *The King's Speech* when the phone rang.

"It's 8:45," I said. "Are you expecting a call?"

"Not me."

"If someone wants to help us sell a timeshare we don't own, I'm going to scream into the phone and give them the raspberries."

"Find out who it is first, Sweetie. I don't want you swearing at one of my friends."

"But it might keep them from calling after eight o'clock."

"Humph! Mr. Warmth. You make Don Rickles sound genial."

The call was from neither a timeshare broker nor one of my wife's cronies. County Detective Bo Stallins needed me at the scene of a triple homicide.

His explanation took no time at all.

"I'm guessin' you know a Margarita Gonzalez?" he said.

"Yeah. She cleaned house for that suspicious death I'm re-investigating."

"A woman named Belinda Cancel stopped at the Gonzalez place over here in Eagleton. She got no response knockin' at the front door, so she looked in the window—saw a body on the floor and called 9-1-1. We got here and found the Gonzalez woman and her two kids dead. Killed execution-style. Each one shot in the head. Woman was shot once in the leg, too. Found your card layin' on the kitchen counter."

"Jesus Christ! That's hard to figure. This was a woman on welfare. She did that cleaning thing once a week and didn't look like she worked anywhere else. Look around the house. She was poor, like really next to down and out."

"Looks that way ta me, too. I don't see no signs of a husband. Know anything about him?"

"Just that supposedly he took off with a younger woman. I don't even know his name."

"Was wonderin' if maybe he was inta somethin', and this was a message ta him."

"Like drugs?"

"Mebbe. Ya never know with these Mexicans. Coulda been done by one o' those cartel killers."

"I only spent a half hour with Margarita Gonzalez. She answered questions about her employer. But I met her immigration attorney. He'll have more information about the family."

"That Ramón Goldbloom?"

"Yeah, how did you know?"

"His was another business card I found."

"Goldbloom's known her for three years. Between him and the Cancel woman, you should get more on the husband."

"I'm gonna call the Goldbloom man next."

"He seemed like a pretty decent guy—for a lawyer. Pretty sharp. You'll get some answers."

"You know this Cancel woman?"

"Never heard of her."

"Tell me more about this suspicious death you're handlin'."

I gave him a quick explanation.

"Think this has any connection?"

"She worked for the guy for a couple hours a week—for however long it takes to clean a single guy's house. She might have done that for almost three years; she wasn't clear on it. I can't see how the two connect, but who knows?"

"I'll copy you on all the reports."

"Good, but better yet, I'd like to look around with you tonight. You mind?"

"Shoot, I'll take all the he'p I can get."

"See you in about thirty minutes."

———

I arrived at Margarita Gonzalez's house to find a parked convoy of police vehicles—two marked sector cars, two unmarked CID units, a crime scene SUV and the morgue wagon.

I gave my name to the uniformed deputy at the front door and was logged in at the murder scene.

Five cops, a deputy medical examiner and his assistant crowded into the tiny house created something that looked like an orderly mob—certainly like no cocktail party I ever saw. I found Bo Stallins standing in the doorway between the living room and the eat-in kitchen. Bo had plenty of time as a detective under his belt and worked scenes like a real pro. He had me by a good two inches but was long-legged and sinewy like a marathon runner. His short hair had gotten considerably grayer since I met him six years ago. After a brief look around, I voiced my opinion.

"Everything's pretty tidy in this room. Doesn't look like she surprised a burglar or was victim of a home invasion."

"Wait'll ya see the back rooms. Somebody was lookin' for somethin'."

"They ransacked the bedrooms?"

"We're guessin' either she knew the killer or she was pretty easy about lettin' people inta her house. No evidence of a break. Once they got in, well, they didn't act too hospitable."

"Get a time of death yet?"

"I'll let ya ask the doctor."

I stuck my head round the doorway. What I saw would make a mortician's blood run cold. Margarita Gonzalez lay on her left side next to the kitchen table, in front of the locked back door. An old-fashioned tubular chrome dinette chair lay on its side, possibly indicating Margarita was seated when shot and fell to the side, taking the chair down with her. A merlot-colored puddle of congealed blood created a large irregular oval under her head on the white and green linoleum floor. Dr. Morris Rappaport and his assistant Earl Ogle worked on a teenage girl crumpled in front of the kitchen counter. She too had been shot once in the head. The entry wound was in the center of her forehead. With so much blood on the floor, working in the small room without stepping in it looked like a major obstacle. To the doctor's right, the older teenage son was propped against the wall listing to his left. From the blood splotch and smear on the wall, I assumed he had been killed while sitting there. His coup de grace was a hole between his eyes.

The sickly, almost sweet smell of spilled blood and the involuntarily bodily releases that always accompany a violent death enhanced the carnage. Things you never get used to.

"Morris," I said.

The middle-aged Jewish doctor, originally from New Jersey, turned to look at me. "Samilah, you get around more now than when you worked in Prospect. But you would, wouldn't you, now that the whole county is your bailiwick."

"Yeah, lucky me. Next to you and Earl, I'm most likely to be called the Grim Reaper of Blount County."

"Quite the honor. I suppose you're looking for a TOD."

"It would be helpful."

"Best guess at this point—three to six hours ago."

"So as early as three p.m."

"A guess only. Will you be handling this case?"

"Not exactly. Ms. Gonzalez was involved with another case of mine. Bo and I will share information. There's only an outside chance these deaths are connected to my case, but who knows?"

"I don't envy you people. Look at this." Mo swept his hand around the little kitchen. "Who could do these murders? I can't say any more."

I stood closest to the boy and looked closely at the wound in his forehead. "Big hole. What do you figure, Mo, .44 or .45?"

"Probably. I'll know exactly when I recover the bullets...and if they're all from the same gun."

Bo spoke up before I could comment. "We's speculatin' before ya got here, Sam, about how this mighta gone down. Me and Cliff here," he poked his thumb at Detective Cliff Harvey, a relatively new member of CID, "we's thinkin' they mighta wanted some information from the woman. When she didn't come across, the killer shot one o' the kids to loosen her tongue. Looks like they did it twice. Then they shot her once in the thigh ta get her attention. Mebbe that made the woman talk, thinkin' it might save her own life. But since she took a second shot to the left temple, the killer killed her anyways."

"That's a good theory," I said. "The only sure thing about this is what we know about the killer—or killers—he or she, if we're being politically correct—is or are cold-blooded bastards. There's no stippling around the wounds, so these kids were executed from a few feet way—enough distance where you'd have to look them in the eye if you wanted your shot to hit between their eyebrows. You tell me what kind of a person can do that to a pair of innocent-looking kids—and then kill their mother for sport, and blithely walk away."

"I hear that," Bo said. Cliff Harvey just nodded.

I hadn't met Harvey before. He was in his late thirties, looked like he spent time in a gym and at least thirty bucks to get his dark blond hair cut. He was one of those detectives who must have dumped all his clothing allowance and more in an expensive men's shop. I was anxious to see what kind of investigative skills he possessed.

A quick blast of cold air slapped the back of my neck, causing me to turn around and look to the source. The unlucky deputy chosen to secure the outside of the home stepped inside.

"Hey, Bo," he said, "I got me a Mr. Gold-bloom here. Says ya called him 'bout yer vic."

Stallins turned and said to no one in particular, "Oh, Lord have mercy, what's he doin'? I jest wanted a word, not for him ta come down here."

I held up a hand and spoke to the deputy, "Hang on a minute. Neither of you can come in here right now."

To that, Ramón said, "Mr. Jenkins? What are you doing here? What's happened?"

"I'll be right with you, Ramón."

Then I turned to Bo.

His voice was barely above a whisper. "Pretty decent guy, ya say? Looks like a little weasel ta me."

Obviously, Ramón had been out for the evening. He wore a fancy black coat with a lamb's wool collar over a shiny, pearl-gray suit and electric blue shirt with a white collar and cuffs—looking more like a pimp than a cultured attorney.

I smiled while looking at Detective Stallins. "I guess those are his party clothes."

Bo raised his eyebrows. "That's the man ya hope never dates yer daughter."

"Aren't you being a little harsh?"

"Am I now?"

"Are we agreed that like him or not, he doesn't need to see any of this?"

Bo shook his head. "Like I said, I didn't want him here in the first place. Jest called ta see if he knew anything—unnerstand?"

"Yeah. I'll take him somewhere and tell him a little about what happened and let him talk about Margarita. If he's got something you need right away, I'll call."

"Sounds good."

I walked over to where Goldbloom and the deputy stood.

To the officer I said, "I've got it from here."

He looked a little disappointed. "Then I guess I'll go back outside and git cold again."

I remembered being a uniformed cop on a foot post and the midnight tours I spent walking deserted streets in single digit weather and could commiserate with him. "Sorry about that."

He nodded and left.

Ramón asked, "What happened to Margarita?"

"It's a mess in the kitchen. You don't need to see it."

"What happened? That detective said she was killed."

"Her and the two children."

"My God. How?" He closed his eyes and wrinkled up his nose. "And what's that smell?"

"It happened a few hours ago," I said. "That's what a murder smells like—times three."

His face looked strained, and he shuddered briefly. "My God. These people get to be like family. Can't I see her? Them?"

"You don't want to do that."

"Oh, man." He closed his eyes again and shook his head.

"I'll tell you as much as I know, but not here. Let's go somewhere else." I looked at my watch and saw it was already five to ten. "All the restaurants will be closed in a few minutes, and I don't want to spend time in some gin mill with country music blaring in the background. The only alternative is that little coffee shop at the Exxon station on 321."

He shook his head. "That's too depressing. I don't want that. But I could use a drink."

"I've got a bottle of scotch in my office."

"Just like a private eye in the movies."

"That's Private Investigator, and yeah. The office isn't far away."

"I'll follow you."

———

It was 10:10 when we pulled into the lot off Home Avenue. I unlocked the office door and held it open for Ramón. When I flicked the switch, the overhead lighting assaulted us.

"It doesn't seem this bright during the day," I said. "Let's see if I can fix that."

I turned on the lamp at Janetta's desk and the one on the spare desk in the main room. Then I lit the desk lamps in John's room and mine.

Back near the entry door again, I said, "I hate fluorescent fixtures. Let's try this."

I killed the ceiling lights, and the four incandescent bulbs provided a warm yellow glow in the main room

"Better." I said.

"Yeah, better." He shrugged off his overcoat and dropped it on the spare desk. "I hate overhead lighting."

I pointed to Janetta's chair, which looked like the most comfortable one in the house. "Sit down in the big chair, and I'll get you that drink. Want ice or water?"

"Both."

"Coming up."

I took the bottle of Glenfiddich from my desk drawer and moved it to the counter where we kept a mini-fridge and glasses. In a jiffy, I poured two drinks and then placed the glasses on the desktop next to my guest.

"Excuse me, I need to make a phone call," I said.

He nodded.

I called my wife, telling her how I'd be helping Bo Stallins with a new homicide. We agreed that there was no need for her to wait up.

Back at Janetta's desk, I took a seat at the corner opposite Ramón Goldbloom who looked more like a South Bronx flesh peddler than a struggling lawyer.

"You look pretty fancy tonight. I assume Detective Stallins interrupted something while you were out."

He nodded. "I got together with a client and his family. They were celebrating his new citizenship. They're nice people, and one of his sisters is very attractive."

"Always good when you can multi-task, huh?"

He shrugged. "I'm not married and don't exactly get many opportunities to meet nice women."

"I'm sure." I held up my glass. "Salud."

He raised his glass and took a small sip. "Not much to celebrate tonight with what happened to Margarita and her kids."

"You're right. I'm sorry Bo Stallins ruined your evening. And I'm sorry about your client and her children. You seem to connect with these people. That must be hard for you. She seemed like a nice woman. I'm sure her kids were nice too."

He nodded, and it looked as if he was fighting off tears.

"Yes. They were all very nice. And I'm afraid I'm getting a little choked up. Sorry. I guess I'm just not a tough guy."

"No need to apologize. Would you like to discuss this?"

He sighed. "Part of me wants to say yes. I may help you find out who did this. But another part of me says no. I don't want to violate anyone's confidentiality."

"I understand. But might not Margarita want me to catch who did this to her...and her children? Avenging their murders would be important, and I'm guessing she would waive her confidentiality agreement with you."

Poor little Ramón looked like he had the weight of the world on his shoulders. He stared at his glass of whisky for a long moment while I hoped he wasn't a killer.

"I never thought I'd get to be a scotch drinker."

"Medicinal purposes," I said.

He scowled at me. "Yeah, right."

"Surely you don't believe that confidentiality thing extends beyond the grave?"

"I'm not talking about confidentiality between Margarita Gonzalez and me. I'm thinking about someone else expecting and being entitled to that same legal privilege. You can't expect me to violate the canons of law. And the Bar Association would have a fit."

I gulped down half my scotch in frustration. "I should know better than to ask a lawyer, a shrink or a priest to help do something as outrageous as finding a person who just murdered three helpless people. Silly me."

"Gimme a break. I'm bound by law. I could get disbarred for what you're asking."

I shook my head. "Sure. Maybe we'll get back to that some day. You think about it. I'll just bet there's a legal way around it. If you don't think about it, I will."

"Look, you said you'd tell me what happened to Margarita and her children. Please. I need to know."

"Sure, I can give you details of Margarita's death whenever you're ready. But, sooner than later, Bo Stallins and I will need to talk to you about Margarita and her family. That will not violate any canon of law, right?"

"I understand. I can give you information on her husband."

"Good. I'll need that and other things. For now, just tell me his name. Then I'll find out if he had anything to do with any of this."

"Francisco. The son was named after him."

"What do most people call him?"

"Margarita called him Paco. I think the people where he works call him Cisco."

"What does he do for a living?"

"He was in the Army for a while but now works for a roofing company. He's a crew foreman. But Margarita said he does other things, too. I have the name and contact information in my files."

"Other stuff like what?"

"I understand he also dabbles in the entertainment business. Margarita said he wanted to be a talent manager. So far, he was handling a couple of singers who make the rounds of the Latin clubs."

"I didn't know there were any. If you can recall any names, I'll call you for that, too."

"Call me whenever you want. I'll be in my office all day

tomorrow. Stop in, and I'll give you her file to read—as long as you never say you saw it."

That looked like some real progress. "Okay," I said, "I will. Now are you ready to hear the gory details?"

"That bad?"

"Yeah. You'll probably want another scotch, either now to fortify yourself or later to get over what you hear."

His eyes got very wide. "Maybe both?"

CHAPTER FIVE

I tiptoed into the house a little after midnight and felt no more like going to bed than dressing up in white tie and tails and doing my impersonation of Fred Astaire. I drank another scotch, thinking it would make me tired, read a Virgil Flowers mystery for about an hour and finally felt my mind smooth out enough to attempt sleeping in a bed. Shortly after the living room clock struck 2:30, I fell asleep. Six a.m. came much too soon.

Eating breakfast with my wife has always been a treat. In the summer, I can look forward to her I-just-woke-up tousled look and one of her flimsy nightgowns. Even during the cooler months, she looks great in a winter robe. Since I didn't get much sleep and I needed to hit the road quickly, we didn't fix one of our more elaborate breakfasts. Munching on scrambled eggs and toast, she brought up a good point.

"Now that catching an *assassin* has become part of your world, don't you think getting a bullet proof vest from Bettye's quartermaster would be a nice addition to your winter fashion statement?"

"They are somewhat bulky, you know. I'd probably need all new sport jackets."

"Better to buy new suits and jackets than a coffin."

"You're getting very practical in your old age. If I wear a vest, will you make fun of me when I look in the mirror and ask you if it makes my butt look big?"

"Oh, shut up, and eat your eggs before they get cold."

"Who started this conversation?"

"Just be careful out there, Sweetie. I don't want to see a flag at half staff outside the Sheriff's office."

———

I got to the office around eight, wanting to organize my thoughts for the interviews I arranged with Leo Turner at 9:30 and Angela Scarano four hours later. I wanted to conduct them in reverse order, but Scarano just couldn't reschedule an appointment with her hairdresser. Things weren't going my way.

Terri Donnellson rolled in at 8:25 looking like a refugee from Siberia. Even wrapped in a long, bulky coat, a scarf long enough and thick enough to efficiently moor one of the Princess Lines' 'Love Boats', and with her head covered by a knitted wool hat with earflaps she might have purchased from a Nepalese Sherpa, she still looked attractive—a little bizarre, but still mighty cute.

She dropped her purse and gloves on the spare desk that we all officially called hers, while I listened to Mr. Coffee gurgle his way toward the twelve cups I started brewing only minutes ago.

"Did you bring this cold weather from New York with you, Boss?" she asked.

I was sitting at Janetta's desk reading yesterday's News-Sentinel. I looked up and tried to appear put out. "No, Mizz Donnellson, obviously not. But you southerners blame me for everything weather-related since the blizzard of '93. By the way, thanks for coming in on your days off."

"You're welcome. I'm glad I didn't freeze between home and here." She unwrapped her scarf and dropped it on the desk.

"It's twenty-two degrees. What are you going to do if it really gets cold?"

"Make sure I never go north again."

"Good thing the Army never stationed you at Fort Wainwright in Alaska."

She exaggerated a shiver. "I would have died." And then took off her coat. Like a little girl, she stuffed the scarf into a sleeve.

"Mmm," I said. "Sounds like the coffee is done. Grab a cup, and warm up."

She hung her big coat on the clothes tree. "Damn thing is so heavy, it might tip this over." She still wore the absurd hat. Her dark bangs showed from beneath the rag wool while two braided ties hung below the earflaps. Only a very pretty woman could pull off wearing a lid like that and not get arrested for perpetrating an indecent act upon humanity.

"And while you're at it, Terri, take off your chapeau. We don't want the immigration people deporting you back to the Himalayas."

"You don't like my hat?" She tried to sound outraged but couldn't manage it.

"Love it. I just don't want you to get overheated."

She smiled and took the 716th MP Battalion ceramic mug she left in the office off the counter and poured herself a cup of coffee.

"Boss, I just love how incredibly insincere you can be. It warms my heart more than the coffee."

"Glad to be of service."

As the spoon she used to stir the coffee clicked against the sides of the mug, she said, "What have you got for me to do today? I hope it's inside work."

"Big inside job. All telephone and computer work. You and Janetta can build a lifelong profile of our victim's time in Texas."

"Okay. Sounds good."

"As soon as she and John get here, we'll go over what we know about the guy so far."

She sat facing me in her swivel chair, nodded and sipped coffee.

"Bo Stallins called me last night with a triple murder that may be connected to this. D'Amato's cleaning woman and her two kids were shot—assassinated really. If I worked in New York or New Jersey, I'd think the mob put out a contract on the poor people."

"And it *may* be connected to this?" She sounded surprised.

"I don't know enough yet, but I don't like the coincidence."

"Gotcha."

The door opened, and John Gallagher walked in stomping his feet. We didn't have any snow on the ground, so I assumed the heater in his old Saturn wasn't working again, and he needed to stimulate circulation.

"Goddamn, it's colder than a witch's..." He stopped in midsentence. "Oh, hi, Terri. Hi, Boss. You guys are in early."

He dropped a white Hardee's bag on Terri's desk and started to hang up his coat.

"We better buy another coat rack," he said. "Or a bigger one. It's getting colder, and people are still talking about global warming. Unbelievable."

"John, don't start this conversation, or I'll send you to the Arctic Circle where the polar bears are wearing bikinis."

"You know, you're getting to be a real liberal in your old age."

"Get a coffee and eat your daily ration of cholesterol. I want to tell you about a new murder and what we need to do."

"New murder?"

"Three actually. Spread out your food and invade Terri's space. We'll wait for Janetta. Everyone needs to hear what we've got now."

———

Janetta arrived a few minutes later, shed a puffy quilted purple coat that looked like something once owned by the Michelin Man and made a beeline to the coffee pot. After we all settled in, I recapped what I knew about the Gonzalez murders, the interviews I scheduled for myself and how I wanted John to coordinate with Bo Stallins and see if somehow Margarita Gonzalez was otherwise connected with Paul D'Amato besides just cleaning his house once a week.

"What do you know about the Mexican woman's skell husband," John asked.

"I'm not sure he's really a skell. All I know is, he left Margarita for a younger woman, maybe one of the singers I'm told he's hanging out with. Poor Margarita wasn't exactly in competition with Penelope Cruz for the title of best-looking Latina. Maybe this guy was nothing more than a self-styled Casanova. Ramón Goldbloom, Margarita's immigration lawyer, says the husband's name is Francisco and works—or worked—for a roofing company full-time. The talent manager thing is probably at best a fantasy. I might get more when I read Goldbloom's file on the family. A complete background on Francisco would be a good idea."

Terri frowned. "Ramón Goldbloom?"

I shook my head. "Don't ask. Just accept the stranger things in life."

She shrugged and sipped from the military police mug. Janetta smiled.

"A lawyer is gonna let you read his files?" John asked. "Does this guy like you?"

"Everybody likes me, John, just like everybody hates you."

"See how defensive he gets?" John said with more than his share of enthusiasm.

"Knock it off, you Irish weasel, or that one-way ticket to the North Pole will be a reality."

"Just for that, I'll tell Janetta and Terri what I learned from the ex-wives, but not you."

"I'm shattered. Tell the ladies, and I'll stick my fingers in my ears."

"Gentlemen," Janetta said, "do you think you can stop fighting for a few minutes so we can get down to business?"

I couldn't resist. "See, John, now even Janetta hates you."

Janetta closed her eyes and shook her head while speaking—much like Bettye did for five years. "Sam Jenkins, will you stop?"

I dipped my head. "Yes, ma'am. John, it's your dime."

"Right. Well. While I was on the road doing *lots* of other things, I called the two women—two wives, that is. Both totally different. One wouldn't say spit, and the other would only hint around."

I sighed for dramatic effect. "And we're doing all this for only twenty bucks an hour."

Janetta corrected me. "*You're* doing this for twenty an hour. Terri and I make a lot less."

"Hmm. Second time you corrected me. Let's let John talk."

He squirmed around to get more comfortable in his seat. "First wife—Annette D'Amato. Used to be a Cavelli. Met him in college—before he went to med school. Got along good—according to her. She graduated and got a job while he went on

69

to med school. She started out kinda low on the totem pole at an ad agency in Austin but worked her way up. Didn't sound like a high-power place you'd find in Manhattan, but I guess she did alright. They got married after Demento graduated and got a spot as an intern in some hospital. I didn't know shrinks got to be interns. Anyways, she said that after the required hospital thing, he went into a private shrink's office with two other guys to learn the ropes. It was an established practice."

"Maybe, John, you should can the Demento thing. I can see you knocking on a door and asking a potential witness if they knew Dr. Demento."

"You think I'd do that? You continually hurt my feelings, Boss."

I rolled my eyes. "My sincere apologies, John. Let's carry on. So, sometime later, *Dr. D'Amato* went out on his own?"

"Of course. We knew that. She, the first ex-wife, claimed he did real good—*doctorwise*. But the marriage didn't. Well, it lasted nineteen years but ended in a divorce."

"Messy?"

"She wouldn't say that. Kinda danced around my follow-up questions. Then, when I pressed her a little, she avoided them like the plague."

"What did you ask that scared her off?"

"The reason they called it quits. I mean, nineteen years is a big investment. She claimed *they grew apart*. Sounded vague to me, so I asked if either he or she found someone else. She said she didn't cheat on him, but didn't know anything about what he did. What kind of answer is that? She'd have an idea, wouldn't she? After that, she wouldn't budge."

"Was she collecting alimony?"

"No," John said with a big grin. "Maybe better. She got a onetime pay-off—$250,000."

"Whoa! Nice piece of change," I said. "Much like a life insurance benefit. What did she do to deserve that?"

John shrugged, then added, "Didn't say what, but I'll bet she signed a confidentiality agreement."

"I'd keep my mouth shut for a quarter of a million," Janetta said.

"Me too," John said. He unwrapped a second biscuit with scrambled egg and Canadian bacon before continuing with his report. "I asked her about children. Claimed they decided against having any. But if he got to be more gay than bi..."

I nodded. "We need to know if D'Amato saw a shrink. I believe most of these therapists do. Once we learn that, we need to get them to talk about him."

"Won't be easy," John said.

"Yeah. You get any more from Annette?"

"You heard what I got. Number two was better, but not much."

"She get paid off, too?"

"Didn't hear about any cash settlement or alimony details."

I nodded. "Terri and Janetta can track down any Texas court documents today."

"Good idea," John said. "Second wife was a doctor, too. Lillian Reich. Never changed her last name. For business purposes."

"What kind of doctor?"

"Pain management."

"Probably had plenty of customers," Janetta said.

"So she claimed," John said. "Also said that prior to getting married, she and Demen...D'Amato gave each other plenty of referrals back and forth. If she thought she had a hypochondriac or someone with *psychosemantics*, she'd send them to him to work on their heads. If he was treating someone addicted to pain killers, he'd send them to her for some alternatives to go along with rehab."

"And this professional relationship blossomed to something more personal?"

"Yeah, I guess. But their marriage only lasted six years. Also, no kids. But they were no spring chickens when they got hitched."

"So why did they break up?"

"She wouldn't spell it out, but she hinted about him not paying enough attention to her. Reading between her lines, it sounded like he wasn't interested in sex with her, but maybe with someone else."

"A he or a she?"

"I wish I knew."

"I'll check the court records on that one," Terri said, "Maybe it will spell out more than irreconcilable differences. Or maybe it will be very simple. No contest. They just dissolved the marriage."

"We'll see," I said. "And that brings us back to D'Amato in Tennessee."

"Where we're getting some juicy tidbits," John said, "but nothing leading us to a killer or suicide note."

———

I never liked Leo Turner. But I've already said that. And I no more wanted to interview him and ask for his cooperation than I wanted to go over Niagara Falls in an open beer barrel.

Turner lived in a rural section of Maryville on a quiet side street off a semi-main thoroughfare called Amerine Road. To get there, I drove past cornfields long ago scalped of the stalks, with only rows of foot-tall stubble left. I passed a fenced-in pasture where a trio of miniature donkeys stood under a centuries-old red oak looking cold and about as ambitious as I felt.

I made my final turn onto the road where Turner lived and pulled up in front of a drab little house on a nondescript street that could have been in East Tennessee or Manitoba. The house was only marginally bigger than the place where Margarita Gonzalez and her children died.

I slid out of my truck and turned up the collar of my coat. A stiff breeze had picked up, and just overhead, a crow was flailing around with an awkward grace, attempting to make headway against the blowing wind, but not making much progress.

I walked up the short concrete path and knocked on the door. A few seconds later Turner opened up.

"Right on time," he said. "I expected that."

I nodded. "Leo." I didn't ask and I couldn't care less how he was doing.

Inside, he didn't offer to take my coat but pointed to a well-used couch in a sparsely furnished living room. It wasn't particularly warm in the house, so keeping my coat on presented no hardship.

Turner was a thin to medium-sized article just over the half-century mark. He had dark, but thinning hair and a five o'clock shadow that appeared each day at 9:30 in the morning. He had cold, pale blue shifty eyes that even Mother Theresa wouldn't trust, but a handful of nervous fingers betrayed all the bravado he wanted to project. He sat in an upholstered chair across from me and quickly picked up a cigar the size of a rolling pin. He looked more like an old-fashioned street corner hoodlum than a recently retired police detective. Any good cop would have thought of him as a nasty piece of work. A discredit to the badge.

The smirk that crossed his face did nothing to endear him to me. "The only reason I'm talking to you is because I haven't gotten my first pension check yet. They're not breaking any records processing my retirement, and I'm guessing the new sheriff can hold it up even more if I didn't cooperate."

I shook my head. "You made your deal with the Feds. Talk to them about the delay. The Sheriff's not like that."

He gave a nervous snicker. "But you're not her, and you would. Everybody knew you were in tight with guys from the FBI."

I smiled and shrugged, recognizing a slight advantage. "Maybe, but only if you light up that stogie. A bad habit you picked up from Ryan Leary?"

"Yeah, right." He placed the cigar back on the lamp table next to his seat. Then his small blue/gray eyes narrowed as he looked at me. "Maybe I'll shoot craps and take my chances with the pension system. It's my money. They say it can take up to ninety days, but this is ridiculous. They can't hang me up forever."

For a cop who'd just been forced to hang up his handcuffs and wasn't exactly sure where his next dollar might come from, Turner tried to act smugger than the only stallion in a corral full of fillies.

I didn't want to start a contest of top the testosterone with Turner who was, on his best day, an unpleasant item who had never shed his share of the Wyatt Earp syndrome so many cops suffer from but lose after two or three years on the job.

"Leo, I'm not here to break your chops or rub your nose in anything," I said in my Dutch uncle voice. "As I told you on the phone, an insurance investigator questioned your decision, and I've got to revisit the case and try to prove you were right."

Another snicker. He picked up the cigar again and began rolling it in his hands. His security blanket. "Or wrong."

"We've got to let the chips fall where they may," I said.

"Everyone's made a bad call in their careers. No one can harm you for an honest mistake."

"Why is that hard for me to believe?"

"Because you know I don't work that way. I don't sandbag anyone."

He rolled his eyes. I wanted to smack him—with a snow shovel.

"Look, if you've got something to hide, tell me to get out, and I'll be on my way. If you just kissed off the shooting as an accident because you wanted to be good to the surviving family or you were just feeling lazy that morning, I'll understand. Then we'll move on. I don't work for either the insurance company or the family of the deceased. I'm just looking for the truth. Short of taking a bribe, this is nothing to prosecute you for."

He slapped the cigar down on the table again and slumped back into the overstuffed chair. The navy-blue track suit he wore—one with double stripes down the arms and legs—made him look thin. The defeated expression on his face made him look old.

"Okay," he said. "What do you want to know?"

We went over the story again in great detail. I asked why he didn't initiate any of the forensic work that a rookie detective would have seen as necessary. He offered no excuse.

"Hey," he said, "maybe I thought he *might* have killed himself, but I'm not sayin' he did. But suppose I did? He looked like a decent guy. His sister looked like a regular, decent woman. Would you want to let the media get hold of that and plaster a story all over? Page one: 'Maryville Doctor Commits Suicide'. What family needs that? And if the guy paid into his insurance policy all those years, why not let his next-of-kin collect? If he was dyin' of cancer, the thing would have paid off after he croaked, right?"

"Was he dying?"

Turner looked more than a little agitated and nervous. "Hell, I don't know. I'm only sayin'."

"Did the sister tell you much about D'Amato?"

"I didn't talk to her much. And you were right on the other account. I didn't want to open up a can o' worms with what I saw as a pretty obvious suicide. I didn't want to waste my time running down leads that would just prove out what I suspected."

"I've heard something about him owning a .45 automatic. Did you find one when you looked around his house?"

He hesitated a moment, not exactly looking embarrassed, but not willing to admit cutting another corner. "Well, I really didn't look around much. No reason to. Know what I mean? The only gun I saw was a six-inch Smith & Wesson .38 right next to the body."

"You didn't see any possibility of murder?"

"Murder? You kiddin'?"

"At this point, I don't know. I'm finding out things about this guy I don't like. And I've got no great ideas where these things will take me."

"What don't you like?"

"I need more information to talk intelligently about them."

"Yeah, right. I'm not in the loop."

I ignored that. "It looks like the worst case might be the family will get denied the death benefit. But it's old news, and there won't be any embarrassing publicity. We'll see what happens."

"And you're sure the Sheriff won't try to jam me up?"

"Under the circumstances you described, I think sweeping this under the rug would be best for the department."

He picked up his cigar again. "I guess you're right."

After spending an hour and a half with Leo Turner, I confirmed exactly what we suspected, but learned nothing new that would lead me to a successful, concrete conclusion about the actual cause of Paul D'Amato's death. I never expected Turner to roll over and say, 'I took a bribe to call it an accident.'

By the time I got myself out of Turner's neighborhood and to the main drag—Sevierville Road— heading into downtown Maryville, my phone sounded off. Before Mick Jagger could tell me that he saw a red door and wanted it painted black, I answered.

"Mr. Jenkins? Ramón Goldbloom. Or is it Detective Jenkins? I don't think you mentioned your police rank."

"You can make it Sam. I've never been very rank conscious."

"Okay. First names are good with me. Did you want to stop by today and look at the Gonzalez file? As I said last night, I'm in the office all day."

"I just finished an interview and have until 1:30 before I pick up another appointment in Louisville. I could stop by now. You got time to talk about it?"

"Yes, I can. Hey, look, I felt like a wimp last night. I'm sorry. I shouldn't have acted like that. Emotional...know what I mean?"

"You did nothing wrong. No one gets used to things like a triple murder."

"But I didn't see them like you did. I still feel like a wimp."

"Well, get over it. You're not a wimp, and if you're inviting yourself in on the case, there's no time to look back. Got that, Counselor?"

"You want me to work the case with you?"

"*Working the case* may be a little strong. I'd like as much help as humanly possible. How's that?"

"I thought we settled that confidentiality thing last night."

"And I thought the jury might still be out on that."

"Do you want to look at the file I'm comfortable to show you or not?"

"I do. I'm heading your way right now."

"Okay. Where are you now?"

"I just pulled into a church parking lot off Sevierville Road around Asbury Heights. I don't like speaking on a phone while I'm driving."

"Good, I'll see you in a few minutes."

I shook my head. "Before I hang up, what are your ideas?"

"I'll give you a bunch of names."

"Like who?"

"Like people I know have been involved with Margarita."

"And you know this how?"

"Any time I stopped at the house, and she had a visitor, I took their name and wrote down their plate number. Any time I drive past *any* client's home for *any* reason, I pay attention. If I see a strange car, I write down the plate number."

"Pretty clever."

"Thanks. I think so."

"These people may lead us to someone else. And that someone else may be the killer...or know who is."

"Hmm," he said. "That would be good."

"It certainly would. I'll be there in a few minutes."

An hour and a half later, after speaking with Ramón Goldbloom, I headed for Angela Scarano's home, situated on a picturesque little bay off the Tennessee River in Louisville.

The sun was not shining. The sky was the dirty gray color of a neglected battleship. The breeze was blowing and felt as cold as Attila the Hun's heart. On the way to Casa Scarano, I passed several lovely homes with water views. The TVA had lowered the river level in early December to allow for the rain and snow runoff expected that winter. The shoreline had receded by at least thirty feet, and the endless strip of brick-red mud bordering the green water near Louisville Point stuck out like gherkins on a Boston cream pie.

But I was in prime real estate country and wondered if a half million bucks would matter much to someone who owned one of the upscale haciendas in that neighborhood—if in fact they owned more of it than the bank.

I parked on a cement driveway apron big enough to have covered Jimmy Hoffa and a hundred other goombahs that crossed the wrong wise guy. I can't help thinking like that when I'm visiting a wealthy suspect with a name that ends in a vowel.

As I approached the front entrance, I realized the home had more than basic curb appeal. The brick and stonework were top-notch. They used high-end Pella windows or their equivalent. Everything had been constructed as if the lives of the workmen depended on it. Oops, there I go again.

If Mr. Scarano wasn't in the building trade, he could afford the best.

———

A thirty-something bottle-redhead wearing a UT sweatshirt, and jeans answered the door. Trained observer that I am, her yellow rubber gloves made me think she might be the cleaning woman—she was too young to be Angela Scarano.

"Hi, can I help you?" she asked.

"Hello. I'm Sam Jenkins, Blount County Sheriff's Office." I held up my badge to show her I wasn't kidding. "I'm here to see Mrs. Scarano."

She barely cracked a smile. "She's expecting you. Come in."

I wiped my feet on an outside mat that might have cost more than all the wool Berber in my living room and stepped into a foyer with buff-colored Mexican tile on the floor.

"Follow me," the redhead said, "She's in the living room."

We wandered past enough rooms to house all the furniture from one of the larger Ethan Allen galleries and found ourselves in a living room with a cathedral ceiling and a glass wall overlooking a deck with an Olympic-size pool and a lawn sloping down toward the Tennessee River. For eight months of the year, the view must be spectacular.

As I entered the room, the redhead withdrew, Angela Scarano bent over, mashed a cigarette in a large ceramic ashtray and stood in front of an off-white sofa long enough to comfortably accommodate the offensive line of the Tennessee Titans.

Angela was short—no more than five-two or three and looked her age—late fifties. Her hair was as black as a Labrador retriever's and her skin as fair as unbleached flour. But Angela was no albino. Her eyes were dark and hard, and her carriage and demeanor showed me a person unfamiliar with the words *warm* and *friendly*.

"Hello, Mrs. Scarano. I'm Sam Jenkins from the county sheriff. Thank you for seeing me."

She spoke with all the emotion of a North Korean dictator issuing a death warrant. "Yes. Would you like to sit?"

No, lady, I thought I'd stand on my head.

"Thank you," I said.

I took a seat in an ivory leather-covered easy chair. A glass-topped cocktail table separated us. Angela took a seat on the sofa.

Before I could refresh her memory of the purpose of my visit, she asked, "Why are you reinvestigating my brother's death after all these months?"

Her tone wasn't exactly adversarial, but neither was it a friendly question.

"As I mentioned when we spoke on the phone, his insurance company has challenged the original classification of accidental death. The sheriff has asked me to review Detective Turner's findings."

"I heard the same from *that* woman."

"What woman is that?"

"From the insurance company. A Miss Barnett."

That surprised me. Or was saying that kidding myself? "When did you speak with her?"

She took a few seconds to think. "Day before yesterday."

"Really? She called you?"

"She knocked on my door."

"What else did she say?"

Angela puffed out a little air to show me that Velma Barnett had not amused her. "It's her contention that my brother took his own life."

That sounded like a fine opening for me to imply I was on her side. I let a smile cross my face before speaking.

"That would be convenient for the insurance company, wouldn't it? As I understand, suicide would negate paying the death benefit."

"Typical of an insurance company. Paul paid premiums for years. Now that he's passed, they're looking for a cheap way to avoid their contract. So typical."

"Isn't it though?"

She reached for a pack of Marlboros sitting on the cocktail table and tapped out a cigarette. After lighting up, she tilted her head back and blew smoke toward the ceiling. It all looked like something from a black and white movie. Betty Davis talking to Robert Mitchum and not liking it one bit.

"Mrs. Scarano, is it possible that—Oh, look." I pointed

toward the river, off to her right. A flock of Canada Geese just landed, and I wanted to use the occasion to drift off topic.

"Yes," she said. "We get them here often. I only wish they'd stay on the water. They make a terrible mess on the lawn."

More time for me to get friendly.

"You have a lovely home here. Did you build it?"

"Yes. Well, my husband did, of course."

"It goes perfectly with the waterfront setting. Is he an architect?"

"No. He designed it and built it though. He's in commercial construction."

Maybe I really should check for bodies under the concrete apron.

"His talent shows," I said.

"Thank you. You were saying?"

So much for scoring those friendly points.

"Yes. I wondered if Paul ever felt depressed or did anything to lead you to believe he was despondent over anything."

She tapped a long ash from her cigarette into the tray with a little too much enthusiasm. "What are you implying?"

"I'm asking, not implying. Could it have been possible—even remotely—that he could have shot himself intentionally?"

"Absolutely not." She took a long drag on her coffin nail and sent more smoke upward, but not at the acute angle of before. A few more questions not to her liking and I'd probably get a blast in the face.

"Even after a divorce and relocation and having clients who were not exactly the most upbeat people? He never got depressed?"

She waved my assertion off as ludicrous. "The divorce was years ago, and he was a psychiatrist, for God's sake. They don't treat the upbeat people of the world."

"Many people in Paul's line of work saw therapists themselves. Did he?"

"No one I know of."

"Did Paul ever speak of any enemies? Irate patients? One of the disturbed people he saw who may have been so off kilter that he or she may have wanted to harm your brother?"

Puff, puff. The look on her face said she was barely able to tolerate me. Too bad, huh.

She shook her head with a modicum of annoyance. "He never spoke of anyone like that."

"Did Paul and your husband get along well?"

If looks could kill, I'd be floating face down among the flock of Canada Geese. She leaned forward and ground out the cigarette with a vengeance. "I don't like your questions or your tone, Mr. Jenkins."

I thought I was being as nice as pie.

"Sometimes, Mrs. Scarano, many people don't. It's just the nature of my business. But as I told my mother, I was put on earth to be a good cop, not everyone's friend."

She stood abruptly. "I'd like you to leave now. I can see you're working to support the insurance company's claim, aren't you? Well, if you have any more questions for us, you'll have to speak to our attorney."

I stood and took the car keys out of my jacket pocket and spun the ring around my forefinger twice. "I'm working for the Sheriff, attempting to find the truth—and I will sooner or later. Someone won't like the outcome of this. I'm not sure if it's going to be you or Lone Star Mutual, but it will be the truth. If you never collect a nickel from them, at least you can take that to the bank. Thanks for your time, Mrs. Scarano. I can find my way out."

———

I left the Scarano property and found a convenient place to pull off the road and call Janetta.

"Is John there?" I asked.

"He's on the road. Terri's here workin' on the Texas angles."

"I need you to run a background check for me. Did Terri show you all you need to know for you to cover all the biggies? Motor Vehicles, local and NCIC criminal history, credit checks, and all that good stuff?"

"We made a list with places and numbers. I think I can handle that. But if I need help, she's right here."

"Good. Do a double package on Angela Scarano and her husband, Anthony. Use the address from her driver's license to get ownership details on the house. And see if you can tie him to a commercial building contractor's license. Try the state first and probably Knox County next. This guy may be connected to organized crime."

"I'll give it a try."

"And call Ralph Oliveri at the FBI in Knoxville. Ask him to check their intelligence files for anything on any Scaranos. Maybe the local Feds have something not in the official records."

"Will he do that for me?"

"Tell him it's for me and give him a few sketchy facts about the case. He'll grumble about doing me favors, but he'll come through."

"Okey dokey."

"That should keep you busy and out of trouble for a while."

"No fun stayin' out o' trouble."

"I've said that all my life."

CHAPTER SIX

My last job of the day was touching base with a VA counselor named Chet Lightner who hung his professional hat in the old county building on Court Street in Maryville. I found him on the main floor across from the old courtroom.

"I already talked to your partner." He picked up a business card very much like my own. "John Gallagher."

The VA offices looked more like a small military museum. Donated photos and collections of shoulder patches, ribbon bars, and assorted medals and qualification badges in frames hung on every square inch of wall space. A few bayonets, trench knives, steel pots, and short-timer's sticks hung or were tucked in any space otherwise available. A wave of nostalgic patriotism almost washed over me.

"I know," I said, "but we've got to take things a bit farther. I'd like to speak with the veterans who Dr. D'Amato treated."

His expression, narrowed eyes and furrowed forehead, told me I was entering uncomfortable territory.

"I don't want to know anything about their emotional difficulties," I said. "I need their help getting a handle on the doctor's behavior. Perhaps during their sessions, D'Amato might have let his hair down or they just picked up vibes from him. I need to know if he exhibited anything that might lead someone to believe he was despondent enough to take his own life. And, I've got to tell you, we haven't yet ruled out the possibility of murder." I shrugged. "Maybe someone knows if D'Amato seemed afraid of something or ever mentioned someone with whom he had problems."

Lightner shook his head. He was about fifty years old, a little overweight and wore his brown hair in a crew cut. I had no problem believing he may have been a career NCO or just someone who did his military time and wanted to help other veterans collect their allowances from the GI Bill or get treated for any service related difficulties that lingered on.

"You're thinkin' murder? Since when? Gallagher didn't say anythin' about murder," he said.

I sighed and shook my head. "Yes, since I no more think the shooting was an accident than JFK shot himself with that Italian carbine. It's either suicide or homicide, and I need a lot more information to figure out which."

He let out a long breath. "I been through this with Gallagher. How about that doctor-patient confidentiality?"

"It's doctor-patient, not patient-doctor. As I said, I'm not trying to get information on your clients and pry into their lives. I just want their help."

"Suppose they refuse to cooperate?"

"We don't beat potential witnesses into submission, Mr. Lightner. I'd like the opportunity to speak with each one. Think of it as one old soldier talking to another. You can check the files. I'm enrolled here. I want my free spot in a military cemetery. If D'Amato's clients have nothing to say or refuse to help, there's nothing I can do but sulk."

"Lemme think for a minute." He scratched his forehead; his eyes looked troubled, and I guessed that he wished he'd never met me. "I'd have to ask them first. Can't just give ya a list."

I shrugged again and reluctantly said, "I can live with that."

And I'd never give up the name of the secretary who promised John a list of patients.

Hopefully, his list and the doctor's roster would be the same.

"Wait now, there's somethin' else might help ya," he said. "Dr. D'Amato not only conducted one-on-one interviews, he held group sessions once a week. On Thursday nights. Maybe I could get ya ta speak ta them as a group. If it's okay with the new doctor and the members, that is."

"I'd like to do both, if I could."

"Okay, I'll get back ta ya."

———

The next morning, we all sat around the outer office thinking about our progress or lack thereof. Terri would only be with us for another day and then back to Prospect PD for four midnight tours. For the time being, she and Janetta would continue on the background investigations. Unfortunately, telephone and computer searching sometimes took an inordinately long time to accomplish the most basic chores.

"Hey, John," I said. "How far did you get into D'Amato's financials?"

"Just a quick look. Why?"

"D'Amato and Gonzalez both getting croaked can't be totally coincidental. She told me she hadn't worked for him since April. Look for checks or ATM withdrawals in the amounts he had been paying her each week. See if the dates are consistent. Was April the last one? Or was her date of April off?

If she kept working for him up until he died, maybe she saw something or someone that made her a target and the case for his murder rather than suicide gets stronger."

"Good thinking, Boss. Soon as I get a chance."

"I also want to go back and look around the D'Amato house again. I know you talked to some of the neighbors, but I'll try to find the people who weren't home when you did the neighborhood canvas."

I wasn't second-guessing John. I just wanted to talk to the retired cop myself and see if I could shake something loose.

244 Blackberry Ridge Drive sat on the right side of a well-maintained gravel road in a gated community on the very east end of Maryville. I parked on the road and walked down a steep driveway that led to a cottage-like home anchored on two sides to the only level ground I could see. The other two sides perched upon tall twelve-by-twelve wooden columns footed twelve to fourteen feet below driveway level in a hollow that fell steeply away from the house. Mature tulip poplars, sweet gums and oaks covered the slopes and low grounds. With the exception of the bottom of the driveway, that small portion of ground supporting the house and about forty square feet where a shed stood, there was no usable land. The board-and-batten house was painted tan and trimmed with green. I mounted the covered porch and knocked on the front door. No one answered. A black and white feral-looking cat stepped onto the porch, looked at me and beat a hasty retreat to who-knows-where. I knocked again, this time a little more vigorously, but got the same results. Feeling defeated by circumstances beyond my control, I turned around to walk off the porch and found a man who looked like he'd never see sixty again watching me from the gravel driveway. The stainless-steel Smith & Wesson 9MM automatic in his right hand concerned me a little.

"I'm with the Sheriff's office," I said. "I've got a badge in my right front pants pocket."

He nodded. "Go ahead."

I unsnapped the leather case and held up my shield.

"Nice-looking badge. You have photo ID to go with that?"

"Sure. Left rear pocket."

"Okay. Why don't you turn around so I can see what's coming out from behind you."

I put the badge back where it belonged, did a slow about-face, took out my wallet and then turned to face the sexagenarian gunslinger. He was about five-nine or ten, in pretty trim shape and had more salt than pepper on top with a receding hairline. He wore a heavyweight dark green jacket over blue jeans and a pair of no-nonsense hiking shoes.

"Take the ID card out," he said," and hold it up, please."

He took a step closer and held out his hand.

That placed me a little off balance with something in each hand, but in the interest of good community relations—and he did have that gun—I stepped forward and offered him my official Special Investigator's credential, but didn't bother to show him the secret decoder ring Bettye might have issued me if she knew Captain Video. By now I was assuming this guy was the retired cop, so I didn't get porky and say, 'Look but don't touch.'

"Special Investigator, huh? You must work with that other old guy who came around here a couple days ago."

To see if I could penetrate his poker face, I cracked a charming smile. "That's me, Sam Jenkins. The other guy was John Gallagher."

"Yeah. I remember."

He handed back my ID card and stuck the pistol into his waistband. His icy blue eyes did their best to look right through me.

"You still working on the Paul D'Amato thing?"

"Right, and not getting very far. Would have been a lot easier if someone who gave a hoot had done this work at the appropriate time."

"That's what I told your partner. Hard to believe the dick who caught the squeal kissed this off with so little work."

"If you knew the *former* dick, you wouldn't be surprised."

"Yeah, I found out his name. He's one of the assholes involved with the chief deputy arrested in that brutality and serial killing business, right?"

"Correct. And can I assume you're Bill Horne, the retired Milwaukee sergeant?"

"Guilty. Twenty-five years on the job. And I know your name, too. You're the guy who cleared that mess and got screwed for it."

"I'm guilty, too. I guess the people who own the house now are out working?"

"No. They're retired. Live in a condo or something in Knoxville. They come down on weekends or whenever. They asked me to keep an eye on the place."

I gave him another high wattage smile. "And you do a bang-up job of it."

He returned the smile. "What can I tell ya? You looking for somebody in particular?"

"Grabbing at straws really. The good doctor's sister—his beneficiary, by the way—talked to me for ten minutes and gave me the boot. Got offended by a few of my questions."

"Yeah, screw her. Paul was a bit on the odd side, but I guess harmless. I met her, and she looked like she could get nasty—real easy."

"You ever meet the brother-in-law?"

"Ooof! That one. Had plenty of bucks, but one look and you could see he was a first-class mutt."

"How so?"

Before answering, he said, "Hey look, you sound like you need a few more answers. It's as cold as a bitch out here. Let's go up to my house and get warm."

———

Bill Horne's driveway intersected the roadway fifty yards to the left of the former D'Amato property. The tightly packed gravel extended another hundred yards down into the wooded lot and ended at a three-car garage. A short walk along a concrete strip brought us to a screened-in porch and the front door. He hammered on a brass, colonial-style knocker, and a woman opened the door. She looked his age, was thin—maybe a little too thin—with mostly gray hair. She wore the clothes of a style worn by much younger women: a wooly gray turtleneck sweater, washed off blue jeans and loafers with white socks.

Bill made the introductions. "Marian, this is Sam Jenkins from the Sheriff's Office. Someone is finally looking into Doctor Demento's death."

Marian frowned. "Bill, you shouldn't call him that." Her face brightened. "Nice to meet you, Mr. Jenkins." She then extended a hand.

I smiled, and we shook hands. "Call me Sam. It's nice to meet you."

She pointed to her right. "Please come in and sit down. Would you like coffee or tea?"

"No thanks. I'm fine. I'd just like to pick your husband's brain—and yours too—if you don't mind."

She smiled again, perhaps happy to be included in the discussion. "Sounds good. You boys make yourselves comfortable, and I'll be with you in a moment."

Bill and I sat in a living room decorated in high quality Early American reproductions—not the clunky Bicentennialstyle pieces that gave Early American furniture a bad name, but authentic-looking stuff representing the first three quarters of the eighteenth century.

Bill looked at me and shrugged. "If you don't want coffee, how about a beer?"

I laughed. "What makes you think I drink on duty?"

"Ha! You know where I worked for twenty-five years. Remember that old Schlitz commercial? The beer that made Milwaukee famous. Cops drank a lot of that beer—on duty."

"Are you having one?"

"Hell yes."

"Marian won't mind?"

"We've been married almost fifty years, whadda you think?"

"Okay. Beer it is."

"Be right back."

Bill brought in two bottles of beer—not Schlitz—Spaaten Oktoberfest and two glasses.

"Damn nice beer," he said. "Too bad you can't get it all year round. When it comes out in the fall I buy a couple of cases."

"Smart guy. I picked up a six pack and got stiffed when I tried to get more."

As we were pouring the dark amber German beer into our glasses, Marian walked into the living room with a footed glass almost full of what looked like white wine.

She sat on a couch next to her husband and said, "We've seen you on TV when you were the Prospect police chief. Bill loved the way you handled the press."

I tried to look flattered. "Wow. Nice to know I've got at least two fans."

"So, now you work for the new Sheriff, and she's got you snooping around a cold case," Bill said. "How can I...we help you?"

"Let's go back to where we left off. What did you think about D'Amato's brother-in-law?"

"Like I said. A typical mutt. Dressed the part. Looked the part. There was no doubt he wanted people to think he's connected." He did the old cop trick of pushing his nose to the side to signify he meant connected to organized crime. "I don't know if he was or not, but he tried pretty hard to make us think so."

Wanting to get more information than give it out, I shrugged and said, "Who knows? I'll have to check him out with a friend in the business." I took a sip of beer and pressed ahead. "It's no secret that Leo Turner botched this one up. Now Gallagher and I have to find out what really happened. D'Amato's insurance company is contesting the accidental death angle, and I can't blame them." Another sip of beer brought me to, "You've been around the block often enough to know this should have been investigated back in June, and Turner should have ordered an autopsy. Now I don't even have a viable incident scene. I've got to reconstruct what I can and hope for the best."

Bill took a long pull on his beer. "I wasn't there when it happened, but like I told your partner, I spoke to Paul just before his death, and then when his family wanted to clean out the house, they came to me."

"Okay. That's a good start but let me ask you a couple of pointed questions first. I've got someone telling me that Paul spoke of blowing his brains out with *his* .45. Didn't you tell John Gallagher that Paul showed you a 1911 GI automatic?"

He nodded. "Yeah. He bought it off some guy walking around a gun show in Knoxville. But it wasn't a government issue gun. It was one of those Colt Series 70 .45s. You know them?"

"Sure, a civilian model. But here's my problem. The shot that killed him was from an S&W .38. That's the gun left on the table next to the body. None of the cops who responded found or probably even looked for another gun. I don't even have any test results for gunshot residue on D'Amato's hands. And that .38 can't be traced to him on paper or by hearsay."

"Strange. Paul didn't seem like a gun collector. He told me he only bought the .45 for home protection. We are kind of out in the woods. If anyone needed help, it would take the locals a bit of time to get here. So, I didn't think anything of it."

"No one I've spoken to seems to think Paul knew diddly about guns. Did he ever show you a six-inch Smith .38 target revolver? Or did he ever ask your advice about guns? Like what ammo is best or what's the best way to clean them or whatever? Most people think cops or ex-cops are experts on guns."

"Yeah, I know. Most people who find out you're a cop ask that stupid question, 'Have you ever used your weapon to shoot someone?' Assholes! Excuse me, Marian, but that gripes me."

Marian placed a hand on Bill's forearm and nodded, indicating that she understood.

"The two uniformed cops who responded to the initial call said there was a cleaning kit on the table, making it look like an accident that happened while he was cleaning a loaded gun. The problem is that no one noticed if the kit was for the .45 he owned or the .38 that killed him."

"Jesus Christ," Bill said. "Investigation 101. What the hell?"

I shrugged and took another drink from my beer glass. "What can I tell you? Do you guys have any idea where the contents of D'Amato's house went?"

"They sold the place mostly furnished," Marian said. "As for the small stuff, the personal items, the sister and brother-in-law just wanted them out of there."

"Yeah," Bill added. "Cheap bastard. The guy pulled up in a hundred- and fifty-thousand-dollar Mercedes, and he didn't want to pay for a dumpster. And he was too much of a hot shot to empty the house and the shed himself. Like I told you, he was a mutt."

Marian said, "The sister, Angela, asked me if we knew anyone who would clean out the place and take the good stuff as payment for the job."

"What did you say?" I asked.

"There's a guy who does work around here—handyman work. You know, kind of like anything legal for money—home repairs, yard clean-up, hauling stuff to the dump, you name it." Bill said. "We gave them his name. He did the job. Took him almost three days, but he cleaned everything up and did some work to fix a few problems with the back deck. Got cash for that though. He made the place ready to give to a real estate agent."

"And this guy is?"

Bill looked at Marian. "What's Jimbo's number?"

"I'll get it," she said.

"Jimbo?"

"Jim Falvey. We've got his card. It's a hoot. Says: 'Dirty Jobs Done Dirt Cheap.' He's a pretty good guy. If you need any real building or remodeling jobs, he does quality work. Talented guy. Just doesn't look the part."

Marian came back into the living room and handed me the card Bill had described.

"One last thing," I said. "We came up with a couple of things that I can't elaborate on that deserve some more attention. Did either of you see or hear about any unusual activity at Paul's house? Like people coming and going—short visits, long visits? Anything out of the ordinary for a guy who was supposedly something of a loner?"

Horne got a strange look on his face. "You mean like he was dealing drugs or handing out bogus prescriptions? No. I know the routine. I heard that sometimes he'd see VA patients or clients or whatever a shrink calls the people he deals with at the house. So, once in a while there might have been a different car there. The place is set pretty low off the road so we'd have to have been out walking that way to notice. The cleaning woman drove an old mini-van, a real rat. She was there on a regular basis. Oh, yeah, and a few times, maybe more than a few, I did see an unmarked PD car there."

I raised my eyebrows. "An unmarked PD?"

"Yeah. Could have been something bought at a county auction, I guess, but definitely PD—Crown Vic with cheap hubcaps. It was only a couple years old, so I assumed it was a detective unit still in use."

"Interesting. What color?"

"Light, sort of a metallic gold."

"Did D'Amato ever mention needing a cop for something or an investigation he was involved in?"

"Not to me."

———

I called Jim Falvey and arranged to meet him at his home on Butterfly Gap Loop, a place I learned was just on the isolated side of remote.

I pulled into the driveway of an all-white single-wide that backed up to a fairly tall and steep hillside. The sound of hammering came from behind the mobile home where I found a man breaking apart wooden pallets and nailing the slats as subsiding on a large, framed shed sitting on a concrete slab. I said hello, and he stopped working and extended a hand.

"Hey, buddy," he said as if were old friends.

"Hey yourself. Jim Falvey?"

He nodded.

"I'm Sam Jenkins from the Sheriff's Office."

"Good ta meetcha. Call me Jimbo."

"Okay, Jimbo. I understand that back in August or thereabouts you were hired to clean out a house once owned by Paul D'Amato?"

"Yep. That's me."

Old Jimbo looked to be on the high side of fifty, hadn't shaved for at least two weeks and owned a belly large enough and round enough to make John Gallagher look like Twiggy's twin brother.

"And you got to keep just about everything except some furniture and whatever was in the kitchen. That right?"

"Yessir. Got several truckloads o' good stuff. Took the rest to the dump. I've gotten a few house jobs like that lately. That's why I'm building this here shed. I just need me some more room."

"What do you do with all the stuff you keep?"

He tilted his head and looked at me like I should have known the answer to that.

"Yard sales. I set up tables out front every weekend."

"You still have anything left from the D'Amato house?"

"Yessir. Whatcha lookin' for?"

"How about a laptop or any computer equipment?"

"Nope. Nuthin' like that."

"Cell phone?"

He shook his head.

"Anything gun related?"

"Didn't get no guns."

"How about anything to do with guns? Holsters, ammo, cases, boxes, cleaning kits?"

He pointed an index finger at me. "Come ta think of it, I did have me a pistol case. A leather zippered thing, but I sold it. And I still may have a cleanin' kit. Looked almost new so I put a good price on it. Probably too high and that's why it didn't sell."

"Can I see it?"

He removed his grubby baseball cap and scratched his reddish-brown hair. "Lemme think now. Just gotta figger out where it's at."

Jimbo walked ten feet to his left and opened the double doors to an aluminum shed half the size of what he had been building. Boxes and loose items crammed the little building.

I looked around while Jimbo did the digging.

To the right and up high, I watched three crows swooping up and down in the sky over a big tulip poplar that must have been two hundred years old. They began squawking up a racket for reasons known only to them then suddenly they cruised into the branches and roosted without another sound.

After a few minutes of rummaging, Jimbo drew my attention when he emerged from the shed holding a red rectangular metal box about fourteen inches long by five inches wide and two inches deep. The brand name *Outers* was printed in yellow on the lower right-hand corner of the top. Jimbo handed it to me, and I unfastened the brass clip that held the top down and opened the lid. Bingo! The box held a small glass bottle of solvent, a cardboard box of cloth cleaning patches, a twelve-inch-long aluminum rod with a black plastic T handle, a couple of screw-on jags and my favorite, a brass bristled bore brush for a .45 caliber handgun.

"Okay," I said. "This is what I was looking for. How much were you asking for it?"

"I figgered it was worth five dollars. New they's a lot more."

"I'd like you to sell it to the Sheriff's Office. If you do, I'll need you to sign a receipt for the money and write a short statement about where you got it."

"For five bucks, I can do it."

―――――

On the way out of Butterfly Gap, my cell phone sounded off.

Mick Jagger got off the first stanza of *Paint it Black,* and then Janetta told me, "Your pal Oliveri called back with the information you wanted. He wouldn't give it to me though."

"Yeah, that's Ralph. If he told you, then you would owe him a favor, but he wants me to be the indebted one. That's okay. I'll call him. By the way, did you or Terri have any luck getting on D'Amato's medical insurance?"

"Not a bit. Those people are tighter than a pair of yoga pants. Telling them it's in connection to a possible homicide meant nothing."

"I hate insurance people. Maybe we're not the best ones to get that information. Tell John to call Velma Barnett and see if he can schmooze her into finding a way for Lone Star Mutual to use their influence and get what we need."

"Okay," she said. "I'll give it a go."

"Oh, one last thing, one of you needs to call Central Records at the Sheriff's office and do a location search for any activity at the D'Amato address or anything close by. Anything that would have required a police presence—even something minor that wouldn't show his name as the complainant. I'm especially looking for any reason a detective may have been in the area prior to his death."

"Sounds like a job for John or Terri. But I'll listen in so I'll know what to ask in the future."

"Great. Talk to you later."

I pulled into the parking lot of one of the three million Dollar General Stores that have sprung up on all the back roads in Blount County over the last few years and called Ralph Oliveri.

"Ralphie, you have news?"

"News, yes, paisan, and maybe a nice big bag o' worms for you. This is no smoking gun, but after you know a little more about your friend Tony Scarano, you might have to look a little harder at your unexplained death and focus on possible murder."

"Oh, jeez, why do you do this to me?" I love to play with Ralph's mind.

"What? You give me names and ask for intelligence. I search my ass off and bring you Uncle Sam's finest info on these mooks and you bust my shoes."

"Oh stop. You know I owe you and appreciate your help. And I always pay my debts. Look at the big scheme of things and how much you're doing for mankind."

"I haven't heard a line of crap like that since Johnny Cochran defended O.J. Okay, Paly, listen and learn."

"I'm all ears."

"Your victim is nowhere in our confidential files. You already have everything I learned about him. The sister, Anthony's wife, Angela, is just a wife. She's been with him for more than forty years, and nobody can tell me she doesn't know exactly what was and is going on businesswise with old Anthony. But, as far as anything solid, she's clean. Then we get to Anthony Scarano, or obviously more commonly known as Tony. He hasn't always been living and working in our neck of the woods. Ten, twelve years ago, they moved here from the metro Miami area. He's definitely connected, but not a made man or even close to it. He's always been in construction— mainly commercial properties 'cause that's where the big money is, but he's also dabbled in high-end residential homes if his goombahs steered a client his way. As a general contractor, the Miami wise guys *steered* a lot of work his way. You understand what I'm saying? He, in turn, used sub-contractors from the *family's* list of favorite sons, and everybody concerned kicked back some of their profit to the local boss man. Nothing revolutionary, but that's how Anthony made a living. At the time, the boss was fat Jimmy Capotorto, a/k/a Jimmy Cap or Jimmy the Cap, as in capo. Ever heard of him?"

"Sure, not one of the traditional old-fashioned bosses—a fat slob who was getting pushed out of some of the more lucrative rackets by the ethnic Florida hoods. Didn't he get whacked around the time you're talking about?"

"Exactly, Jimmy was capped," Ralph laughed at his pathetic excuse for a pun, "by one of his own guys—his bodyguard to be exact, but nothing was ever proved. After that, one of Jimmy's main people, Tomasino Bitonti, a/k/a Tommy Bucks or Tommy the Zip made it known he was interested in taking over and bringing the Miami Mob back to the status it once enjoyed under the old Mustache Petes. Tommy had been a button man brought over from Sicily to do a couple of hits. Apparently, he liked life on the beach and stayed around. When Tommy got the nod to take over, he began cleaning house, and Tony Scarano got the boot. But Scarano was connected enough through actual family relations to get relocated to beautiful downtown Knoxville where he operates today doing business as T and A Construction."

"What class. T and A as in Tony and Angela, but with an obvious double meaning. I love these goons."

"Don't we all?"

"So what's Tony up to lately?"

"Nothing illegal that we know of unless you count hiring undocumented Mexicans to work his jobs at relatively low wages. Tony coordinates with the local *patron* and always finds plenty of help at bargain basement prices. We don't have the strong unions down here to object to illegal aliens taking jobs from US citizens as they do elsewhere. Tony does his thing, and based on current administration policy, we have no bitch."

"Ralphie, that's interesting as hell but gives me nothing but basic suspicion about the honesty of a lifetime criminal. I had hoped you could tell me Tony had a good reason to whack his brother-in-law. Is he experiencing a cash flow problem where he could use a half mil in insurance money to help out?"

"From all I see, he's doing okay. He isn't in arrears to any legitimate organization. He bought his Mercedes-Maybach for cash last year. Angela drives a big, paid for late model Mercedes two-seater and does not run all the credit cards up to the max. Tony seems to be doing quite well—seemingly without the help of his goombahs *steering* customers his way."

"As always, thank you. I appreciate the effort, but right now I can't see how this can help me solve Paul D'Amato's death and the obvious murders of Margarita Gonzales and her two kids, which I think must be connected. Have you got any words of wisdom to help me out?"

"Sorry about that, Sambo, but us FBI types are obviously not so street-smart as you ex-New York hot shots. Lemme know how you make out."

CHAPTER SEVEN

O n the way back to our office on Home Avenue in Maryville, I stopped at the Justice Center on US 321 to log in my new evidence and see what my favorite sheriff was wearing.

I smiled at Bettye's secretary. "Hi, Cynthia. Is Ma'am Sahib in?"

She frowned at my foolishness. "She is."

"She alone?"

"Yes." Still no smile.

I took two steps to the Sheriff's office door. "Don't bother announcing me. If I catch her doing anything she shouldn't, I'll scold her."

Cynthia's frown deepened. "I've never operated like this before, Mr. Jenkins, but I've been told that you do not need an appointment, and you're always welcome. I just can't imagine why."

I wasn't going to let her think she could hurt my feelings. I smiled again. "Neither can I. You'll have to ask Miss Bettye."

I pushed the lever down and entered Bettye's version of the

Oval Office. She looked up from a document she had been reading and removed her glasses.

"Hey, darlin'. You look like you're up to no good. What's the big smile for?"

"Hey, yourself, lady. The smile is for you 'cause you brighten up a cold and dreary day."

"Well, thank you very much, but I'll say something you might—cut the crap, Sport. What are you up to? What are you doin' to earn the money I pay you?"

"Wow. If I had feelings, they would be hurt. First Cynthia said something dreadfully disrespectful, and now you're being a cold fish. I'm out in the dead of winter working like a common gumshoe, and you women give me a hard time."

She showed me the familiar look that said she might tolerate me.

"Do you want me to speak to Cynthia?"

I shook my head. "Of course not. Secretaries generally don't like me. I suppose it's because of my irreverence for protocol."

She laughed. "Good thing you don't work at the White House."

"I could probably get along with some presidents. I liked Tricky Dick. It would be the Chiefs of Staff and Secret Service guys who would have a hard time with me."

Bettye laughed again silently and shook her head. "What brings you to the big ol' Justice Center today?"

"I wanted to log in some evidence I've gathered in this cockamamie unattended death investigation of yours."

"Anything significant?"

"Sort of. At least I think so. It's nothing that would make a prosecutor do a Highland jig, but it makes me think that Dr. Demento didn't die by accident or suicide."

Bettye raised one eyebrow—I can't understand how anyone can do that. "What does that leave?"

"Three guesses and the last two don't count."

"Murder?"

"Maybe it also leaves me to believe that a few cops dropped the ball on this one. Although the one most remiss has already been given the sack."

"Leo Turner?"

I nodded. "Leo's report said accidental discharge of a firearm while cleaning said firearm. The pronouncing doctor didn't go along with that and didn't like the smell of the whole thing. All he would agree to certify was that Demento was indeed dead. I just found the cleaning kit. The fatal shot to the head came from a .38 revolver. The kit only had all the accessories to clean a .45 caliber pistol—which a couple of people said he owned. The .45 has yet to surface."

Bettye frowned. "Why do you call him Demento?"

"One of his neighbors tagged him with that. He's a retired detective and said the victim was quite an oddball."

"A retired detective. I should have known. Is he from New York?"

"Milwaukee."

"Just as bad. What about this cleaning kit? Could he clean a .38 with a .45 caliber tools?"

"Maybe...if he struggled. I used a .45 brush to clean my .38 caliber competition gun, but I attached the brush and rod to an electric drill. That way the oversized brush could do its thing more efficiently. Most of your average gun owners wouldn't do that—too much effort. It's possible that he owned a .38-sized brush and smaller cleaning patches, and someone threw them away, but it's not probable. Why wouldn't whoever cleaned up after his death just put that stuff back into the kit with the rest of his things?"

"A murder isn't going to make that insurance investigator happy."

I shrugged. "That's life in this little city. By the way, is she still around? I asked Janetta to tell John to get her to do us a favor."

"I don't see much of her. The people in CID say she's out more than she's in. With a cell phone and a laptop, why does she need room here?"

I shrugged again. "Beats me. Maybe she's a cop buff. Anyway, other than my miraculous discovery today, we're not finding any concrete evidence pointing one way or another. I wish we had started investigating while the body was still warm. And how's Bo doing with the Gonzalez murders? Those must be connected in some way."

"Don't use me as your middleman. Ask Bo yourself. But before you do, give me a rundown on your investigation in case anyone asks."

"Okay. We've got a guy who, according to the locals, acted blatantly depressed—constantly in a blue funk. I'd like to know if he was seeing a shrink, but the medical insurance people are reluctant to let us see any of his claims. That's what I wanted Velma to help out with. This guy was into some kinky porn—gay probably, but since he was married twice—to women—maybe bi-sexual. While he may have been mentally troubled—even possibly unstable—he continued to work as a councilor for the VA. So far they are reluctant to tell us who his patients were so we can ask their opinions. But, we may be able to work around total cooperation from the VA. Then we have a brother-in-law whose wife stands to inherit not only the proceeds from D'Amato's house and estate, but a half-million-dollar insurance payoff, and he's a former organized crime connected guy from Miami."

"Lord have mercy."

"You got that right, Blondie."

"Any hope of sorting it out?"

I used my James Mason voice to answer. "There is always hope, my darling. Am I not the world's greatest detective—rival of Mr. Sherlock Holmes and the great Nero Wolfe?" Then back to my own voice to finish my thoughts, "That reminds me. I've got a job for you. See who drives or used to drive a light metallic gold unmarked Crown Victoria. Or if one like that sold at one of your auctions."

She showed me one of those smiles of hers that could light up a coal mine. "Don't you work for me?"

I shook my head. "Pfui. It would take me a year and a day to cut through your bureaucracy. Get one of your in-house minions to do it. Easy peasy. I need to know this."

"I don't know why I put up with you."

"Yes, you do. What other detective comes in here and tells you that you look beautiful?"

Bettye was wearing a winter-weight navy blue two-piece suit. I couldn't see her skirt, but if it was like the others she wore, it ended about a half inch above her knees. The single-breasted top allowed me to see a hint of cleavage—although like some other girls I know, I think Bettye might be able to show cleavage in a turtleneck.

"Why Darlin' aren't yew jest so sweet?" she said, putting a little extra *country* in her voice. "I'll call ya if I find anythin' on that car. Now git out. I've got me some work ta do."

I stood up and bowed. "Yes, ma'am. I'm on my way."

———

On my way out, I waved to Cynthia and headed toward the CID squad room. A sergeant named Hugh Bledsoe sat at the team commander's desk.

"Whadda ya say, Chief."

"Howzit goin', Hughie?"

"What can I do for ya t'day?"

"I'm looking for the insurance investigator who's using one of the rooms up here. Seen her lately?"

"No. Don't see much of her. I can leave a message."

"Sure. John Gallagher has probably done that, but it couldn't hurt to do it again. Thanks."

———

After puttering around for the rest of the day and not making much progress, I went home to let my wife commiserate with me.

"How can I make you a gourmet dinner and solve your cases, too?" she asked. "There are only so many hours in a day."

"If you can't make my professional life easier, what will make my private time worthwhile? Something smells pretty good."

"That's Greek-style beef stew. You know the one, with onions, garlic, red wine, Greek oregano and LOTS of cinnamon. You also probably smell the roasted asparagus. And as you can see, there are noodles ready to go into that water."

"Sounds great. I see you're already sipping some of that red wine from Santorini I bought last week. I'll grab a glass and join you. And because you're so nice, I'll tend to the noodles."

———

The next morning John was in his office, Janetta was doing something at her desk, Terri was back at Prospect PD, and I was making a list of what we had on the D'Amato case and what ideas we'd already been kicking around for further the investigation. At about 9:30 Velma Barnett let in a blast of cold air through the front door.

I was sitting at Terri's desk, the one closest to the entrance. After getting blown halfway across the room, I looked up at Velma. "Morning."

She stood there looking like an old west gunfighter who just stepped into a saloon. "I understand you're looking for me."

So much for civilities.

"We are. I'd like to give you some information you may not have and then ask a favor."

She was unable to keep the suspicion off her face—if she even wanted to try. "What do you need?"

She kept standing with not even a hint of a friendly look on her face. She hadn't even opened her coat.

"I thought you or someone at your company could find out who D'Amato bought his medical insurance from, who his doctors on record were, and maybe even what he'd recently been treated for."

While I was speaking, John Gallagher left his room and joined us in the main office.

"Hello, Velma," he said.

She lowered her eyes and stared at him. "Gallagher."

Mizz Warmth.

She turned back to me and, after a long moment, responded to my question.

"That sounds like you might want to find out if he was being treated for depression. You finally thinking suicide?"

"Maybe. We're not sure. We certainly don't have anything close to probable cause to believe that, but it's looking less and less like an accident."

"Good. The company will—"

I interrupted. "Why don't you sit down? It's easier to talk with eyes at a level. Saves me from straining my neck. John, grab a chair, and join us."

"Sure," he said. "Anybody want coffee?'

I shook my head. "I'm good."

Velma wanted one. "Black, two sugars."

She turned the side chair away from the desk I was using and sat.

"Like I started to say, the company would love to hear that he killed himself. I don't have any idea if they can get health insurance information through normal channels, but maybe my boss can use the Good Ol' Boys Network to find what you need."

"Good. Had the original detective done his due diligence, he would have learned that Paul D'Amato wasn't the most upbeat person—possibly clinically depressed. As far as I know, no one checked his medicine cabinet for anything as common as aspirin, much less anti-depressants." I paused and scratched my head trying to look like I was deciding if I should give her some confidential information. "I'd also want to know if he had been treated for any sexually transmitted diseases—especially HIV."

"You think he was gay?"

John joined us and set a cup of coffee on the edge of the desk near Velma.

"Here ya go. Black, two sugars."

"Yeah, thanks."

I'll bet he would have been terribly disappointed if he bought her lunch and got such a warm display of appreciation.

I picked up my end of the conversation. "I *know* he had more than a passing fancy for hardcore porn—much of it gay porn. Who knows? He had two ex-wives who are conspicuously closed-mouthed about why they divorced him."

A menacing smile crossed her face. Velma was liking how our conversation had turned. "So maybe he had AIDS and decided to end it early. And with no autopsy results, we won't know unless we see his medical records. Can we get the body exhumed and do an autopsy now?"

A ghoulish thought.

"Since Detective Turner dropped the ball—either negligently or intentionally—we wouldn't have enough cause to request it without permission from the next-of-kin. You don't have to be one of the greatest thinkers of the century to know Angela Scarano wouldn't sign off on that one."

"That bitch wouldn't help if she thought it might lead to a verdict of suicide."

"Certainly not. She didn't seem to like me."

Then John jumped into the conversation. "Suicide's only one possibility. A couple of things that Sam found could suggest murder."

I wished he hadn't said that.

Velma slammed down the coffee cup. "Oh, Christ on a bike! The company will *not* be happy to hear that. What makes you think somebody offed him?"

"Consider this just a piece of one of our working theories and not something we're focusing on, but I found a couple of little things," I said. "People knew that he owned a .45 automatic. One of his neighbors saw it. As you know, a .38 revolver killed him. That presents the big question: where did the .38 come from and where did the .45 go? We couldn't trace the .38 revolver any better than you could."

"You prove someone killed him, make an arrest, and Lone Star is in for a half million-dollar payout."

I tried to mitigate John's comment. "Let's give your boss some hope. His brother-in-law is a pretty well-to-do contractor here in Knoxville, but in a former life, he was definitely connected to the mob in Miami. That opens up all kinds of interesting possibilities. And if the brother-in-law had any involvement with D'Amato's death, and if his wife, and him by extension, benefitted from the insurance money wouldn't that negate the payment?"

Velma tightened her lips and nodded. The evil smile of anticipation came back. "Probably. Yeah, probably. I like that."

"Get us the info we need, and we'll keep you posted.

"Yeah, okay. Thanks."

————

After Velma left, Janetta said, "Think she'll win the Miss Congeniality contest this year?"

"That's one cold-blooded woman," John said.

"Yeah, she's supposed to be a good investigator, but she's got the personality of an eel."

Janetta shook her head. "You can say that again."

I looked at my watch. "It's almost 10:30 and we're no further ahead on this thing. Let's stop what we're doing and do some coordinating. We've got so many loose ends and more things pending than we know how to handle. If anyone needs coffee, get it now." I looked at John using my evil-eye cop stare. "If anyone needs something to *eat*—maybe they shouldn't."

John began fidgeting as he always does when I try to embarrass him.

"You know, Boss, I wouldn't mind something—a doughnut maybe. I could go down to the new Dunkin's and be back in—how long? Fifteen minutes? You want something? Janetta?"

Janetta beat me to the punch. "John, if I ate as many things as you, I'd have hips like an old plow horse."

"No, John," I said. "I don't want something to eat. Less than an hour and a half earlier, you ate a breakfast with more calories, fat and cholesterol than nine people eat in a week."

He tried to look shocked. "No!"

"Yes!'

"You think I should cut back?"

I closed my eyes and shook my head. "No, John, I think you

should go across the street and get your oil changed. Maybe the guys at AutoPro can pull all the grease and petroleum out of your arteries. Jeez!"

He hung his head like a little boy caught with his dirty fingers in a peanut butter jar. "Okay. Okay. No doughnuts. I'll wait for lunch. It's only an hour or so away."

I sighed. "Thank you."

After that, we settled in around Janetta's desk, and I started.

"Let's make a list of what we have hanging—the stuff we need but are waiting for someone else to give."

John opened up with, "The medical stuff you asked Velma to get."

I looked at Janetta. "Your handwriting is much better than mine. Will you take notes?"

"A drunk writing in Sanskrit writes better than you."

"Yeah, thanks. Moving right along." I said. "I've got to hear from the guy at the VA about talking to D'Amato's patients. I'll call him when we're done here. It would be best if he gave me the names of people who are willing to talk to us. But, John, how about the list of people that D'Amato saw on a regular basis? Did the secretary who you bamboozled into sending you a list come through?"

"Yeah. She copied a file and emailed it to me. I just got to print it off."

"Good. Give me a copy so I have something to do while I try to get names from Lightner at the VA. I hope he can get me tied up with the new shrink who took over D'Amato's therapy group. They meet tonight. "

John said, "I'll print it as soon as we finish."

"Bettye also has to find out who drove a gold unmarked PD car Bill Horne saw parked in D'Amato's driveway a few times. I'm sure she'll call as soon as she knows something."

"How about the Gonzalez murders Bo Stallings is working?" John said. "We need to learn any new stuff he's got. I'll call him."

"Good," I said. "If it gets too complicated to discuss on the phone, we can have a sit down with him."

"You talked about the friend of the Gonzalez woman," Janetta said. "No one has spoken to her yet."

"Yeah, good thinking. Sometimes a woman will tell her friend things she wouldn't mention to anyone else. We just need more people to keep up with all the potential leads."

"Back in the old days," John said, "a homicide team could be eight detectives and a sergeant. And still they got more overtime than any other squad. We need more people."

"Good luck with that," I said. "Bettye has to scrounge up the money to pay our salaries and expenses. That's what you get when you're a non-budgeted unit."

"Maybe we can get Terri back before her regular days off," Janetta suggested. "I could give her a call and see if she can work any additional hours."

"She'd be good to interview Margarita's friend. You know, woman to woman. Give her a little time to wake up after a midnight tour and see what she wants to do."

"I've got to get back to the doctor's financials again," John said. "I let them alone to do other stuff."

"Let's let Janetta do that," I said. "No offense, buddy, but she's an accountant, and you can barely balance a checkbook."

"Oh, that hurts."

I ignored John and turned to speak to Janetta. "When I spoke to Margarita, she told me the last time she worked for D'Amato was in April. Let's see if he wrote her any checks after that. May has thirty-one days, and he died on June 20th. Maybe he wanted a clean-up or two during that time. If she was there closer to the time of death, maybe she saw something or someone who got her and her kids killed by the same one who did D'Amato. If someone killed him."

"That reminds me of the old saying," John said, once again smiling like the village idiot. "Thirty days hath September, we eat turkey in November. Buck, buck, buck."

I shook my head, once again amazed at what often comes out of Gallagher's mouth. "That's an old saying, huh?"

"Sure. You must know it. It's been around since we were kids. Helps you remember how many days are in the months, 'cept when it's a Leap Year."

"Oh, I'm sure that little ditty would clear up any confusion about the number of days in a month. Jesus Christ, John, I think this meeting is over."

Janetta asked, "John, have y'all ever talked to a VA counselor?"

"You know, Janetta," John said, "There's something I wanted to clear up ever since I moved south. I thought y'all was supposed to be plural. But when I go to Walmart, the cashier might say, 'Thanks. Y'all come back.' And I'm alone. What gives?"

"A common misconception for you Yankees. Y'all can be singular or plural, but *all y'all* is always plural. Now, if you're from one of the old-timey mountain families like us Galloways, you might say you'uns and we'uns, too. Got that?"

"Hmm," John said. "We didn't have those problems in New York."

Janetta shook her head. "Don't you get me started about how you New York people talk."

I didn't want to give John time to respond. "So," I said, "if I get the go-ahead from Lightner and talk to the VA group tonight, after I finish with them, who do we go after first? I say Francisco."

"Do we get a vote?" Janetta asked.

"Probably not," John said. "When he wants to go after some-body's scalp, that's what he wants to do. It's called *funnel* vision."

"Funnel vision?" I asked.

"Yeah, you know, when everything is funneled into one bowl...or place. You never heard about that?"

"Since you know about all of these psychological phenom-ena, maybe you can take over Demento's group encounters."

"I don't think so, Boss. But you gotta admit that when you get an idea, your word is law. Right?"

"Oh, thanks, John. Have I not, in all the years you've known me, been a proponent of participatory management?"

"Sure, but you usually say, 'Thanks for your input, but we'll do it my way.'"

"Well, okay, does anyone think we have more on the Scaranos—who will probably bring a lawyer with them—or Francisco the runaway father who we can hoodwink the hell out of?"

"I guess Francisco," John admitted.

"What do I know?" was Janetta's thought for the day.

"Super. I'm going to call that VA guy."

CHAPTER EIGHT

I left the Home Avenue office feeling like I wanted to scrap the whole affair and retire...again. All my professional life I hated to backtrack an investigation and start from scratch. Now, to help Bettye, I agreed to resurrect a fairly recent but still cold case that seemed more like a frozen one and second guess someone else's investigation. I was not a happy private eye, or part-time Special Investigator or whatever someone—not me—wanted to call me. I wanted to hang out with my wife, make exotic dinners, drink at least a bottle of decent wine with each meal and not wake up at 3:45 in the morning wondering what I didn't do or what I needed to do the next day to clean up someone else's mess.

When I stepped into the parking lot at quarter to four that afternoon, I looked up at the gunmetal gray sky. The wind blew the last remnants of autumn leaves and whatever dust and debris that lay on the ground up and around in mini tornadoes. I turned up the collar of my coat and opened the driver's side door of my truck.

When I spoke to my wife a few minutes earlier, telling her I would be home early but needed to attend a six p.m. meeting of a VA support group, originally organized by the late Doctor Demento, she sounded sympathetic. She even offered to provide to me a wee dram of some ridiculously expensive West Highland single malt whisky prior to a more than decent early dinner that she would begin to prepare.

What more could I ask? How about an answer to how Paul D'Amato died and with more than a little luck, the name of the person or persons who killed Margarita Gonzalez and her children? Was that too much to ask?

———

As usual, Kate had the entire dinner situation well in hand. An enameled cast-iron Dutch oven sat on one of the large burners simmering something called Basque clams and rice while a tray of root vegetables—red onions, carrots and parsnips—roasted in the oven. I picked up the cover of the Dutch oven and peeked inside.

"Don't do that," Kate said. "You're supposed to leave it tightly covered until it's done."

"Sorry. Still looks quite good."

"I was going to make you a pot of chili with roasted cauliflower and Brussels sprouts but thought you may get embarrassed in front of your audience tonight."

"Ha. Very funny. Every man needs a smartass wife or two in his life."

"A little humor is well within keeping of a good relationship. Besides, who else has a wife who would put up with all your shenanigans?"

"It's a good thing you're so good-looking, or I'd think bad thoughts about your behavior."

"Fat chance. Hey, while you're standing there, why don't

you fix two glasses of that scotch I told you I'd have ready for you...us. I've already put an appropriate wine in the fridge."

"Sure. I'll need some decent fortification before I stand up in front of who knows how many people who may just tell me to bugger off."

———

The VA support group met in the recreation room of a church on Sevierville Road that also provided a facility for one of the local AA groups that held non-smoking meetings.

I parked my truck close to the door. The dark gray clouds of the afternoon still capped the night sky, hiding any traces of the moon or stars. Light but annoying snow flurries felt like a sandblaster in the twenty mile per hour wind. I thought of the most blatant cliché in literature: It was a dark and stormy night.

I made it to the side entrance without getting blown off course, entered the building and went looking for a counselor named Larry Kessler, the new shrink and moderator of the group. With the help of an older man who acted like the one in charge of the facility, I found the room I needed.

I arrived fifteen minutes early and saw twelve people, nine men and three women, milling around two dozen folding chairs arranged in a circle in the center of the room. I asked the first warm body I encountered to point out Doctor Kessler.

I estimated him to be in his early thirties, about five-ten and trim enough to assume that he probably tithed ten percent of his salary to Planet Fitness. I would have said he was a good-looking guy if he hadn't shaved his head, but left his face with a perpetual four day stubble. I introduced myself. He smiled and offered a firm and friendly handshake.

"Good to meet you, Mr. Jenkins."

"You, too. But I'm guessing these meetings are on the informal side. Call me Sam."

He smiled again, first with a grin, and then his dark brown intelligent eyes joined in. "Yes, we do keep it informal. Have you ever been to a group session like this before?"

I shook my head. "No. I'm afraid my generation of veterans wasn't greeted home by an enlightened public or a VA that treated the not so obvious injuries until many years after our war."

"Vietnam. Yeah. Guys in my business certainly sympathize with those in your place. I'll say I'm sorry, but I'd be speaking for my parent's generation. Hey, I hope you don't mind, but I accessed your VA file and military records before agreeing to invite you to speak with the group. I won't be violating any confidences to say that some of the members don't respond well to non-veterans. Just a natural occurrence. Just as recovering alcoholics don't want advice from well-meaning non-drinkers. But I see that you've been around the block—around the world would be more correct. You've got more combined active duty and reserve time than anyone else in this group."

I tried to conjure up a self-deprecating grin. "And if anyone asks, I didn't spend all my time in the rear with the beer."

"Ha. Yes. So I learned. Good. You'll get along fine here. Let me give you a quick rundown on what I envisioned. Like any group session, it's first names only. If they give another one of the members their family name, that's their business. We also don't refer to rank and almost anything is fair game for discussion. If something is bothering someone, they can spout off and have agreed to listen to whatever opinions or commiserations that are offered. I'd like you to make your pitch before they get into their regular business. They all know what happened to Paul D'Amato. Some of the newer people didn't know him, but most of the members have been around long enough to have worked with Paul one way or another. Do you have any questions before we kick off?"

"No. I'm just going to present a few facts regarding the investigation and ask for any information—however small—and see where it goes. I'll be brief, but that will depend on the responses from the group. When things grow quiet, I'll leave you to your normal business."

"Sounds good. You're welcome to stay afterwards. You're a vet just like the rest of us."

"Thanks. Let's see how it goes."

By the time Larry Kessler and I finished chatting, another ten people had joined the original crowd. Some held capped take-out coffee cups, others plastic soda bottles and some stood in their spots empty-handed. There were all shapes, colors and sizes. They wore varied outfits, but the most commonality came from being the right age to have participated in one of the Middle Eastern wars. At that point, I learned that Larry was appropriately a take-charge guy.

"Okay, folks," he said, loud and clear, "grab a seat. I'd like to get started."

The former military personnel took less than sixty seconds to understand that *Take your seats* didn't mean finish your conversation first or go to the latrine and come back five minutes later or engage in any form of unauthorized grab-ass before providing your undivided attention. The assembly of twenty-one quietly filled almost all the chairs in the circle. Larry and I stood behind two of the unoccupied seats.

He began with, "We discussed what might be going to happen tonight during our last session, so I won't repeat myself. But to start, I'd like to introduce Sam Jenkins from the county Sheriff's Office before I turn this over to him. I'm not trying to blow smoke up anyone's ass, and I know this is going to sound like a personal endorsement, but I think if you know something about him, you'll see that he's one of us. I've only just met him, and he didn't tell me anything I'm going to say." He shrugged. "I have an *in* at the VA office, and I looked up his record."

I scanned the crowd. No one yet appeared impressed, and the women didn't swoon as if I was the second coming of Tom Jones. Larry took a folded sheet of paper from his back pocket.

"Sam spent almost five years on active duty with the Army and sixteen in the Reserves. Some of his awards and decorations include three Bronze Stars and an Army Commendation Medal all with V devices, three purple hearts, a Vietnamese Gallantry Cross, a combat infantryman's badge, master parachute wings, a SCUBA badge and too many weapon bars on his expert badge than I cared to count.

"You don't need to hear any more from me. Please welcome Sam Jenkins."

Before I could say hello, a man directly across from me spoke, "I guess you're a gen-uine old-time war hero, huh?"

It sounded a little more than pretty sarcastic to me. I couldn't allow myself to think *so far so good*.

I tried to appear modest. "When I got out of advanced training and was still in a stateside assignment, I put in papers requesting a transfer to as many interesting commands in Europe that I could think of. Most of the clerks looking over the 1049 Forms laughed. We all know how the military operates. Since I expressed so much interest in Europe, they sent me to Southeast Asia. What can I tell you? I was lucky enough to come home in almost one piece."

Another guy on my right side of the ring of seats made a comment. For a reason unknown to me, he looked a little angry. "Most guys your age can't help themselves. They tell us how they would have done it over in the sandbox."

I nodded and saw his point. "I know what you're saying. When I came home and got off active duty, plenty of the World

War Two vets looked down at my *dirty little war*. I heard all about the *big war* and how they fought it. I'm not here to tell you war stories or bitch about the hippies who gave me the finger when I returned to the states and landed on the west coast in my spiffy uniform, thinking I looked like the cat's ass. I wouldn't begin to tell you how to fight in the desert because I never did. I'm here to ask you for any help you can offer while I'm trying to determine what happened to Paul D'Amato. Do I have any takers? Or should I leave now?"

More than twenty pairs of eyes moved back and forth for a long moment before the guy who spoke first made another comment, "What do you want to know?"

"Before answering that, I want you all to know a basic truth about what a few colleagues and I are trying to do. You all know that Paul D'Amato died of a gunshot wound in June. The investigating detective stated that it was an accident. So far, during our re-investigation of this incident, what we've found tells me that an accident does not look probable. The insurance company with whom Paul did business sent an investigator here to see if she could gather enough facts for them to call it suicide. They would do something like that to save themselves from making a big payoff to Paul's beneficiary. To make sure Paul's family gets a fair shake, the Sheriff asked my partner and me to reopen the case. Look, I'm not going to sugar coat anything and stick up for the detective who did the initial work on this case. He was at least lazy and at most guilty of malfeasance. His case was just full of holes.

"I work for the Sheriff, and by extension, I work for Paul D'Amato—even though he's dead. Paul's not here to enjoy the fruits of my labor, but I owe my allegiance to him and to find the truth. I don't work for an insurance company, for Paul's family and certainly not for a newspaper who may print a story about the disposition of this case in a two-inch column on page six.

"I said an accident looks improbable. Suicide is a possibility —no one would like to hear that, but we've got to let the chips fall where they may. But there's also a third possibility that we've got to explore."

A new voice from my left said, "Murder?"

I nodded. "I've been doing this kind of work for a long, long time and my experience and what we've so far uncovered tells me that it's something just as possible as suicide."

A young woman asked, "How can we help?"

I pushed my hands and arms out to my sides. "Just give me honest answers to a few questions. You don't have to prove anything—that's my job. Most things are solved by getting information from the average person on the street, not all the forensics and scientific crap you see on television. You can't be held liable for your answers as long as they are given to the best of your knowledge and are truthful. I'm sure you've all heard the term *raw intelligence*. I'll take whatever you think may be pertinent and then analyze it."

Larry stood up. "Most of you knew Paul D'Amato. If you want to share anything you know that may be of importance, let's please get back to our normal procedure of standing and introducing yourselves."

As I looked around, many heads nodded. I wanted to drive a point home. "You may tell me your first name, but I will consider anything said here tonight totally confidential. Are we perfectly clear on that?"

The same heads nodded, joined by a few more.

"Okay, the first thing I'd like to cover concerns your personal time with Paul. I don't want to know what you told him about you, but rather what you heard or observed about him.

"Did anyone get the idea that Paul was depressed or perhaps even despondent?"

One hand went up.

"Yes, sir," I said, pointing at the owner of the hand.

He stood. "My name's Jerry. I was in the Air Force."

I got with the program. "Hello, Jerry."

He began with, "I saw Paul personally as well as in the group, and I gotta say, he seemed generally unhappy. He was like professional and all, and we talked about me, but he looked like he was always on a downer." Jerry sat down.

I nodded. "Thanks, Jerry. Anyone else get that impression? Anyone want to elaborate on that?"

Several more hands went up, and I listened to their comments. They were all similar to but no more complicated or definitive than that expressed by Air Force Jerry.

I followed up with all the standard lines like: Did he ever mention getting grief from an anonymous individual? Did he ever mention anything about genuine enemies, even in abstract terms? Did he ever personally mention that he was taking medication? Etcetera, etcetera.

I got enough participation to know that they were all interested and staying awake, but no one offered anything I could call a revelation—until the very end.

———

"I'd like to go a little outside the box I've constructed for a minute because I think another incident that happened recently may be connected to Paul's death in some way," I said.

"You may have heard or read about the murders of a woman named Margarita Gonzalez and her two children that happened in Maryville. This occurred just after we began re-investigating Paul's death. Margarita worked as Paul's house cleaner for a few years. Did he ever mention her, even offhand, or if you went to Paul's home office for a session, did you see her?"

A young man, not yet in his mid-twenties, raised his hand, and I called upon him.

"I'm Jason. I was in the Army."

"Hello, Jason. Thanks for your input."

He spoke in an animated fashion, using a lot of hand movement to punctuate his statements. "We used to have a guy named Gonzalez in this group. He used to be Army, too. He told me he did a one-on-one with Doctor Paul. Maybe the name's just the same and he's no relation, but I thought I'd mention it. Maybe he could give you some info."

"Thanks, Jason. Do you remember his first name?"

"Sure. He said he liked to be called Cisco."

I felt a slight jolt pass through me and raised my eyebrows. "I know last names aren't forbidden here, but it's not usual for someone to use theirs. How did you learn it?"

"We went out for beers a few times after group sessions. Neither one of us or the other guys who went were alkies, you know like in AA, so we guessed it was okay."

"Did Cisco talk about Doctor D'Amato outside this group?"

"He mostly talked about himself. Said he'd been in the Army a while—like two hitches—seven years. Said he'd been a Ranger for his last three years. He sure told a lot of stories. Don't know what was true, but, man, he liked to talk."

I filed away what little I learned and left the group with a final thought. "I've given Larry a stack of business cards. Please take one. If you think of anything that may be helpful, give me a call. And please remember anything you tell me can remain confidential, and if anyone ever needs help with something not related to this, I'd be happy to give you a hand with a little free legal advice."

So, I now could place Francisco Gonzalez, possibly *the* Francisco Gonzalez, ex-husband of Margarita, with Paul D'Amato. I wondered what else went along with that relationship.

And I left the group happy that Larry Kessler didn't object to Jason breaking the protocol of the group by divulging a surname. I guessed the desire to learn the truth overshadowed a rule.

———

The next morning dawned in the single digits. I expected to find skim ice on the coffee John always left in the pot the evenings before. I upped the setting on the office thermostat a degree so as not to overtax the heat pump that provided warm air to our portion of the building. Immediately, the auxiliary electric heater kicked in, and I watched imaginary dollar signs spinning on the kilowatt-per-hour meter attached to the wall outside our door.

We were making progress, but now that we possessed more hard facts, timing became crucial. We couldn't question the key players in our little whodunit because we didn't yet know what *it* was. Until we had answers to our questions before we asked them and could blow someone out of the water if we caught them in a lie, we could only keep many of the things we needed to do on the back burner. We had been horsing around for days, and now we needed to assemble as many pieces to our melodramatic puzzle as humanly possible and press ahead with great vigor.

We needed all the girl talk Terri Donnellson could pry out of Belinda Cancel about the Margarita Gonzalez/Paul D'Amato relationship. We needed Cisco a/k/a Paco a/k/a Francisco Gonzalez to 'fess up to his part in the saga. We knew little about him other than what Ramón Goldbloom gave us. He had been in the Army, he now worked as a roofer, he wanted to be a talent manager, and he had ditched his wife and kids for some unknown reason. I also needed Angela Scarano to drop the tough guy act and tell the truth about where she and Leo Turner fit in the big scheme of things.

Terri would be a key player on our side. She was a smart and street-savvy cop who could schmooze her way into Belinda Cancel's heart and make her feel like she and only she could help us solve the murder of three people and avenge her friend and two children.

What we learned from Belinda, I wanted to use to grill Cisco Gonzalez and learn if and how he fit into either or both incidents. If Cisco was a tough nut to crack, we may end up floating dead in the water. Or he might provide us with what we needed to clear both cases.

In any event, the time for Mr. Nice Guy was over. We needed to push and push hard. Toss good community relations and political correctness out the window and get a clearance or two. Damn, but wasn't my adrenalin flowing.

Janetta arrived first while I busied myself cleaning up the mess Gallagher left in Mr. Coffee.

"Hey, Boss," she said, with more bubbles in her personality than the frigid morning should have allowed.

"Good morning, Ms. Galloway. Before that Irish miscreant gets here with enough breakfast to feed the US 2nd Division, you and I have to get our shapely butts in gear and plan for a day that promises to be littered with success. No buggering about. No allowing things to happen around us. We're gonna make things happen. Understand?"

While taking her coat off she said, "You want me to say you have a shapely butt?"

"Pfui. My butt is immaterial. This investigation has dragged on too long. I've been complacent, acting like witling, a sluggard, but all that will change today."

The front door opened, and John Gallagher stepped in along with a gust of cold air.

"Jeezooi!" he said. "If I wanted this kind of cold, I could have stayed in Kings Park and bitched about Long Island winters."

"John, Janetta, get settled in, and get ready for some serious work."

John dropped a large white Hardee's bag on Terri's desk and shed his parka. "Whatta you all excited about? It's too cold to work before coffee and some breakfast."

"I've had coffee and eaten breakfast. We're gonna crack this business wide open in two days at most."

Janetta looked at John. "What's goin' on?"

"I've seen this before," he said. "He gets like this when he's cranked. He used to do stuff like this all the time back in New York. You gotta just let him go. Most of the time he knows what he's doing, and you can't stop him. The guys in the old office used to call him Madman or Mr. Machine, or sometimes just a lunatic, but he used to get results. What can I tell ya?"

"It might only be nine o'clock, but after him, I'll need a drink," she said.

"You'll get used to it," John said. "He sounds like he's nuts, but he might be a genius—most of the time."

"Hey!" I said. "Just talk about me like I'm not here, why don'tcha?"

"Relax, Boss. Don't get all wacky on us. We're here to help out and do whatcha need. Right, Janetta?"

"Uh, yeah, right."

I took a breath. "Good. I've got this all mapped out—like the D Day landing. I need to get our act together because I intend to rip a few new ass....a few new, uh, get a few people to start speaking with straight tongues."

"Sounds good, Boss," John said, sounding enthusiastic. "Somewhere in this *confusement* is a solution to the case."

129

"Yes, John, let's cut the *confusement* and get down to brass tacks. What do you think?"

"Sure, Boss. What do you need?"

"I need to know what went on in Margarita Gonzalez's head, and since she can no longer tell us, there might be only one way to find out. Janetta, did you get a hold of Terri?"

"I did. Yesterday. She'll be in here around noontime. Then she'll track down Belinda Cancel and ask whatever you'd like."

"Good. How about D'Amato's bank statement? You find anything to contradict Margarita not working after April?"

"Maybe. He wrote her a check for a hundred dollars, the usual amount he paid her to clean the house a couple of times after April. But there was also a five-hundred-dollar ATM withdrawal two days after the last check was cut. All twenties, of course. I was wondering where that was destined to go. He didn't usually withdraw that much at once."

"Excellent. Excellent. I wonder if Margarita got the cash for something other than cleaning house. Or who else got it? If he was going to make a purchase, why not put it on a credit card like all the other purchases he made?"

"You think Margarita was blackmailing him over something —something she found in the house?" John asked. "Or how about buying more for his porn collection?"

"Sounds like a lot of smut," I said. "You think someone would pay that much for filthy pictures? Doesn't make much sense. How different can one batch of porno be from what he already had? The blackmail thing sounds more likely. But since we can't ask either Margarita or Demento, we'll have to make our own conjectures."

Gallagher showed me his stupid grin. "There you go again, Boss, trying to sound intelligent using words like *conjecture*."

"Shut up, John. This is good. Yeah, very good. I'll bet Belinda can fill in all kinds of gaps. When is Terri getting here?"

"I told you," Janetta said. "Noon."

"Nuts. But okay, let's work with what we've got. Where's the hard copy of the info on Francisco Gonzalez that Gold-bloom gave us?"

"I've got it right here," Janetta said.

"Good. As soon as Terri is finished talking with Belinda and we get a basic knowledge of what she heard from Margarita, I want Belinda here, and we'll pick up the ball. Then we'll look for good ol' Cisco and put him into *The Room of Truth*."

Janetta looked a little puzzled. "Room of Truth?"

"Don't ask," John said.

CHAPTER NINE

Terri walked in at ten minutes to twelve. That ridiculous Nepalese or Peruvian or whatever Sherpa hat sat atop her head.

"What is going on here?" she asked. "It's noon and only twenty-two degrees. Are we heading for a new ice age?"

I got up from her chair and looked at her while she took off her coat.

"Maybe," I said. "People who want to deny the existence of global warming or climate change say the abnormally cold winters here in the south mean nothing is warming. But what do they know? Are you going to wear that hat while you're inside?"

"What? My hat? No." She pulled the wool beanie off and ruffled her hair with her left hand.

"Better," I said. "You, my dear, are now the key copper in this Agatha Christie-like horse manure with which we are dealing. I need you to get the crucial oral evidence from Margarita Gonzalez's only known buddy that will cinch up this case and let me—and John—and Janetta—and you—nail the person or persons responsible for all the deaths on our plate."

"Wow," she said. "Not too much pressure, huh?"

"Great detectives excel under pressure. I have every confidence in you. Use your intelligence guided by experience."

"All that for twelve-fifty and hour?"

"Think of the priceless experience you're getting, and what's money when your reputation is at stake?"

"What's money? I haven't got a couple of pensions and Social Security checks coming in every month like you, Boss. Can I pay Alcoa Utilities with my reputation?"

"After something like this, you'll be the hottest item in Tennessee law enforcement. All we need is for you to grill Belinda Cancel, establish a rapport, make her trust you, and then get down the basics and bring her here for a few more questions. After we clear the suspicious death and three murders, the Sheriff might give you a raise."

"It would have to be a pretty big raise. Even with my Prospect PD salary, this winter is making me think about declaring bankruptcy. The money I get from the Sheriff lets me buy a few dozen packages of Ramen noodles to keep me from starving."

"You want food? I'll get you the best lunches money can buy in Blount County. Get me what I need, and I'll make sure you're well fed."

She closed her eyes and shrugged. "Oh, great. And if I don't, I'll die of hunger."

———

By 2:30, Terri still hadn't called. I took that as a good sign because if Belinda Cancel didn't want to cooperate and told

Terri to go skip rope, she would have phoned to see if I had worked out a Plan B.

A few minutes later, John emerged from his room with news.

"I finally got through to Bo Stallins. He was up in Louisville handling a mercy killing/suicide in a little place off Topside Road. Old couple. Looks messy to Bo, but really kinda simple. Wife had terminal cancer and lots of pain. The husband left a detailed note. Hospice had her on morphine. He gave her an OD and downed all the antidepressants a doctor had given him along with a bottle of vodka. He asked his daughter to stop by, I guess, when he figured it would be all over. She found them and called 9-1-1."

I shook my head. "Sad. Let's hope we're never in that position."

"Yeah. Don't you wish that when your time is up you just went to sleep and didn't wake up? No anticipation, no pain, just didn't get up again?"

"That would be nice, but so would be visits from Santa Claus and the Easter Bunny."

"Man, that's pretty gloomy."

I didn't want to get into a philosophical discussion. "What did Bo say about progress on the Gonzalez murders?"

"Not much. He sounded sort of embarrassed. They're getting nowhere."

"Nothing? Did they talk to the ex-husband?"

"Yeah. Said they had him for hours but got nothing. He was like a zombie."

"I suppose the shock of your two kids getting executed would leave the toughest character screwed up. I still want to talk to him. We can approach him from a different angle—as Demento's patient."

"Bo won't mind. He'd like any help we can give him."

"Did he interview Belinda Cancel?"

"His partner, Cliff Harvey, did. Said she was no help."

"I sure hope Terri isn't just spinning her wheels."

That thought wasn't out of my mouth thirty seconds when a car door slammed in the parking lot. After a brief moment, Terri Donnellson opened the door and held it while a short, dark-haired woman entered."

"Belinda," Terri said, "these are the men I'm working with: Sam Jenkins, John Gallagher," she pointed to each of us," and that's Janetta Galloway, the office manager. This is Belinda Cancel."

John and I said hello. Janetta smiled and gave a little feminine wave. Belinda did not offer to shake hands.

I picked up the conversation. "Ms. Cancel, thanks for agreeing to speak with Officer Donnellson and for coming here on a cold and nasty day."

She nodded, but refused to smile.

"But it's warm in here. May I take your coat?" I thought a little of the old Jenkins charm might cheer her up.

She looked surprised that, I supposed, a cop might be polite. "Thank you."

She spoke with enough of an accent that anyone would assume English was not her first language. But her English was a hell of a lot better than my Spanish.

After placing her coat and scarf on the rack next to the door, I pointed to the empty chair next to Terri's desk. "Please sit. Terri, use your chair. John and I will get others."

Once all four of us sat assembled around Terri's desk, I provided an opening. "Okay, ladies, we're here to help. Terri, why don't you begin?"

"Right. I believe you're going to be impressed with what Belinda has to say, and she's agreed to repeat everything she's already told me. But I know how you two operate, so why don't you get acquainted and ask some of the questions that come to mind."

I nodded and started off, knowing that John would jump in if he saw an appropriate time.

"How long had you known Margarita Gonzalez?"

"I can get you an exact date from my records, but approximately a little more than three years."

Belinda Cancel was in her mid-thirties. She wore her dark brown hair pulled back and tied in something like a bun. Her red lipstick contrasted with her fair complexion. She didn't wear much makeup, but perhaps a little too much eyeliner. Her dark gray pantsuit would have been appropriate for an office or courtroom. She presented a professional, no-nonsense appearance.

"And how did you two meet?"

"I'm a counselor at La Union Hispanica in Maryville. Are you familiar with it?"

"Yes, you're on East Broadway. But I'm originally familiar with it from New York."

"You're from New York?" She looked surprised. "I am too."

"Yes. Both John and I lived and worked on Long Island. Where did you live?"

"Brentwood."

"We're familiar with Brentwood. Neither of us worked in the Third Precinct, but because of our assignments, we covered the entire county."

"You were with the police?"

"Yes."

She nodded.

Brentwood being one of the largest Puerto Rican communities in the world prompted my next question.

"You don't look Mexicana. Puerto Rico?" Actually, she had that fine-featured old country Spain appearance.

"Yes. My parents came from Utuado. Do you know it?"

I did. Many of the Hispanic people I had arrested as a patrolman were originally from there.

"Yes, I do."

"Ah. From there, they went to The Bronx and then Brentwood."

"And you've settled in East Tennessee. Good for you. Quite a bit less crowded than Long Island, isn't it?"

Belinda showed us her first smile. "You know it is."

"I'm assuming that La Union Hispanica does the same job here as in New York—providing more or less public assistance to Spanish-speaking people who need help with something."

"Exactly. We can't provide money like the county's Public Assistance Department but just about everything else."

"And so Margarita came to you for help with...?"

"Yes, she did, but then we became friendlier. We are...were about the same age, and I liked her and felt sorry for her. Her husband had left her for a younger woman—so she said—and was not paying child support, and at one point no longer visiting his children and not helping her with household money. She had no money left. I took her to Social Services, helped get her assistance—welfare money, if you will."

"When exactly did the husband leave her?"

"Around three years ago, he started not coming home nights. Then he might disappear for a day or two. He told her he had to get away to get his head straightened out, whatever that means. Then when he left her for several days at a time, he told her he went back to Georgia to see friends from the Army. He said he started disliking civilians—how they treated him—and needed to speak with military people who could understand him."

"Do you know who suggested that he go to the VA for help?"

"I asked Margarita, and she suggested it to him."

"But he still left home—left his wife and children?"

"He moved out in what? I guess you could say in stages. Then totally."

"Did you introduce her to a divorce lawyer?"

"She wanted to see one, but never got a chance. She didn't have enough money, and we didn't have any volunteers to do that kind of work pro bono."

I nodded. "And did you introduce her to the attorney Ramón Goldbloom?"

"Yes. Ramón helps us a lot. He is a good person. Margarita had a green card. She got it while her husband was in the Army, but she wanted to become a citizen. Ramón specializes in that kind of help."

"Do you know how they came to live in Tennessee?"

"When Francisco first left the Army, they lived in Georgia. He learned how to do roofing. Then someone he knew from the Army told him about this big company here who needed Spanish-speaking people to supervise workers. The company did roofing, gutters and siding. He brought the family here, liked it, and got that job. I think he still has it."

"Thank you." I paused, thinking how to tell her something that she might find troubling.

"We want to be honest with you, Ms. Cancel. We don't want any surprises down the road that you didn't expect. We knew Margarita worked off the books sometimes while collecting public assistance and receiving food stamps. Some of her wages were reported and some not. That didn't and does not now concern us. People do what they have to do to provide the basics for their families. We are not the primary investigators dealing with the murders of Margarita and her children, but as Terri has undoubtedly told you, we are dealing with the death of Doctor Paul D'Amato, the man Margarita worked for on a regular basis. However, we think both cases may be connected.

In other words, if we learn the truth about how and why D'Amato died, we may learn who killed Margarita and her children."

"I see."

"Since Terri has already heard what you have to say, I'm going to ask her to talk you through your story. I don't like to take notes while someone is talking, so would you mind if we recorded our conversation?"

She shook her head. "No, I don't mind. I have nothing to hide, and I hope *you* can be some help in getting justice for Margarita and her children."

She placed lots of emphasis on the *you* in her sentence. I wondered who she thought might not be much help.

While John got up and walked over to a cabinet where we kept the outdated audio recorder we occasionally used, I asked another question, "Did other detectives from the Sheriff's office speak with you, Ms. Cancel?"

Out of the corner of my eye, I noticed Terri roll her eyes. Belinda's dark eyes narrowed, and furrows appeared on her forehead. She did not look happy.

"Yes, I spoke to one man." Her speech quickened, and her accent thickened.

I watched as she rummaged in her purse. Finding what she wanted, she tossed a business card onto the desktop close to me with as much contempt as a Jew who received a Christmas card from a former Nazi.

"Yes, that's the one," she said. "He asked me questions."

I read the name on the card. "Detective Clifford Harvey. I'm guessing something went terribly wrong."

Belinda appeared visibly upset, fidgeted in her chair, and I hoped her remembrance of Cliff Harvey didn't cause her to lose enthusiasm for the mission at hand.

"Oh, that one," she almost spat out the words, "he wanted

my help, and he talked down to me like I was some kind of a puta latina. He called me *sweetheart* and *sugar*. I am no one's *sweetheart,* and how dare he call me *sugar?* I showed him respect, and what did he do? He treated me like I was some kind of alien trying to sneak over a wall and get into Texas. He had no right to disrespect me so, I told him nothing."

I raised my eyebrows and blew out a little air. "You're right. He was out of line. I'm not his supervisor, but I can apologize on behalf of the Sheriff for Detective Harvey's conduct. I am sorry."

Belinda shook her head and looked like she passed the point of extreme anger and would settle down. "It is not your fault. He is a fool. Excuse my language, but he is a *pendejo*, an asshole. I am not some kind of whore. I am a natural-born citizen. I have an important job. I have been to college. How dare he?"

Belinda's fair complexion had turned almost red but was returning to normal. By all appearances, she was one angry lady.

"If you want," I said, "I will talk with the Sheriff about this. She is a very smart woman. She will deal with this and make sure Detective Harvey does not offend another person."

She shrugged. "And what will happen then? He'll have another cop stop me and give me a traffic ticket. Or worse. I can't win with someone like him."

"I'm sorry you think that. I promise you that what you envision will not happen. Perhaps I should handle this another way. Would you like me to try?"

She shook her head in frustration. "Do what you wish."

"No, Ms. Cancel, it's what you want."

"He should have respect for another human being. He should learn. If you can do that, okay."

Thanks to Cliff Harvey alienating Belinda Cancel and having to listen to her complaint, I felt like I needed a stiff drink.

With luck Terri, John and I could bring her around and hear the story to which Terri had alluded.

———

John set up the recorder and made it ready to go. Belinda had calmed down, refused the coffee Janetta offered her, but took a bottle of cold spring water. When she was ready, I turned on the recorder and gave a standard preamble stating the date, time and persons present.

Then Terri began with a question. "Please tell us the first thing Margarita told you that concerned or bothered her."

Belinda shook her head, not refusing to answer, but more likely in disbelief of what she had been told. She took a deep breath and began, "She called me asking what to do. She told me about this Doctor D'Amato she worked for. While once cleaning his house—this goes back more than a year now—she found a folder—according to her description, a large accordion envelope—of filthy pictures. Pictures of naked men. She asked me what to do, go to the police, maybe. I didn't know, but I asked a lawyer who helps at La Union doing criminal defense work. He told me that owning such pictures was not a crime as long as no children were involved. He suggested that Margarita forget what she saw and continue to clean the doctor's house, if that was what she wanted to do, and say nothing."

"And then what happened later on?" Terri asked.

"More than once, while cleaning the doctor's house, Margarita was present when a man—someone she knew to be a policeman, a detective, came to the house and handed the doctor an envelope. The doctor, in turn, gave the man an envelope or sometimes a stack of paper money not in an envelope. The man would then leave."

"Did she know what the envelopes contained?"

"She did not."

"Why did Margarita think the man was with the police?"

"She had seen him on the television news and in The Daily Times. He was one of the detectives who worked with a high-ranking officer and the District Attorney."

"Did she know his name?"

"No. She only knew his face."

"And then, after that, what did Margarita tell you?"

"She said that at various times when she would arrive at the doctor's house—maybe a little early—she would see a young man already there but getting ready to leave. Not always the same person. Some of them looked as if they had just bathed."

"Did the doctor say anything to Margarita when she saw these visitors?"

"Not about the young men. He only told her what he wanted her to do, what he wanted her to clean if there was something necessary—something more than what she might always do."

Terri was on a roll and kept feeding Belinda the right questions. "Then you told me about something Margarita found, something she saw, Belinda. Something that upset her very much. What was that?"

Belinda closed her eyes and remained silent for a long moment. Then she shook her head and finally looked up at Terri, then at me and then John.

Before Belinda could answer, the phone rang on Janetta's desk. She snatched the receiver off the cradle before the second ring and quietly answered. I had hoped that the interruption hadn't broken Belinda's concentration. After only a brief moment Janetta hung up, looked at me and nodded.

I looked at Belinda and said, "Please continue."

She nodded. "She found her husband, Francisco."

That one surprised me. "Her husband?"

Terri raised her hand six inches above the desktop signaling me to shut up.

"Yes, her husband," Belinda said. "On the doctor's computer." Again, she paused, took a couple of deep breaths and continued. "On the computer. She was in the doctor's study, his computer room. She had been dusting, and when she cleaned the keyboard of his computer, the screen came on. And there was her husband—naked! He was smiling, looking straight at someone's camera. Margarita told me she almost died—almost fainted. She was not very computer savvy, but she knew a little. She advanced through the photos and saw more pictures of Francisco posing nude, also doing some disgusting things. And then she saw other men the same way, and she stopped and switched off the monitor."

"What did she do next?" Terri asked.

"She told me that she felt sick, could hardly think and maybe she couldn't finish cleaning the man's house, but she did. And then she came to me."

"And then?" I asked.

"And then," she said, "we planned. I asked Margarita what she wanted to happen. She said she had to confront her husband. She could live knowing he left her for some other woman, but she couldn't live with knowing he did this and how he might be with his children at some time in the future. She wanted to get a lawyer and divorce him properly. She wanted a judge to force him to pay for child support so her boy and girl could have good clothes and good food and pay her something to keep a good home for her children.

"But she wanted to have proof before speaking to Francisco. She wanted me to tell her how to get that proof before confronting Francisco and then giving it to a divorce lawyer."

Belinda had worked herself up into a near frenzy and was close to hyperventilating. We gave her a moment to compose herself and regroup. Janetta, who had stopped whatever she had been doing, joined the conversation.

"Belinda," she said," can I get you anything? More water? We have whiskey if you want a drink. What can I do to help you?"

"Nothing. Thank you. I'm okay. This was so terrible, but you need to know." After a moment of silence, she began again. "I told Margarita I would help her. I suggested that the next time she went to clean the doctor's house, I would go with her. She could tell him I was a cousin, and I came to help her because she had to finish quickly and do something at her son's school. I planned to go to the man's computer while Margarita distracted him, and I would download those disgusting pictures on a thumb drive—then show them to Francisco and demand an explanation."

"How did that work out?" I asked.

"I did the computer work. No problem. Then I suggested that I would be there with another person when she confronted Francisco."

"That could have been dangerous," I suggested. "Cisco had been a soldier. He could have—"

She cut me off. "Francisco was a...I use this word in the literal sense, not the filthy way. He was a *bicho*, an evil thing."

When an angry Puerto Rican wants to call a man a *prick*, they use the term *le bicho*. I thought Belinda meant it both literally *and* in the worst possible way.

"I didn't think of the danger," she said. "We were three. Margarita arranged for her children to be at their friend's homes. I brought another woman from La Union Hispanica. Her only job was to keep her phone close by and call the police if it became necessary."

"Apparently Cisco didn't try to harm you. Tell us what happened," I said.

"We used my laptop and showed him the photos Margarita found. He acted angry at first, yelling at her—asking where she got the pictures. When she told him, he finally calmed down and wanted to explain. He claimed that he only posed for those pictures to make money—for Margarita and the children. He swore that he was not a homosexual. That seemed to be important to him—big macho soldier. I didn't believe anything he said. He had stopped giving her money. Apparently, Margarita didn't believe him either. She told him she wanted a divorce and wanted him to sign whatever her lawyer gave him with no argument, or she would let the world know about what he had done. He didn't like that and got angry again. But soon he left. Later on Margarita told me he came back and cleaned out everything he had left at the house, but he did not cause any trouble."

"Have you heard anything about him since he left Margarita for good?"

"People I know have seen him at a club in Knoxville. They call it El Baile Latino. He thinks he's some kind of a talent scout. Maybe he is. I don't know. I think he's just trying to meet women...or maybe men...who think they can sing."

"What did you do with the thumb drive?"

"Me? I copied it and kept one safe in case something happened to the original. Margarita kept that one."

"Did Margarita know you had a copy?" I asked.

"No. I thought it best to keep the second copy a secret."

"Did Francisco try to get it back?"

"He asked for it, but she refused. He left without it."

"Do you think he might have killed Margarita to get it back?"

"Anything is possible, but no. I think he is basically a coward, and I don't think he would have killed his children. But I must tell you, Margarita did something very stupid. She told me about it after it had been done. Had she asked my advice, I would have advised against it—strongly."

I was almost afraid to ask. "What happened?"

"The next time she went to clean the doctor's house, she confronted him about the pictures of Francisco. She offered to sell the thumb drive back to him for five hundred dollars or she would give it to the county mayor, thinking he had something to do with the doctor's job."

I shook my head, John let out a long breath, and Terri said, "Oh, my."

"I'm sure you know that was extortion," I said. "If the doctor hadn't died before Margarita, we would be looking at him for the Gonzalez murders. Now I wonder about the doctor's family. What more did Margarita tell you?"

"Only that she arranged to meet the doctor in the parking lot of Food City on East Broadway. She wanted a lot of people around so she would feel safe. He paid her in cash, and she gave him her copy of the thumb drive. He only asked how could he be sure that she didn't have another copy."

Belinda had been doing a lot of talking and feeling a lot of emotion. She paused to drink from the bottle of water and slowly replaced the screw-on cap.

"And Margarita told him?"

"She said he couldn't be sure. She was mad and defiant and wanted him to be nervous."

"She didn't have a copy, but you did. That took a lot of nerve on her part. I wonder if he told anyone else that he suspected there was a second...or even a third copy."

"How could I know this?"

"You couldn't. But it wouldn't matter to someone who wanted to keep their fetish a secret, would it?"

"Are you angry because we made a copy of the pictures? We wanted something to give to the lawyer she used for the divorce.

We thought it would force Francisco to pay her money... legally."

I shook my head. "No one is mad at you or Margarita. I just hope no one knew who you were and now might think you held on to a copy of that thumb drive."

That was possibly the first time that Belinda took the situation to be as serious as it really was.

"Do you know why Margarita sold her copy? What would she show a divorce lawyer?"

"She said she didn't care any longer. She just wanted them all out of her life and wanted to become a citizen."

I asked her one final question. "This reminds me of that old question, what came first, the chicken or the egg?"

She looked confused. "I'm sorry. What?"

"Who knew Doctor D'Amato first? Did Francisco arrange for Margarita to get a job cleaning house, or did Margarita suggest that Cisco see the doctor for some Army-related psychological problem?"

"That's easy. Francisco arranged for her job."

"Okay. Now we'll need to borrow your copy of the flash drive. Can you give it to Terri this afternoon?"

"Yes, of course. I have it locked up at the office."

———

Terri drove Belinda back to La Union Hispanica on the other side of Maryville. John and I sat around shaking our heads and thinking that our can held more worms than a compost pile and that maybe we should open a bait shop and sell a few to fishermen.

"I wish Bo knew all this before he questioned Cisco," I said. "Maybe he wouldn't have bought the grieving father/zombie act for too long."

"And now we know what the doctor's five-hundred-dollar withdrawal was for," Janetta suggested.

"And we can guess where some of those two-hundred-dollar withdrawals went," I said.

"It's going to be interesting to see if we can ID the other people in Demento's photo albums," John said.

"Yeah. With each bit of new information we get, three new questions come up."

"Why don't we take a shot at Cisco real soon," John asked. "Bo's good, but he ain't us. Especially now that we can beat Cisco over the head with what we know."

"No, buddy he isn't us. Few of them are...Modestly speaking, that is."

Janetta snorted. "You two modest? Ha."

"Just for the record," I said, "I'm ignoring that remark. But, for the same record, I want it known that we're taking another shot at Angela Scarano, too. I'll tell her to bring her lawyer and advise her to forget any insurance claim fraud charges and start thinking about accessory or conspirator in multiple homicides. Maybe that will shake her up a little."

"It would shake me up...a lot," Janetta said. "But, hey, it's almost six o'clock. Are we going home tonight?"

"Best idea I've heard all day. Let's lock up and blow this joint."

"Oh, before we go," Janetta said, "I should tell you about that phone call I took while you were talking to Belinda. That was Bettye. She said she had someone trace the car you were interested in. They did sell it at auction because it had high mileage. But at the time the retired Milwaukee detective would have seen it at D'Amato's home, guess who was driving it?"

"It's too late to play games," I said. "Who?"

"Your old pal, Leo Turner."

CHAPTER TEN

Before going to the office first thing the next morning, I stopped at the Justice Center to see Bettye. I arrived at 9:15, giving her enough time to settle in with a cup of coffee, but too early for anyone at police headquarters to get down to serious business. Not to be denied one of the pleasures of her professional life, Cynthia Wilkins couldn't resist telling me that Bettye was expecting the county controller and the department's budget director at 9:30, which implied, 'Make it snappy, Buster.'

I also couldn't resist flexing the power I held with Cynthia's boss.

"My business is extremely important. I might be finished in five minutes or, depending on the Sheriff, I may take longer. Let those two take a seat. I'll be out as soon as possible."

After giving my lecture and being fairly confident that it might cause a wanted poster with my picture to be hung in the office of the National Secretary's Association—$10,000 dead or alive—I'd have female bounty hunters from all fifty states on my trail. I knocked twice on the door to Bettye's office and entered before she could reply. I caught her with the coffee cup almost up to her lips.

When she saw me, she smiled. "Mornin', Sammy. What's happenin'?"

I returned the smile and tried out my Ebonics act that is almost as good as Stanley Rose's. "You happenin', baby. I got me some im-potent bidness wit' you." Then I looked around her office and with an exaggerated smile continued, "What kin' o' po-leece depar'ment you runnin' here? I ain't seen me one donut in dis whole gat-dag buildin'."

She set her cup on the desk. "I don't know about the rest of the building, but neither Cynthia nor I want to wear any dough-nuts on our hips. Would you like me to ask her to bring you coffee?"

Back using my own voice, I said, "No thanks. I'd be afraid she'd spike it with arsenic...or Ex-Lax."

She shook her head but refused to comment for fear of encouraging me.

"I'm guessin' you were told I've got a big meeting at 9:30. What can I do for you...or are you planning to do something for me?"

"I have a question Janetta didn't ask you last night. It's concerning the gold Ford you say Leo Turner used. Was that exclusively his wheels, or did anyone else use it?"

"That was assigned to him personally. Ryan Leary made sure his people always got the new vehicles. Leo took the car home with him."

"I thought so but needed to be sure. I'm about ninety percent certain that Leo Turner did some kind of business with Paul D'Amato prior to his death. Janetta called Records and learned that no one could find any legitimate calls at D'Amato's house or in the immediate area. So, lacking good old police busi-ness, what were those two doing?"

Bettye did the one eyebrow thing again. "That's a good question. I assume you're going to find out."

"Sure, but I want as much information under my belt as possible before I confront Leo. He's been around the block enough to clam up and say the L word. I don't want that. Catching him in a lie would be great. Then I could hang something over his head and have something to bargain with. As I've always said, with interrogation, timing is everything."

"I remember. You're scary when you interrogate someone."

"It's an art every cop should master. And it's a lot of fun."

"Aside from having Leo in your sights, how are things coming along?"

"Things are beginning to move along nicely. I hope to get this D'Amato case—and maybe the Gonzalez murders—cleared up in a couple of days. Keep your fingers crossed that what I have planned works out well."

"You know I will, but right now, if you don't need anything else, I see it's 9:30, and I'm goin' to throw you out again. As much as I'd love to keep you around more, I do have real business a'waitin'."

I shrugged. "Always second best. I don't know why I work so hard for you."

She smiled and fluttered her eyelashes. "Yes, you do."

———

When I pulled into the office parking lot, I noticed something that looked blatantly like a rental car—a base model, white Chevy Malibu—parked near the entrance. When I opened the door and finished wiping the Ice-Go from my shoes on the welcome mat, I saw Velma Barnet standing in the middle of the room talking with John Gallagher.

"Morning," I said, while continuing to shed my coat and hang it on the rack.

Velma nodded and returned something someone might have mistaken as a civilized greeting, "Yeah, morning."

John said, "Velma brought some info on D'Amato's medical history."

"Nothing much," she said. "He has no history of being officially treated for depression or any other psychological problems. And no treatment or medication for HIV, AIDS or other STDs. But that doesn't mean some other shrink friend didn't treat him pro bono or off the books. Who knows if he got script under the table and bought the meds for cash—or self-medicated somehow. If you want to get something more concrete pointing toward suicide, you'll have to start checking local pharmacies."

John and I looked at each other.

I responded to Velma's statement. "Thank you and your boss for digging up that information. As far as trying to get records from a pharmacy, that could be a problem—two ways. They claim some amount of confidentiality with a customer's history. We could probably get around it with a court order, but judges are sticky about showing them probable cause. With what we've got right now, we'd be seen as just on a fishing expedition. We'll keep it in mind as a last resort, but that job of canvassing pharmacies might be rather daunting based on the number of people we've got to work the case."

"Oh, great," she said. "Is this looking like Lone Star is going to have to pay up?"

"I hate to disappoint you and the company, but as it stands now, this is looking more like a homicide than anything else. We should know more in a couple of days."

She shook her head in what could easily pass as genuine anger. "This is not going to go over well at the company. I just about promised them that I'd bring back a definite ruling of suicide. Shit! Any chance that brother-in-law did it or took out a contract?"

"Unknown at this time," John said. "But we're going to look into that."

"Unless I get a very good idea pretty soon, there may not be any reason for me to hang around here. I may as well go back to Texas where it's not so goddamn cold."

I shrugged and tried to look like I cared. "Sorry we couldn't provide better weather."

"Yeah, right." She tossed a business card onto Terri's desk and started for the door. "Give me a call when you know what you're doing." And then she was gone.

John looked from me to Janetta. "Wow. Miss Personality. Imagine being married to that?"

"No!" I said.

"How can one person be so hateful?" Janetta asked.

———

"John," I said, "It's too cold to be doing roofing jobs, and it's too early to be hunting chippies at a Spanish dance club. Let's track down Francisco the Ranger. Right now, he's got my vote to be the featured item at the Turd of the Month Club. We need to have a nice long talk with him."

"Sounds good. We gonna bring him here?"

"I was thinking about that. If we did, we'd have to chase Janetta away."

"Why would I have to leave?" she asked. "I've got things to do. Where would I go?"

"We can't really interrogate a guy with you working a few feet away. We're going to bring up some very questionable behavior. If you were close enough to hear, he'd be embarrassed to death and clam up...or maybe not. Who can be sure? Anyway, it wouldn't look very professional. Go across the street to AutoPro and ask Lee to change the oil in your car. Go to the mall. Go to lunch. It's been my experience that women can always find ways to kill time."

"Wouldn't you rather go to the Justice Center and use one of those sleazy little rooms with a beat-up old table and chair and a bare light bulb hanging over his head? You could scream at him and use a rubber hose or do whatever old-time detectives do."

"Not a bad idea, but we scrapped the rubber hoses when we stopped wearing fedoras, back when Nehru jackets, love beads and leisure suits were in fashion."

"You're right though," John said. "This office is too friendly. An interview room would be better. Call your cousin, the Sheriff, Janetta, and ask her to arrange for a comfy place for us to do our thing."

———

Before leaving the office, I called Bo Stallins.

"We've gotten some info that looks important to your Gonzalez murders," I said.

"Glad someone's makin' some progress. Whaddaya know?"

I had rolled things over in my mind a lot since learning that Cliff Harvey could have known the same information days earlier had he not alienated a crucial witness. The easy way to handle it would have been dumping it in Bettye's lap and moving on, but maybe Cliff Harvey needed a little reeducation more than being humiliated in front of the Sheriff. Bo Stallins was the lead detective on the case. That ultimately left the responsibility of success or failure on his shoulders. Effectively, his partner might have screwed him out of an important clearance-by-arrest and left the case relegated to the unsolved status with Bo writing obligatory updates every twenty-eight days. Bo needed to know what John and I found out and how we came upon it.

"I've got good news, but also some bad news," I said.

"Uh oh."

"Nothing drastic, but I've got to tell you something that won't make you happy."

"Now that you've got me thinkin' the worst, spit it out, brother."

"Like I said, we've got important stuff...and you should have had it days ago, except Harvey screwed up."

"Oh, man, what happened?"

I told Bo what Belinda Cancel had said about Cliff Harvey's lousy bedside manner and the information she ultimately gave us.

"Gat dag it!" he said." "Cliff's a pretty good detective, but, man, cain't he jest put his foot in his mouth sometimes. Sam, I'm sorry. What do you want to do? Tell the Sheriff?"

"Depends on Harvey. I'd rather not involve Bettye if he shows a little remorse and acts like he learned something. But, if he behaves like a nitwit, I don't plan on taking any crap from him. Hey look, Bo, anyone can make a mistake, but if what Belinda Cancel says is accurate, you're going to need to keep a choke collar on him. What she described wasn't a mistake, and he needs a serious attitude adjustment."

"I hear ya. Want me to take care of it?"

"I'm not trying to kiss this off on you. You're not his supervisor, and I won't suggest you rat him out to Bledsoe or Joiner. I'll talk to Harvey—cop to cop—hoping he'll see a need to change his approach to some people. If that doesn't work, I'll see Bettye. Everything is up to him."

"Lord have mercy. Sometimes it jest pays to stay in bed."

According to Ramón Goldbloom, Francisco Gonzalez lived on a side street off Old Knoxville Pike in South Knoxville. We found no evidence to lead us to believe that he still didn't. I didn't want to spook him by calling first, so we took the drive north on East Broadway that changed names to Old Knoxville Pike, but remained alternately known as Tennessee Route 33. All that could easily confuse any GPS.

The house sat on the corner of Thirty-three and the side street directly across from a clothing manufacturer's warehouse and shipping facility, surrounded by an eight-foot cyclone fence topped with steel arms tilting outward at a forty-five-degree angle and strung with four rows of barbed wire. On top of all that, rolls of razor-edged concertina wire provided one more deterrent to burglars. We were not in one of the more prosperous neighborhoods of Knox County.

John knocked on the front door of the house where Goldbloom and other records showed to be the digs of Cisco Gonzalez.

A heavyset woman in her fifties answered the door. If nothing else, John and I look like cops. As soon as she laid eyes on us, her expression immediately turned from neutral to concerned.

"Yes?" she said cautiously.

"We work for the Blount County Sheriff," John said, holding up his snazzy silver and gold-colored badge. "Is Francisco Gonzalez home?"

"Is he in trouble?" she asked with a fairly heavy Hispanic accent.

"No," John said. "We just need to ask him more questions about his family. Do you know what happened?"

"Yes. Madre di Dios. It was terrible, no? I feel so sorry."

"Is he here?" I asked.

"You have to go around to the side." She pointed to her right, our left. "There are steps. He rents the upstairs. His car is here. He must be home."

"Thank you," John said.

We walked to the left side of the house and along an unpaved driveway with sparse gravel under dead or dormant grass and weeds. It looked as if the place had been converted to a two family with a full-length dormer that stretched across the back of the house. A wooden staircase led to a door on the second floor.

A shocking blue Subaru Imprezza WRX sport sedan sat on the frozen ground just east of the steps. I noted down the plate number, took a quick snapshot with my phone and walked around the car looking into the dark tinted windows. Except for some splash dirt from the light snow on the roads, the car looked very clean inside and out. It sported a large and functional hood scoop and a ridiculous spoiler that rose more than a foot above the trunk lid. A right-out-of-the-showroom instant street rod.

We trudged up the steps. The farther up we went, the wind from which a row of tall hedges protected us on the ground made everything feel colder. I knocked on the door. The salsa music we heard through the door died just after I knocked. A long moment later, a young man wearing a black tank top answered the door. His shirt was skintight and showed that he probably spent lots of time lifting weights. His black Levis were as tight as the shirt. Facially he was an extremely good-looking man in his thirties. His hair was still cut short enough to please an Army first sergeant. If he had ever gotten a break in show business, he could have been cast as a heartthrob on one of the soap operas broadcast on Telemundo.

"Cisco Gonzalez?" I asked.

"Yes, sir, who are you?"

I showed him a badge. "Investigators, Blount County Sheriff's Office. If you don't mind, we need a little of your time?"

"Is this about my children and Margarita? I already told two other investigators all I know. We were separated. I haven't seen them in a long while." He spoke with a slight accent that would have made Ricardo Montalban jealous and made girls feel giddy.

"You're going to get cold standing in the open doorway," I said. "It's freezing out here. May we come in?"

"Yes, I guess so."

He turned and stepped into the small living room. We followed. Cisco must have had the thermostat set on eighty. I wondered if the blast of hot air would cause my deodorant to fail. Cisco sat on a padded rocking chair. John and I parked it on a wood-framed sofa. A set of weights—barbells and dumbbells—and a bench press bench sat on the floor next to us.

"What is this all about?" he asked.

"We're getting close to knowing something," I said. "I think you might be a big help. We'd like you to come into Maryville with us so we can show you a few things we don't have with us. We'll drive you there and back."

"How long will this take?"

"Probably not long. You ready to go?"

He hesitated answering then, "I need a warm coat, yes?"

"Si." I said. "Mucho fria out there, amigo."

He smiled and went to a closet to grab a winter jacket.

We descended the steps and when we hit the ground, I said, "Nice wheels you've got there, Cisco."

"Thank you, sir. It's a nice car, I think."

"Just get it?"

"It's a 2010, but new, a leftover, almost two years old. I got a good deal. Not a car for everyone. They had it sitting on the lot in Knoxville for a long time, I think."

"I hear they're pretty fast.'

"Oh, yes, very quick."

"Expensive?"

"This STi, the special edition, is more than the standard model, but not so much."

Probably had to pose naked a few times to come up with the down payment. I hope your kids had new sneakers.

"We're parked out front," John said.

It took us almost thirty minutes to get to the Justice Center. As we approached the CID squad room, I found Lieutenant D. L. Joiner standing next to a detective's desk discussing something.

"Hello, Sam," he said.

"Hello, LT. I understand you've got a room we can use."

"Sure. Interview Two is ready. Need anything?"

"Thanks. We're good. But if you would, tell Bo Stallins that we're here, and I'll get with him when we're finished."

"Will do. Holler if ya need anything."

I nodded and led Cisco to the interview room. John brought up the rear.

On the road back to the Justice Center, I noticed a change in Cisco's whole being. He became quiet, almost sulky. John and I attempted to engage him in conversation, establish a rapport before any serious questioning, but he responded with only a *Yessir* or *Nosir*. In the long hallway from the squad room to the little ten-by-ten cubicle where we would chat, he didn't walk or stroll. He marched—head up, shoulders back, a perfect 180 steps per minute. He had lapsed into soldier mode. Maybe he considered himself a POW.

We found the door to Interrogation Room Two open. I extended my arm toward the small table and two chairs.

"Have a seat. Make yourself comfortable."

Cisco moved the chair out from the table, planted his

bottom on the padded seat and sat at attention, palms flat on the table, stiff as a board.

We needed to get him to loosen up. I was afraid that if he stayed in that posture too long, he'd be in danger of popping one of the internal springs within him coiled so tightly they were close to the breaking point.

I took the seat across from him. John leaned against the wall to his right. Cisco focused his gaze straight ahead as if looking through me. His eyes took on the familiar look any former combat soldier calls the *thousand yard* stare, something inherited by people who were subjected to prolonged periods of stress and emotional trauma. I never heard of a true cure for it.

"I understand you were in the Army," I said. "Who were you with?"

"3rd Division, sir. 2nd Battalion, 7th Infantry, Reconnaissance Platoon."

"Eleven Bravo?" I asked, using the Army's military occupational specialty code for light weapons infantryman.

"Yessir. Eleven Bravo all the way."

Damn. Audie Murphy, eat your heart out.

"When you were stateside, where did you serve?" I knew where the 3rd Division called home. I wanted to be sure he did.

"Fort Stewart, Georgia, sir."

So far, so good.

"Uh huh. The 7th Infantry has quite an impressive history. How many times did you deploy overseas?"

"Three times, sir, during Operation Iraqi Freedom. First time in 2003, then a long tour—eighteen months—from 2004 to 2006. Then we went back again in 2007."

I let out a long breath. I truly felt sorry for him and any other GI in the same boat. "More than your share of hard tours. Didn't see much of your family while you were in."

"Nosir. That's why I didn't re-up."

But then you left your family again voluntarily.

"With seven years in, I'm guessing you were a staff sergeant?"

"Yessir. Squad leader in the recon platoon."

"Good job?"

"Yessir. Loved it."

I nodded and gave him a fatherly smile, like one old soldier to another.

"Before we speak about what happened to your family, I'd like to ask you about another incident we're investigating. I think you might be able to help us because you knew one of the people involved—the victim."

He didn't respond to that. No comment. No movement. Certainly, no flinch.

"We're looking into the death of a Doctor D'Amato. We've heard that you knew him in his role as VA counselor."

He forced his brow to wrinkle. "Who? I don't think I know him, sir."

Bad answer.

"Paul D'Amato. A psychiatrist. You attended a number of his group sessions with other vets. And you spoke to him one on one. Paul D'Amato."

"Oh, sorry, sir. Doctor Paul. Yes, I know him."

"Mind if I ask why you took advantage of the VA benefit and saw a therapist?"

"Yessir. I mean nosir. I don't mind. After three tours in Iraq —we got into some serious shit over there, sir—I guess I've got to say my head got screwed up. I was having trouble sleeping. I couldn't hold my temper dealing with Margarita and the children. I didn't hit them or anything, but everything they did pissed me off—real bad. They really didn't do anything terrible, but I had big trouble dealing with civilians in general. I figured I could get help from the VA. The Army owed me that much."

I raised my eyebrows. "I understand. It's an old story. Young soldiers catch the brunt of the shit in any war. They shouldn't be asked to do and see things the brass expects of them. I was in the Army, and Investigator Gallagher was in the Navy...And we thank you for your service."

"Yes, sir, just doing the job."

"Sure. Before we go on, would you like something to drink? Coffee? Tea? Soda? Water?"

"No, sir. I'm good."

"Need the men's room?" John asked.

"No, sir."

We continued for almost another hour, getting nowhere. I looked at John and raised my eyebrows, my signal to see if he agreed with me moving forward, away from Mr. Nice Guy and dropping a bomb or two in Cisco's lap. He winked.

"So, during all the times you saw Doctor Paul, he never was anything but cool and professional toward you, even though he hired your wife to clean his home? He never acted friendly or familiar? Always remained distant?"

"Yes, sir. He may have looked a little depressed, but like I said, he always acted professional with me. He never told me about himself."

I sighed for a little theatrical effect. "Really? What if I told you we have seen things to make us believe otherwise?"

"I don't know what you mean, sir."

"I think you do, Cisco. Let's drop the act and cut the crap. We've seen photos of you that came from the doctor's computer. Those pictures were of a *very personal* nature? These are the pictures Margarita found by accident. Remember now?"

He said nothing to that. His almost black, hard-as-nails eyes bored into mine.

"You don't want to comment?"

"Do I need a lawyer?"

"Posing for photos naked is not a crime. Homosexuality is not a crime. I just wish you wouldn't lie about your relationship with Paul."

His jaw muscles began working a mile a minute, grinding his teeth together. Finally, he spoke, "I am no *maricon*, sir." He used a Spanish term for *homosexual*.

"Okay. What were the photos about?"

"I work out. I have a good body. Paul, he liked to look at pictures of men. He said he liked the photos best if he *knew* those men. He offered me money. I thought what the hell, man. I don't work all twelve months a year as a roofer. I can always use extra cash. Why not make money? It's not like other guys haven't seen me naked. Guys were his thing, man, not mine."

"Was this relationship with Paul why you left Margarita?"

"I told you, man, I am no queer. Me and Margarita, that's a long story. No. She just didn't make me happy anymore. With her and the kids in that little house, I always felt up tight—strangled."

"But she confronted you with those photos. I'm sure she wasn't very happy about that. Did she make fun of you? Did she call you names? Did she threaten to tell your children? Did it make you mad enough to kill? Did you kill Doctor Paul for letting those pictures fall into the wrong hands? Did you kill Margarita to keep her quiet and kill the children because they witnessed what you did? Did you panic?"

"No, man, stop! Stop! None of that. Now I want a lawyer. I'm not answering no more questions."

So, I had progressed from sir to man. How quickly basic military courtesy fades when you accuse a man of murder.

"Okay, don't answer any more questions. I won't ask any, but I can and will tell you things you need to think about. Now let's get to it."

We continued for a total of five and a half hours. I tried my best to get inside his head and make him cry *uncle*. I wanted him to think that without us on his side he would face the most horrible experience of his life—worse than any Islamic terrorist could provide. But Cisco wouldn't go for spit. He knew nothing about how Paul D'Amato died. He knew nothing about the murders of his estranged wife and two children. Throughout the ordeal he remained sitting in the position of attention, his eyes focused on a spot on the wall behind me. He refused all our offers of liquid refreshment, food or a bathroom break. When John and I finally agreed that we were bumping our heads into a brick wall, we cut Cisco loose and arranged for a uniformed cop to drive him home.

———

We started heading back to the office in the borrowed detective ride Bettye had just loaned me while we continued to work full time on her cold case. We had been putting too many miles on our personal cars to justify the mileage allowance. Before we got too far, I came up with an idea.

"You got Bill Horne's phone number handy?"

"Yeah. I got all his personal info and statement in the case folder."

"Give him a call and see if he's home. I snapped a photo of Cisco's hot wheels. That thing stands out like an elephant in a flea circus. Let's ask Bill if he's seen it parked at D'Amato's house, especially on the day the doctor died."

John tapped in the number and got a quick answer.

"Bill? John Gallagher from the Sheriff's Office. Are you at home now?"

He waited for an answer and then laughed.

"Okay, we'll see you in a few. The Boss wants you to look at a picture he took...okay. We'll be there in ten—fifteen minutes."

"What's so funny?"

"When I asked if he was home, he said, 'It's cold as a bastard out there. I cancelled my tennis game. Of course I'm home.'"

"Typical cop. A smartass. No wonder you two get along so well."

"What? You don't like him?"

"He's fine, but he's still a smartass."

Fifteen minutes later, we were seated in the Horne's living room with Marian asking if we wanted coffee, tea, beer or some of the batch of chocolate chip-peanut butter cookies that had been out of the oven long enough for them to be edible.

Like a hungry teenager, John said, "I love peanut butter cookies."

She looked at me with an implied question.

"What the heck," I said, "I like cookies, too."

"Coffee?" she asked looking at the three of us.

"Make coffee," Bill said. "You can't eat cookies without something to wash them down. Coffee would be great. It's cold out there. You can't give them iced tea."

"Wow," I said. "Just like going to my grandmother's house."

"Yeah, right," Bill said. "What did you want to show me?"

I took my phone from my jacket pocket, pulled up the picture of Cisco's WRX and handed the phone to Bill. "Ever see this thing at D'Amato's house?"

It didn't take him ten seconds to answer. "Sure. Plenty of times. Who could forget something like that? Stupid kid's car. You know anything about spoilers?"

He didn't give us a second to answer.

"When I went to the pursuit driving course back at the PD —second time around—I asked because at that time everything from a piece of crap like this to an old lady's family sedan had one as an option. The guy running the class told me that they do nothing to improve handling unless you're going over 110 miles an hour. Ha. You go that fast on a public highway, and you'll find your ass locked up."

"How about that?" I said. "So, you saw it there often?"

"Often? What's often? I don't know. I saw it there a bunch of times. I guess that's often. Obviously, you know who drives it. What's his story?"

"Give me a minute, and I'll tell you. How about the day D'Amato died. Did you see this car there?"

"I'd love to make your life easy and say yes, but I just don't know. I know what they'd want in court, and I can't give you that—a definite yes—nope. Sorry."

"No sweat. Worth a try. The guy who owns the car is the ex-husband of D'Amato's former cleaning woman. She's the one killed in Maryville along with her two kids. So now, we've got him connected with all the others. What started out as a death of a doctor has become what sounds like murder times four."

"So you got the bastard?"

"Not exactly."

CHAPTER ELEVEN

Back in the car, heading toward the office again, John said, "How about that?"

"How about what?"

"What Bill said."

"Yeah? He said a few things while you were wolfing down most of the cookies Marian made."

"You heard him. He said that if we ever needed help with an investigation, he'd like to pitch in. That's good, huh?"

"Yeah, I think it is. That way if you take on one of those divorce cases I tell you not to touch with a ten foot pole, you've got a new partner to peep into keyholes with."

"What are you so uptight about?"

"I'm not uptight. I think he's a good guy—probably a pretty good cop in his day."

"So?"

"So?"

"That's what I said."

"So, if we get something that requires an experienced pair of eyes, give him a call. But don't forget Terri. She's got a whole working life ahead of her, and if we can teach her how to be a world-class detective like us, we should do it."

"Okay, I agree. But speaking about world-class detectives and what I said about us being such good interrogators, what happened with The Cisco Kid?"

"Not our finest hour—or hours—almost six of them, and that bastard wouldn't budge. It's like he went into some kind of military trance. I couldn't believe it. I still think he's good for at least one of those murders, but we may need a stick of dynamite to move him."

———

We made a brief stop in the office, basically to drop off the keys to the PD sedan and close up for the night. Janetta had already left.

I dropped off my portion of the case documents on Terri's desk. "John, I've about had it with this case, I hate having to pick up someone else's mess or screw-up. If we had this squeal on day one, we'd have had someone in cuffs in two days. Thank you, Leo Turner, you bastard."

"I didn't know Turner too well, but he never seemed like a good detective. You know, if he couldn't knuckle up a suspect, he couldn't clear a case. It was always like he had one foot out to lunch."

"What?"

"What, what? You don't think he was a piss poor cop?"

"I agree with that, but what was that one foot thing?"

"The old saying. Don't tell me you never heard it."

"Maybe I heard a different version—or two."

"Yeah? Like what?"

"Forget it. I just came up with another reason to think of

myself as a moron. There are not enough hours in a day to work this, and we're forgetting things that may be important."

"Like what?"

"Like the thumb drive we got from Belinda."

"We already know Cisco is on it. He admitted that."

"Yeah, but Belinda said there were also other men—in the same condition."

"Naked."

"Right, and to use her words, doing filthy things."

"You want to look at a whole computer full of naked men?"

"We really shouldn't ask Janetta or Terri to do it. It's you or me, buddy. There may be someone there with more to lose than young Cisco if their skivvy pictures became public knowledge."

"You want to start tomorrow?"

"It may not take too long. I'll take it home and start on it tonight."

"Better you than me."

"You remember Joe Kelski? He worked in Criminal Intelligence for years."

"Yeah, sure. His wife and mine were pregnant at the same time. In fact, they went into Smithtown General the same day and delivered only minutes apart. Our kids were born at the same age."

I couldn't help shaking my head. "Wow. Born at the same age? Who'da thunk it? Anyway, he always used to say: 'Sometimes ya gotta take one for the team.'"

"Still, looking at a bunch of naked guys? That sucks."

"Yeah, like a bunch of amateur male strippers are worse than looking at a thirty-three-year-old woman and her two kids shot in the head with a .45."

———

Kate and I were sitting in the dining room. She wanted to look at the small collection of ceramic snowmen she had added to a wall shelf and the hutch while we ate dinner. George Winston's album *Winter* was playing on the stereo. It made me want to turn the thermostat up two degrees to feel warmer.

"Are you any closer to solving this doctor thing you're working on for Bettye?" she asked.

"The quick answer: No."

I slurped up a spoonful of her homemade gumbo and rice. She took a minute sip from a footed glass of red wine.

"And the long version?"

I sighed. "We know a lot more than when we started, but not enough to definitively say what happened to good old Doctor Demento. Certainly not enough to arrest anyone if, in fact, he was murdered like I suspect."

"How much longer can you give it?"

"It's been kicking around for six months already as a closed case. There's really no rush. The other side of the coin is the Gonzalez murders. They were very cold assassinations. Someone needs to answer for that."

"But that's not your case."

"True, but Bo Stallins and his partner are coming up with nothing. I think everything is much too close to be a coincidence. Demento and Margarita Gonzalez and her weirdo husband are all connected."

"Will you stop calling the man Demento? You're going to slip one day and say that in front of a reporter."

"Yeah. That's what I told John." To keep from hearing more of my political incorrectness, I popped a shrimp into my mouth, chewed and told her, "Great Gumbo, Cutie-pie. You must be Polish-Cajun or something."

She made a face. "Yes, or something. What are you doing next, Sherlock?"

"Next is asking you to pass that basket of French bread. Then I'm going to finish this gumbo and my second glass of vin rouge before I search a computer file of naked men to see if I can find anyone famous."

She wrinkled up her nose. "Naked men? Famous naked men? You certainly work at a strange job."

"You can look if you want. Just don't distract me with heavy breathing."

"Thank you, no. You may be getting older and grayer, but my darling, you still look good with your clothes off. You're the only man I want to see naked."

———

It didn't take me more than twenty minutes to find what I wanted. I popped the thumb drive out of my computer tower, stuck it into my pocket and went downstairs to tell my wife about my success and make a celebratory nightcap before watching TV.

"Bonanza!" I said.

"I'm almost afraid to ask what you found."

"Then I'll tell you before you ask. I found my stick of dynamite, but I may be planting it under a different ass than I first thought."

CHAPTER TWELVE

S aturday morning and we all came into work again. After finishing the morning amenities in the office, I told John to continue gobbling up the biscuits and gravy he brought in from Hardees and listen up to my recent revelation. Janetta wasn't hard to draw into the drama. She continued to sip her coffee and listened attentively.

"You remember me insisting that these four deaths must be somehow connected. I just had a feeling but couldn't figure how."

John continued chewing and nodded. Janetta lowered her cup and nodded.

I held up the little black plastic thumb drive. "This is the key. It's not the smoking .45 we're looking for, but you will not believe who just became players in this fiasco."

"Who?" Janetta asked.

"Yeah, come on, Boss. Don't keep us in suspense," John said as he shoveled more saturated fat and cholesterol into his mouth.

I grinned like a little kid who just caught a ten-pound catfish in a small pond. "Okay, wait for it. You know that this holds Demento's collection of porn on it, right?"

Again, they nodded.

"So, if Cisco Gonzalez isn't guilty—he may be, but maybe not—who is?"

"Like you said last night," John offered, "someone else who doesn't want the world to know he poses nude for the pleasure of some other guy."

"Yes, and take a wild guess at who showed up on the thumb drive, in the buff, and not alone?"

"How would we know that?" Janetta said.

"You wouldn't. So, I'll tell you. How about our old buddy, brutal cop, conspiratorial serial killer and apparent sex maniac, Ryan Leary?"

"Leary?" John said, almost choking on his greasy biscuit. "Leary is in the slammer."

"Yes, he is," I said. "Has been since August. But when did Doctor Demento die?"

"June 20th," Janetta said.

"You think Leary whacked Demento?" John asked.

"Who knows? But somehow the good doctor had a bunch of photos of a quite naked Leary doing things I won't explain now with some pretty young boys and girls and even one of those famous Thailand he/shes who he obviously met on one of his Southeast Asian sex junkets."

"Why do I feel stupid asking what is a he/she?" Janetta said."

"It is just what it sounds like. Very pretty young Siamese boys made up to look like girls. Only once you see all of them, you know they certainly weren't born girls."

"Oh. A young Thai transvestite?"

"Yes. I know enforcement of the statuary sex crimes is pretty lax in Thailand, but I doubt that anyone on the Federal parole board wouldn't look unfavorably on Ryan Leary if this information got out before he became eligible. If having sex with a transvestite or people of both genders was Leary's thing, he should have had his picture taken with those who were quite a bit older."

"Whoa," John said. "Slow down. Okay, maybe Leary had something to do with killing Demento, but he was behind bars, wearing stripes when Gonzalez and her kids were murdered."

"Yes, but wait, there's more. Leary is not the only familiar face I found in the collection."

"Oh, jeez," John said. "Who's next?"

"How about Leo Turner and some woman who wasn't shy about being photographed *in flagrante delicto*—in the very most *indelicato* ways."

"So now you think Turner killed Margarita and the kids?" John said, looking exasperated.

"Probably. Maybe. At least it's a thought, and I think he could be that coldblooded. Nothing I've said is etched in stone but look at these two new characters dumped in our laps. Could you get any more sleazy operators? Leary is capable of anything, and Turner jumps on his bandwagon whenever Leary says he needs a henchman."

"Who says *henchman* anymore?" Janetta asked. "That sounds like dialogue from one of those old cowboy movies my father used to watch."

"What's with you Galloway women?" I said. "Your cousin loved to break my chops. When she left, you took over."

She smiled. "I guess you're just lucky then."

"Huh. I can't wait for my luck to run out."

The words weren't out of my mouth when the phone rang. Janetta answered. "Sam, a Detective Sipe for you."

"Rocky Sipe?"

"Didn't say."

I picked up the extension on Terri's desk. "Sam Jenkins."

"Hey, Chief. You doin' aw right t'day?"

I recognized the voice. "Not bad, Rocky. Howzit goin'?"

Detective Rockwell Sipe worked in the Narcotics Unit at the Sheriff's office.

"Not too bad. Listen, reason I'm callin' is I got me a young feller here we done for possession with intent. When I gave him the ol' story about the only way he's gonna get away without doin' serious hard time was ta give us somebody bigger an' badder than him, he whipped out your business card and says that you told him if he ever needed he'p ta give you a call. This here's his phone call."

"Who is this guy?"

"Name's Justin Samples."

"Never heard of him. He say how he knows me?"

"Not in detail."

"Can you put him on the phone?"

"Sure thing. Hang on. I gotta uncuff 'im."

A long moment later, "Mr. Jenkins, you there?"

"Yeah, this is Sam Jenkins. Who is this?"

"This is Justin, sir. I was at the VA meetin' where you was the other day."

"Justin? Oh, yeah, you stood up and gave information about Doctor d'Amato."

"No, sir, that was Jason. I'm Justin."

"Sorry, my mistake. Detective Sipe says you were arrested. What is it you think I can do for you?"

"Well, sir, the detective, he said I might get me some slack if I could give some info about somethin' big. I can do that."

"And what is this big thing you know about?"

"I can tell ya all about who killed Doctor Paul."

CHAPTER THIRTEEN

That took me by surprise. "Really? How do you know this, Justin?"

"The man who done it told me all about it."

I felt like the Clue Fairy just stuck a big one under my pillow...but I didn't want to get too excited before further exploring Justin's story.

"Listen carefully now, Justin. For this to do you any good, and for Detective Sipe and me to go to the DA on your behalf, we'd need a lot more than just a story about what some guy told you. We need what's called corroboration. What you say may be interesting, but we'd need a lot more evidence to arrest someone and go to court. Understand?"

"Yessir, yessir. How about if I got the whole thing recorded?"

"What do you mean recorded? This guy just let you record his confession? That's crazy."

"Nosir, it ain't. Swear ta God. We was drinkin' some, and I got him tellin' me all about what he done. I switched on the video camera on my phone and let'er rip before he got in my car and left it goin' while we's talkin'."

"You have this phone and video with you now?"

"Yessir. Right here. The detective, he's got all my property."

"Put him on the phone."

"Hello?"

"Rocky, do you have a phone in his property capable of video recording something?"

"I do. Got me an iPhone right here."

"I'll be there in ten minutes."

"In our office. We'll be a'waitin on ya."

———

John and I hotfooted down to the Justice Center. We went through the back door and made our way to the Narcotic Unit's office, tucked away from almost everything else on the backside of the first floor. The secretary we spoke to made a call, and in only moments Rocky Sipe came out to meet us.

Rocky was the senior man in the unit and had been in that assignment for most of his time at the Sheriff's office. He was one of those narco cops who, I thought, could never do anything but deal with hopheads. He looked and acted the part too well to perhaps ever integrate back into polite police work. But who knows? If he became interested, maybe he could put on a three-piece suit and deal with white-collar criminals like Donald Trump. He stood six foot tall, was a burly 200 pounds with more than a few tattoos running up both forearms. He wore a T-shirt even in winter, a dirty Atlanta braves ball cap and always sported a four-day stubble.

Justin Samples was a skinny kid of twenty-seven, an Army veteran dressed in blue jeans and an orange over-the-head Polar

Fleece pullover with a big University of Tennessee T on the left side of his chest. His dark hair was skinned to white walls on the sides with a wide strip of spiky darkness running from his forehead down to the back of his neck. His goofy blue eyes blinked faster than the shutter of a camera set on motor drive. If I had seen him in the 1960s, I would have thought he was a soldier who just got a seventy-five-cent haircut, went AWOL, and hadn't shaved for two weeks. He smiled immediately when I walked into the room.

"Hey, Mr. Jenkins, sir. How ya doin'? Remember me?"

I looked him over carefully. "No, sorry. I'm afraid I don't. You say you were at the VA group session where I spoke?"

"Yessir. Right there in the church, settin' right up front while you's talkin' ta us. I took one o' your cards and remembered what ya said—'bout if we ever needed he'p, we should give ya a call."

"And now you've got yourself in a jackpot, and here I am."

He grinned like I was his fairy godfather.

"By the way," I said, "this is my partner Investigator Gallagher." I poked my thumb over my shoulder in John's direction.

He looked up at John. "How you doin', sir?"

"Never better, kid."

"According to Detective Sipe, you're in pretty deep shit," I said, wanting him to know getting out of major trouble wasn't going to be a walk in the park.

He nodded almost as fast as he was blinking. John and I pulled over a couple of chairs and sat close to the boy.

"You're pretty hyped up, Justin. You on something?"

"Nosir. Nosir. I'm just nervous, I guess."

"Huh. When was the last time you did some drugs?"

He changed from nodding to shaking his head side to side. "I ain't done nuthin' for a long time—Nosir. Not a *long time.*

Maybe, I'm guessin' now—since two o'clock last night, uh, two o'clock this mornin' ta be exact."

"Yeah, right, ancient history."

Out of the corner of my eye, I saw Rocky Sipe grin and then heard Gallagher snort.

"What's the story, Justin? You just happened to be making a video, and some guy walked up and confessed to killing Dr. Paul D'Amato?"

More head shaking. "Nosir, nosir, nuthin' like that. I hate ta admit it, and I hope ya'all might cut me some slack right here and now 'bout what I'm gonna confess, but ta get me the he'p I need, I gotta 'fess up that I was sellin' some of my product to this guy I know. I usually don't do somethin' like that, 'cause what I have is usually only for my own use, you unnerstand, but I knew this guy pretty good—from the VA group, as a matter of fact, and when I met him and he's lookin' kinda funny and ..."

"Whoa, Justin. Slow down. We've got all day. Go slow. Take it easy. You want some water or something?"

"Oh, yessir. I wouldn't mind havin' me a Dr. Pepper or somethin'. Don't much matter what."

I looked at Gallagher and rolled my eyes. "John, would you mind getting Justin a cold regional beverage—something without caffeine—juice maybe."

"Sure. Be right back."

"Okay, Justin, let's take it from the top. Where did you meet this guy when you recorded his confession?"

To augment his other hyper behavior, Justin's right knee began bopping up and down to some upbeat music only he could hear. "Outside the Taco Bell across from the airport. He wanted ta buy somethin' from me."

"Some of that two ounces of cocaine Detective Sipe took from you?"

"Uh, yessir, like I said, I don't usually sell nuthin' and I mean *nuthin'*, but I was havin' a little cash flow problem, and this guy I know, he needed a little blow 'cause he was goin' to try and catch some tail at a club up ta Knoxville. The girls go for guys who can supply a bit o' coke, ya know."

I nodded. "Sure. That's been my experience, too. Why the video?"

"Well, sir, even though I know this guy, well, I really don't *know* him, know him and I don't trust him much. See, he's pretty pumped—a weightlifter and all—really tough lookin' and I ain't but 'bout one-forty and I ain't no badass. But I figger I got ta protect myse'f 'case he says he'll pay for a gram, and then he ups and decides ta rip me off and take everything I had on me and kindalike whoup my ass."

"Sure. That's smart. So, you cranked up your phone before he got there and let 'er rip?"

"Yessir. Just like that. But I didn't need to 'cause he didn't rip me off, and later on, it was Detective Sipe who seen me sellin' a little more product ta someone else and... Well, here I am."

"Yeah. Here you are—needing a favor. And you're telling me this guy who you sort of know meets you in a parking lot to buy a gram of blow and ups and confesses to killing a doctor you both know."

"Truth be told, that's not exactly what happened."

I blew out a little air. "Talk us through it, Justin. Make me believe this is real."

"Swear ta God, Mr. Jenkins, this happened. You'll see it for your own self. Just wait. Now, sir, I's sittin' in my car a'waitin' for 'im. He gets there, comes ta my car and sits in the shotgun seat. Me, I'm lettin' my phone record the whole thing—for my protection like."

"Sure. What happened next?"

"Well, 'cause I know this guy for a while, us bein' vets and all, I guess, I offer him a drink. I got me a bottle o' tequila, and since he's Mexican or somethin' like that and I figger a drink was just the right thing ta do—buildin' goodwill with a customer and all."

"Yeah. Sounds like good business sense."

"Yessir. That's why I done it."

With that, John Gallagher stepped into the room and handed Justin a sixteen-ounce bottle of Tropicana.

"Here ya go, kid," he said. "Bottoms up."

"Thank ya, sir. How much do I owe ya?"

"On the house," John said. "Drink up."

Justin unscrewed the cap and gulped down one third of the pint.

"Feel better, Justin?" I asked. Junkies love OJ.

He nodded.

"Let's get back to the story."

"Yessir. Where was I?"

"In the car giving your buddy some tequila."

"Oh, yeah. So, I say, 'You gonna get some poontang with the blow I give ya?' He says no doubt he'll score. The girls up in this Spanish club always come through."

"Yeah, okay. This is getting to be an epic. When does he get to the Doctor D'Amato part?"

"Oh, right." Justin took another long pull on his OJ. "I mentioned somethin' about you comin' down to the VA meetin' and askin' about Doctor Paul. You askin' if anyone thought he was depressed enough to maybe commit suicide. This guy laughed and said you didn't know what you was talkin' about. He said Doctor Paul wasn't depressed, he was just a faggot and didn't like bein' one.

"Well, sir, we drunk a bit more—almost the whole pint. And let me tell ya, sir, that Mexican shit goes ta my head quick like. Seemed like he was gettin' a bit tight himse'f. Then he says that one time while they's doin' a one-on-one session, the doctor, he kinda like comes on to him—this guy that is. Says the doctor was lookin' for sex. So, this guy, he says he didn't want no part of the doctor no more. That's why he quit comin' to the group sessions and didn't go to see him no more."

"That's it?"

"Nosir. No. He said he went back one more time, but brought a gun with him. When Doctor Paul came on to him again and wouldn't stop, this guy, he shot him after he, the doctor, grabbed for—you know—the guy's package."

I didn't want to look too excited over what I'd heard, but I did let my eyes wander over to John and then to Rocky Sipe.

"And you've got all this recorded on your phone?"

"Yessir, right there next ta the detective."

"Are you sure you've got video that will ID this guy and everything he said? The courts are not big on us getting voice comparisons introduced into evidence."

"Got me some video of him, but mostly it's just talkin'. I needed ta put the phone down ta look natural. I couldn't like actually point it at him the whole time."

"Okay, very good. And what's this guy's name?"

"Cisco. Cisco Gonzalez."

We watched a few seconds of the video, saw the Cisco Gonzalez that we all knew and loved get into Justin's old Camry and then only saw the rear view mirror recorded after Justin placed the phone, screen up, on the dashboard. But the audio portion went pretty much as the young man described.

John and I adjourned to the CID squad room where we wrote up applications for an arrest warrant for Francisco Gonzalez and a search warrant for his rented apartment and his car. Cisco could slip into his tough guy military trance, give me any kind of thousand-yard stare he wanted, but with his confession recorded, he was well-done toast. His only hope was to sign a formal confession and cooperate fully to entertain any hope for a lenient deal from the district attorney.

After proofreading everything, I called the duty ADA and asked for an appointment with the interim DA, Moira Menzies —on her day off.

"How in God's name did you get this?" Moira asked, referring to the recorded confession.

"I didn't. Rocky Sipe popped some simpleton for cocaine possession, and he's using the recording to negotiate a deal. This clears a botched-up unattended death investigation that's part of our favorite detective Leo Turner's legacy. He initially called it an accident. I think this guy Gonzalez may be good for the murders of his ex-wife and two children, too. But that remains to be seen. Please give this Samples kid some consideration when he gets before a judge."

"For a murder that may have forever gone unsolved, yes, I will."

"Thanks. After we collar Gonzalez, I'll let you know where we stand with the other murders. Whenever you have some spare time, I'll explain what we learned today. You'll be surprised to hear who may be involved up to their eyeballs. I don't know anything certain about who killed the Gonzalez family, but we're probably on the right track."

"Okay. I can hardly wait. Now, let's go see the on-call judge. Be nice to him. He came in on his day off and may not be receptive to any of your sarcasm."

"When have you known me to be sarcastic?"

"Oh, spare me."

With our warrants in hand, John and I first stopped to call Bettye Lambert and update her on the cases. From there, we picked up Bo Stallins, Cliff Harvey and two uniformed deputies before heading to South Knoxville.

After scoping out Cisco's place, we staged our vehicles a block away from the home where Cisco rented and formulated our battle plan.

I walked up to the front door of the downstairs living quarters. If the woman who lived there was home, I would evacuate her and anyone else present before making our move on Cisco.

That phase went off perfectly. Mrs. Delgado, the homeowner, quietly accompanied me to one of our vehicles and waited.

The plan was to send John Gallagher, Cliff Harvey and one uniformed cop to watch the rear while Bo Stallins, myself, and the second uniform tried our hand at a frontal assault.

Standing at the base of the stairs, I said, "This is the part I hate. That landing is only big enough for one person to stand clear of the door. But it opens in so that's an advantage. I'll knock on the door. He knows my voice— "

Bo interrupted me. "From what I hear, this ol' boy wasn't too happy with you last time you spoke."

I nodded. "Let's hope he doesn't hold a grudge. And let's hope he's not the one who took the doctor's .45 automatic. With hot loads, those things would punch holes in that hollow core door like a hot needle through wax. Just make sure you guys keep your heads below floor level in case he's still mad at me."

"I hear that," Bo said.

The uniformed cop chose to remain silent, putting all his apprehension into looking concerned.

Some melodramatic writer might call our next move a moment of truth. I was more concerned with keeping my middle-aged ass clear of the door and a possible line of fire. But no two ways about it, at some point, I had to do the inevitable.

I looked from Bo to the uniformed cop, whose name was Barry Meyers and shrugged. I began to feel the cold and damp and shivered. "Oh hell. Remember the Alamo."

And up we went.

The door opened on the right. I stood to the left. Bo and Barry held their Glocks drawn and pointed in an appropriate direction, prepared to pepper the doorway with twenty .40 caliber hollow points. I held my Smith & Wesson revolver alongside my right leg, hoping I wouldn't need to use it. I pounded on the door with the side of my left fist.

"Cisco! It's Sam Jenkins from the police. I need you to open the door."

No response.

"Cisco! Open the door."

A long moment later, "You got a warrant?"

"Yes, we do. Everything is being done properly. I have more questions for you."

"I told you, man. No more questions. I want a lawyer."

"We'll get you a lawyer." I was almost yelling now. "He'll meet you at the Justice Center, but you have to open up first."

"Am I under arrest?"

"You will be, but we plan on treating you like a gentleman. No rough stuff unless you resist. That work for you?"

"I don't like this, man."

"I understand, but you need to make this go easy. I've got a half dozen heavily armed men around the house. There's nowhere to go."

"Why don't you bring me a lawyer now?"

"It doesn't work that way. You come with us then we talk to you and the lawyer. You have to quit stalling. I don't want to break down the door and leave Mrs. Delgado with a lot of damage."

"I need time to think."

"You'll have plenty of time when we get to Maryville. You have a weapon inside?"

"A weapon? No."

"Remember, if the door opens and I see a gun, the men behind me are going to kill you. Don't make that happen. Just open the door and get this done."

Another long moment of silence dragged on.

"All right. I'll open the door. I got no weapon. Hold your fire."

As the door opened a crack, our three guns elevated to shoulder level as we waited for something no one wanted to happen.

Cisco's right hand held the doorknob while the left rested on top of his head. He seemed to know the drill. As soon as he saw the three muzzles pointed at his torso, he spoke up.

"Hold your fire, man. No problem here. Hold your fire."

I pushed the door farther in and stepped through the threshold. "Back up inside, Cisco. Both hands on your head." He quickly complied. "There ya go. Now stand easy."

He stood very still, like a statue, wearing the same tight black jeans, but today he chose a turquoise muscle shirt to show off his physique.

Before Bo Stallins cuffed Cisco, I said, "It's just as cold today. Tell us where to find your coat, and Deputy Meyers will get it for you."

The last order of business was giving John Gallagher keys for the apartment and car so he could secure everything after he supervised the search.

———

Interview Room One was larger than the room we used for Cisco's previous visit. A heavy steel ring was bolted to the table-top, four chairs surrounded the table and permanently affixed recording equipment would provide a record of any statement an arrestee might make.

Once Cisco settled in with his handcuffs fastened to the desk, I asked the big question, "Do you have a lawyer, or do you want us to get you a public defender? You don't have to pay for the lawyer we provide."

"I don't know no lawyer, man, and I don't have much money."

Bo Stallins was sitting in for John Gallagher while John conducted the search of the apartment and the car. When Cisco asked for a PD, Bo offered to make the arrangements.

Before Bo left, I said, "Cisco, your English is perfect, but if you want, we can get you a Spanish-speaking lawyer. Your choice."

"I need the *best* lawyer, sir. They don't have to speak Spanish."

I nodded. Smart choice, I thought. Bo understood as well. When the chief public defender heard about a defendant charged with murder, he wouldn't send a rookie.

I gave Cisco a cold stare. "You don't have to say anything if you don't want until your lawyer gets here, but I'm going to give you a few things to think about that you can discuss with whomever they send," I said. "I'm not trying to trick you into confessing or sandbag you. I don't have to. Our arrest warrant was based on enough evidence that a judge agrees with us—we got you, my friend. Someone else handed you to us on that proverbial silver platter."

His eyes popped wide, and his jaw dropped.

"Don't understand?"

"No, sir."

I was back to being *sir* again. A good sign.

"I'm going to play something for you when your lawyer gets here. Since you're entitled to know what we based our probable cause to believe that you killed Paul D'Amato, I see no problem giving you that information right up front. The guy you bought cocaine from, Justin Samples, recorded the entire conversation with you sitting in his car, drinking tequila and copping dope. There's some video as well. We know it's you."

That seemed to leave him speechless. I, on the other hand, was on a roll.

"Anything we find in your apartment or car that links you to Paul D'Amato is just icing on the cake. Do you think we'll find anything?"

He began to nod but caught himself. "I better wait for my lawyer."

"Of course, but I'm going to offer you the same deal now that I will repeat later for the lawyer's benefit. It will give you something to think about.

"It's very simple, Cisco, especially in a case like this. If you decide to stick to a not guilty plea and go to trial, the DA will basically go for your throat with as many and as serious a bunch of charges that fit the circumstances. Believe me when I tell you that this is a slam dunk. Ask your lawyer. But, if you make our lives easy, the DA can, in return, agree to a deal to help you out. You are going to do some jail time. The amount of time depends on you. You think about it, and I'll bring it up again. Any questions so far?"

"Yes, sir. Why did Samples show you this recording?"

"That's easy. After you left to find a girl or two who would have loved to share your cocaine, he got arrested for possession with intent to sell. To get himself a bit of slack, he ratted you out. He swapped his knowledge of a murder for a possession of drugs arrest. He isn't walking free, but he won't make out bad at all."

Cisco shook his head, and someone knocked on the door sooner than I thought. Bo Stallins opened it and ushered in a well-dressed lady to join the gathering.

I stood up and motioned Cisco to do the same. He jumped to attention like a good soldier.

"Hello, Millie," I said.

She nodded. "Sam."

"Cisco, this is Millicent Austin, Chief Deputy public defender—she's a good lawyer. Millie, Francisco Gonzalez."

She offered a hand that Cisco shook like a perfect gentleman.

"Ma'am. Thank you for coming to help me."

"Have you been answering questions prior to my arrival?" she asked.

"No, ma'am. We were just talking."

"Oh? Talking about what?"

I jumped in. "I was just giving him an advance on the discovery process. I told Cisco a few things that may help him decide what to do when the time comes. I'd like to tell him again, now that you're here."

She looked at me with the suspicion of a condemned person hearing the hangman wishing her a good day.

Millie Austin had been a public defender since she left UT Law School. She was in her late- thirties and saying she was a tough attorney would have been a gross understatement—when seeing her in a courtroom with one of her defendants, she looked like George Patton next to a cowardly corporal. Her thick, dark brown hair ended just above her shoulders, her intelligent eyes were the color of semi-sweet chocolate, and her charcoal gray suit made her look like central casting's ideal Hollywood attorney—someone terribly competent but just as unapproachable. Having the tenacity of a hungry pit bull usually made her clients happy, win, lose or draw.

"Mr. Gonzalez," she said, "I don't mean to insult you, but do you speak English well enough to have understood everything he's said to you? If not, I speak Spanish rather well and will be sure you know exactly what's going on here."

"Ma'am, I was in the Army for seven years. I speak good English. I know what I'm being charged with."

I cleared my throat to get Millie's attention. "Why don't we all sit down? Once you hear what I have to say, you and Cisco can discuss it and decide on a course of action."

"Fine," she said, "you have the floor."

The three of us took seats. Bo Stallins pulled a chair away from the table and sat close to the wall.

"Okay, Cisco," I said, "now we're getting down to real business, and because I'll ask you to provide answers to questions I've not posed to you before, I'll formally advise you of your rights. You have the right to remain silent—say nothing at all. You wanted a lawyer, so we have provided the services of Ms. Austin. I explained before that her assistance is at no cost to you. As Ms. Austin will advise you, anything you say can and will be used against you if this matter goes to court. Do you understand all of that?"

"Yes, sir."

"Good. Would you like me to speak to you and your lawyer or should I take a hike and let you find out what my case is about via the normal channels of discovery?"

Cisco looked confused, said nothing until he looked at Millie. "Ma'am, what do I do?"

"Mr. Jenkins is just sounding very official. He wants to impress us with how well he knows the law. Yes, we want to hear what he has to say."

I smiled. "Good again," I said. "Let's begin by listening to

DEATH OF A DOCTOR

what gave me probable cause to believe Francisco caused the death of one Dr. Paul D'Amato and apply for his arrest warrant. We were about to preview this, thinking you would be a lot longer before joining us, Ms. Austin, but here you are. So this will be Cisco's first time hearing what was recorded."

"Yes," she said. "I was only downstairs in pre-arraignment detention speaking with a new client. It didn't take very long to come up two flights."

I smiled, trying to make Cisco—and Millie—think I was their friendly neighborhood cop, always willing to help out. "Ah, you're like me. You've always got a customer."

She finally broke a hint of a smile. "I've always got a customer because of guys like you."

I shook my head, almost laughing. "Ouch! You got me. Okay, Counselor, let's see what this recording tells us."

I played the recording on a laptop Lieutenant Joiner had set up for me before we arrived at the Justice Center.

When the recording ended, Millie Austin began to make a pitch better suited to be given in front of a jury.

"Please wait," I said. "How about I let you and your client discuss this? Let him tell you...whatever he wants to tell you. Then if you'd like to hear more from me, I'll be happy to present more facts that lead me to believe that Cisco did harm to Dr. D'Amato."

"All right," she said. "When we're finished, I'll call for you."

"Someone will be right outside," I said. "If I come back, perhaps we can record our conversation because I'd like to ask questions for the record and ask Cisco to make a choice or two. That work for you, Counselor?"

She nodded. "Works for me."

Bo Stallins and I left the room to allow a criminal defense attorney to say whatever they say to an obvious killer.

———

"I'm gettin' me a Pepsi," Bo said. "Want anything?"

As I turned to say no thanks, I saw John Gallagher walk in, grinning like he just won the Irish Sweepstakes. I saw what he had tucked under his arm but couldn't resist asking, "What are you so happy about?"

He laid his prize on the desk where I was sitting.

"Demento's laptop. Found it in a draw under some of Cisco's muscle shirts."

"Gives us more coffin nails than a pack of Winstons. How about the missing .45 that belonged to D'Amato?"

"Nothing yet. Harvey and the other guy—Whatshisname— are still looking, but if we didn't find it yet, in all the old usual spots, I doubt they will. Not that many more places to look."

"One out of two ain't bad."

"Yeah. I think The Cisco Kid is chopped meat. What's going on here?"

"Cisco and his lawyer are talking things over. I played the recording for them."

"Who's the lawyer?"

"Millie Austin, Chief Deputy PD."

"She some kind of a cop hater?" John had plenty of experience with public defenders.

"Probably. But she's a smart lawyer. I hope she sees this as something that needs a quick plea agreement. We don't want to spend our old age in court with hearings, motions and all that bullshit."

"Who cares? The sheriff pays for our court time."

"You want to sit around a courtroom hallway, drinking coffee from a vending machine?"

"Better than digging ditches for twenty bucks an hour."

I shook my head and looked up as the uniformed deputy

from the jail unit, who had been standing guard outside the interrogation room, called my name.

"That lawyer asked to see you again."

I stood up. "Come on, John. Bring that thing, and let's hear what Cisco says. Just lay it on the table. Let him have the first word."

John grinned again.

The deputy spoke next. "Tough-lookin' woman, that one."

I nodded. "Yeah. Give her a little edge, and she'd kick the shit out of Hulk Hogan."

He laughed. "I hear that."

When we arrived, the deputy unlocked and opened the door. Millie Austin and her new client were sitting where I left them.

"Ms. Austin," I said, "This is my partner, John Gallagher."

She nodded. "Detective Gallagher." Still all business.

John bowed as if he was meeting the Secretary of State.

He laid the laptop on the table near Cisco who couldn't take his eyes off it.

"You called, Counselor, and we're here. How can we help you?"

"I'm going to make a motion to suppress that recording. It's—"

Before she could finish, I interrupted. "I thought you might. Look, I know you're an excellent lawyer, but I've been around a courtroom a long time, and from past experience, I believe it will fly. I think you do, too, but if you have a crystal ball and know better, give it a try. Sometimes wasting time doesn't hurt." I looked at Cisco who was still staring at the laptop. I doubted he had heard anything we said. It turned out I was too impatient to wait for him to mention the laptop.

"Cisco, you recognize that?"

He looked at me with his mouth open.

"Yes? No? That came from your apartment. Would you care to tell us where you got it?"

"Don't answer that, Francisco."

"Okay," I said. "His answer isn't necessary. We know the origin of the laptop, and we'd be happy to show you the content that links it to your client and the victim." I gave Cisco a malevolent look directly into his eyes. "Shall I show Ms. Austin some of the photos in the documents section, Cisco? Photos that will suggest how well you knew Dr. D'Amato?"

"Come on, man. Don't do this, okay?"

"What's wrong, Francisco?" Millie asked.

He didn't respond to her question.

"Let's skip my last question for a while, Millie, and let me anticipate what you'll say next. If the recording that shows Cisco confessing to the murder of Paul D'Amato is suppressed, the warrant to search Cisco's apartment would have been obtained using *fruits of the poisoned tree*. Right?

"Let's ask Mr. Gonzalez if he wants the photos on this laptop shown in open court, or would he rather take it like a man and negotiate a good deal in exchange for a plea. Please explain that to your client and get his thoughts while we step outside for a few minutes and let you two talk."

John and I stood up. He grinned at Cisco, snatched the laptop off the table, and we stepped into the hall. Less than five minutes later, Millie banged on the door. The deputy unlocked it, and we stepped in again.

"What do you have the authority to offer?" Millie asked.

"Me? Officially nothing. But I will get the catching Assistant DA in here after we have an agreement. I'll push whatever you and I think is reasonable. Once I put you with an ADA, it's up to you to slug it out, but if you and I make a deal, I'll be on your side. Remember, this incident had been swept under the rug by the original detective. If it wasn't for John and me, no one would have ever known a murder occurred. The DA would never get to put a plus in their win column. I think we can get Cisco some leniency if he saves the state time and money."

Millie took a deep breath. "I've never dealt with a cop like you before. You'd actually go to bat for my client against an ADA?"

John snickered and stuck in his two cents, "He gets some kind of kicks when he gets his own way."

I shrugged that one off. "I know enough about criminal law to make a decision about what would be a good disposition for this case. The DA herself has the final decision, but I believe she'll listen to me with an open mind. The rest is up to you and Cisco. If you want to accept my deal, I'll want to ask a few more questions. His answers will not taint the deal process. I'm just nosy and may use his information to clear another case. If you reject that idea and he refuses to answer, okay, no hard feelings, and you guys run with it by yourselves."

Millie Austin shook her head and looked like she faced an exasperating decision. "This is most unusual, but I guess it can't hurt to hear what you have to say."

"Good. First of all, let's agree, for argument's sake, that Cisco killed Paul D'Amato, and let's not squabble. Maybe I can throw you a bone here when I say that if Cisco would like to use the opportunity, he can articulate to you some extraordinary and extenuating circumstances behind what he did. No justification for taking a life, but there may be some extreme emotional distress, on his part, that may mitigate his actions—where D'Amato is concerned. I'll let him decide if he wants to elaborate on them. His choice.

"Next, I think taking a plea would be more in Cisco's favor than having the files on this computer," I patted the laptop sitting on the desk, "opened up in a public forum. If I were him, I'd probably feel the same way.

"Third, I doubt that he knows anything about Dr. D'Amato's brother-in-law, but I do. Would you like me to enlighten you two? It may sway him toward taking the plea if he isn't yet convinced."

Millie frowned. "We're listening."

"Before reestablishing themselves in East Tennessee, D'Amato's sister and her husband lived in Miami. He had a *very close* working relationship with an organized crime family who controlled many aspects of the ongoing criminal activity in that area. He's not wanted for any crimes locally, but he's still a dyed-in-the-wool bad guy. He knows more hoods in south Florida than both of you have names on your Christmas card lists.

"What I'm suggesting is that if on an outside chance—and I doubt that would ever be possible—you get Cisco a walk on this murder charge, you, Ms. Austin, may in effect get him a death sentence."

"Wait, wait, wait a minute! Please don't—"

"No, you wait, Millie. This is a distinct possibility. D'Amato's sister Angela is—make that was—very fond of her older brother. To make Angela happy, why wouldn't husband Tony arrange for Cisco to meet with a fatal accident or just disappear one day? In Miami, there are several factions that engage in various aspects of organized criminal enterprises. While they don't actually work in conjunction with each other, they have a tacit understanding not to tread on each other's toes and sometimes cross paths for mutual benefit.

"Suppose husband Tony, obviously an Italian, asks one of his goombahs to speak to one of the boys from Sineloa and as a nunc pro tunc favor, hint that they should make Cisco disappear? I'm just saying."

At the mention of the state of Sinaloa, home of the infamous drug cartel, Cisco's eyes got as big as jumbo tortillas.

"Okay, you're trying to scare us. What if we don't buy that?"

"Then you don't buy it. John and I still get paid every other Thursday. But before you decide, please ask Cisco. It's his life."

She nodded. "Of course. Finished for now?"

"Sure. If you should decide to work on that good deal with us, then I'll ask my questions. There are only a few."

"Let me think for a minute," she said.

She pondered for a long moment.

"I'm inclined to hear these questions first and then begin negotiations. Any objections to that?"

"Certainly not," I said. "My first topic is how he might help us learn how and why Cisco's estranged wife and two children were killed. Would he be willing to do that?"

Cisco answered before Millie could comment. "Yes, I'll help, but I already told you and the other detectives I don't know anything."

"If that's the case, I can't get blood from a stone. But I'd like to help you remember as much as possible, and I can only do that by asking you questions in a special way.

"Look, Cisco, I got you a great lawyer. She is going to look out for your well-being. If I ask something she doesn't like, she'll tell you to shut up. Then you decide to answer or not. What do you have to lose?"

Cisco looked at Millie with an unasked question on his face.

"Sure," she said. "We all know the rules. Ask away."

"Good. All I want are true answers. Don't say something you think I want to hear. The first one is easy. Did you take Paul D'Amato's cell phone?"

She didn't object, and he didn't hesitate. "No."

"It's common knowledge that Paul D'Amato owned a

handgun he kept in his house. Now it's missing. Did you take it?"

"Handgun? I brought the handgun that I—"

"Francisco, stop!" Millie said.

"Don't get bent out of shape, Counselor. I know he brought the .38 that he used to shoot D'Amato. That's a given. I'm looking for a different gun. How about it, Cisco? I'm not going to charge you with theft of a pistol, but I want to know where it is. When you took the laptop, did you also take a handgun?"

Without hesitation, he said, "No."

"It doesn't sound like D'Amato was cleaning his handgun before you arrived. How did a cleaning kit get on the dining room table and why?"

He gave a sheepish expression before answering. "I got in a panic. Shooting someone like Dr. Paul felt a lot different than what I had to do in the war. I put it there to make it look like he shot himself. I saw it on top of a cabinet once. I looked in there and found it."

"Okay. The next question comes with an explanation you need to hear before answering. So listen carefully. I'll state the question first and then explain something very important. Wait for the explanation. Wait for your lawyer to speak first, and then give me your answer.

"Did you kill Margarita Gonzalez and your two children?"

He tightened up so much he looked as if he was either about to scream or make a run for it. I wasn't sure which.

"No!" he yelled, before I interrupted.

"I asked you to listen first. So listen. If you did cause their deaths, now is the time to tell me. I can see the same extreme emotional distress applying to them as to D'Amato. Your lawyer will explain all this to you again after you both hear what I'm about to say."

Millie patted the table near Cisco's forearm, in an effort to calm him.

"If you killed them and plead guilty to all four deaths, you could ask for a deal to serve time for one murder with everything else written off administratively, and the sentences would run concurrently. In other words, plead guilty to D'Amato and negotiate a deal for that. Plead guilty to Margarita and the children and in effect those are tossed in, and you don't get additional punishment. If you reject this offer, we *must* continue to investigate the deaths of your family. If we learn you're responsible, it's a whole new arrest and prosecution. You will never— never—see freedom again. Believe it.

"Now, let Ms. Austin talk to you about it. We'll wait outside. Take your time."

———

After twenty minutes of sitting in the squad room twiddling our thumbs, we began to get hungry. The day tour had already gone home, and the people working a five-to-one had settled in and begun business. I called the Chinese restaurant down the road in the Browns Creek Shopping Center. I ordered Szechuan tofu, and John wanted his usual—*Moo Goo Foo Goo*—known to the rest of the English and Chinese speaking world as Moo Goo Gai Pan—chicken with vegetables. One of the uniformed deputies working the swing shift on the reception desk downstairs offered to pick up our meals and deliver them to the second floor.

Still trying to kill time while Millie and Cisco did their thing, John offered an opinion.

"That Cisco had some *canoons*, seeing the laptop and not saying a word until you asked."

I chuckled. "Canoons?"

"What? You speak enough Spanish to know that one."

"Perhaps you mean los cajones? Pronounced ca-hone-es, yes?"

John squeaked out of answering when the deputy delivering our grub placed a small shopping bag on the desk.

No sooner had I opened up my container of crispy bean curds and vegetables in a spicy brown sauce than the armed hall monitor standing outside Interrogation One fetched us. Ms Austin and The Cisco Kid wanted to talk.

"Son of a bitch," I said. "Do they have a microwave in here? I hate eating cold Chinese food. What the hell are we anyway, prisoners of war?"

"Sir, there's a microwave in the break room," the deputy said.

"I hope you know how to work it, John."

"Sure. You don't?"

"Shut up, John. Let's go down the hall."

We hadn't been in our chairs more than fifteen seconds when Ms. Austin began by scolding me. "If we can continue without you trying to scare Mr. Gonzalez to death, I think we can come to an agreement."

I spread my arms to my sides, palms up. "Great. Shock Theater is over."

"If he pleads to causing the death of Dr. D'Amato under extenuating circumstances, what can you offer?"

I didn't want to give away the farm on the first round of negotiations, so I tried to paint a picture of definite malice on Cisco's mind to see how the opposition would counter.

"Well, he went to the doctor's home with no legitimate business in mind but killing him—unless he can convince us and an ADA differently. And we can't forget about that pesky jury. He brought a gun with him. Normally people visiting a psychother-apist don't go to a session armed and dangerous. I agree with the emotional distress, but the best I can see is Man One with a maximum sentence. And you will have to explain what made him distressed. I assume that can be done privately in this room with the ADA and then probably *in camera* with a judge to save Cisco embarrassment in open court. I don't know about the DA, but if he keeps his nose clean, I won't oppose parole when his time comes. His military record means something to me."

Millie made a face to indicate she wasn't pleased with my offer. Let the games begin.

"That's the best you can do?"

"Come on, Millie. You know the store is not mine to give away. Without me paving the way, the DA may offer Murder Two—at best—and if you're lucky, with a sentencing recommendation for his cooperation. Moira will know she can win this one. You know her. It's going to depend on her mood. I'll keep my promise and go to bat for your side."

She pondered that for a long moment. "Okay. Can you get an ADA here to finalize this?"

"Not so fast. We've covered D'Amato's death. What about Margarita and the children? What does Cisco have to say about that?"

"Let's let him speak for himself, Sam. He understands exactly what you explained, and he wants you to know he had nothing to do with those murders."

I looked from the lovely Ms. Austin and then stared at her client. "What's the story, Cisco? Once this is over, we'll have at least six people investigating the murders of your family. If we learn that you did it, my friend, you are one vaquero without a caballo. Comprende?

"Yes, sir, I understand. You think I would kill my children? Man, they were my blood. I may have left Margarita. I didn't want to be married no more, but why would I kill her? I'm not admitting to something I didn't do. Go ahead and investigate. I hope you find out who killed my children...and Margarita. When you do, don't make any deals with them. Shoot them."

———

Shelby Johnson was the on-call ADA authorized to listen to Cisco's plea and negotiate a final deal. After the usual haggling, they settled on what I had proposed: Manslaughter 1st degree with a sentence of fifteen years. If Cisco behaved like a model prisoner, he could be out in as little as five years—or what the criminals of the world would call *a nickel*.

Officially, the job John and I had been hired to do was complete. But who wants to leave loose ends hanging in the breeze? I damn sure wasn't going to call her, so Bettye could delegate the job of informing Velma Barnett that Lone Star Mutual would have to fork over one half million buckaroos to Angela Scarano.

My objection to ending our involvement in this saga rested on what really happened between Mrs. Scarano and Leo Turner. Before Angela received a big check or even notification that one would be forthcoming, I wanted to speak to her—and her attorney—again. If she bribed Leo Turner to make that case take a dive, I wanted Leo's genitals in a vice.

Now, all I had to do was convince Bettye Lambert to let John and me continue to work this angle of the case and also wiggle our way into the Gonzalez murder investigation.

CHAPTER FOURTEEN

Bettye had driven to the Justice Center on her Saturday off to see what the outcome of our interview with Cisco Gonzalez turned out like. John finished his *moo goo foo goo* and went home. The Sheriff and I sat in her office.

"Look, Betts," I said. "It's your big chance for a triple homicide clearance, signed, sealed and delivered. And let me tell you, you will get one hell of a lot more for your measly twenty bucks an hour—plus expenses—than any other sheriff in this U-nited States might expect."

"That's why I love ya, Sammy darlin'. Who else would do as much work for li'l ol' me?"

She smiled and put her eyelashes in motion. Flutter. Flutter.

"Nuts. You play me like a hillbilly banjo. I've given you all the ammo you need to put that obnoxious insurance investigator in her place and cost one company from the capitalist insurance conglomerate, the people who hold so many *God-fearin' Amuri-cans* hostage, one half million Yankee dollars. Pfui on them."

"Lord have mercy, Sugar, but don't you sound vindictive."

"I am vindictive. I like to stick it to the Man."

"Think about that, Sammy. For most of your life, you were the Man."

"Baloney. I just don't want Mrs. Angela Beneficiary Scarano, to collect her cash without me watching her squirm a little. And, Miss Bettye, if you play your cards right, I might just be able to nail down an arrest in the matter of Margarita Gonzalez and children. And, if I'm correct, that will involve our old friend, the erstwhile detective Leo Turner—and maybe even Ryan Leary tossed in for good measure."

"And just how, Special Investigator Jenkins, are you going to do that?"

"We start by you personally calling Angela Scarano and telling her that you're *very special* investigator and his faithful sidekick want to take her up on her offer of talking to me again in the presence of her attorney. Ten o'clock tomorrow would be a great time for me. Either in her home or here in Interview One —which in case you've never been there, is very spacious, civilized and conducive to a subtle coercion of the truth from a nasty miscreant like Mrs. Scarano. Can you make that happen?"

"Do I really want to?"

"Of course you want to. Am I not the world's greatest detective? Don't you want a triple homicide cleared on your watch? In the national spotlight, you'll be the hottest female cop since Angie Dickinson starred on *Police Woman*."

"You are so full of manure, you might sprout vegetables any day now."

"That might be true, but you're the one to reap the harvest." I slid a piece of paper across her desktop. "Here's the number. No need to call collect."

———

John and I pulled up to Casa Scarano at 10:10 the next morning —stylishly late. The open garage doors showed the back end of a shiny black Mercedes-Maybach sedan and a sparkling red Mercedes AMG roadster—conservatively $400,000 worth of automobiles when you consider tax, title and all the little hidden extras car dealers sneak into a sale. Also parked on the driveway apron was a big, new Lexus LS sedan with Knox County plates—a paltry seventy-five grand or so.

It didn't look as if the Scaranos were hurting for disposable cash. Their hired hand must have settled for the lowly Lexus.

I parked our borrowed three-year-old dark brown Crown Victoria that needed a wash and followed John to the front door.

The cleaning woman must have taken the day off. A distinguished-looking, middle-aged man wearing a dark gray three-piece suit opened the door.

He smiled. "Ah, gentlemen, come in. Mr. and Mrs. Scarano are in the living room."

"Mr. Farley," I said, "Small world, isn't it? Nice to see you."

"And you as well," he said, keeping the genuine smile on his face.

I had met Roland Foley when I was still chief at the Prospect Police Department and investigating the history of a 9mm handgun found in the possession of a young man who perpetrated a horror on the citizens of Prospect. He killed his mother, a teacher at the Prospect Elementary School, and a number of young children before putting the muzzle end of an AK-47 in his mouth and pulling the trigger. The Sig Sauer P225 Sergeant Stan Rose found stuck in the boy's waistband had once been the property of Roland Farley but sold to a stranger he met walking through a gun show in Knoxville. What Farley had done was perfectly legal if not very intelligent, and he owned no liability. Now we met him acting as legal counsel for the Scaranos.

We found Angela Scarano and an oily specimen, I assumed to be her husband, sitting on that big creamy soft leather couch. Roland Farley took a seat across from them in an easy chair.

Mrs. Scarano stood and greeted us. "Good morning. This is my husband, Anthony." She extended a hand in his general direction.

Husband Anthony stood and extended a hand in my direction. "Tony Scarano. How do you do?"

I nodded and shook his hand. "Sam Jenkins, Blount County Sheriff's Office. This is my partner, John Gallagher."

John shook Tony's hand, too. "Hi, how are you?"

If central casting chose Millie Austin as the quintessential female attorney, the same Hollywood mogul would have picked Tony as the stereotypical mobbed-up guy. He wore a dark gray pinstriped suit that might have cost more than the three pension checks I had coming in each month from the PD in New York, the Army Reserve and the Social Security Administration put together. Top that off with another thousand dollars worth of white dress shirt, silk tie and Italian hand-sewn loafers and his slightly overweight body almost looked exquisite. Had it been springtime, I would have expected a tan Armani sport jacket, contrasting and appropriately expensive slacks with a silk shirt open at the neck with the collar draped not-so-tastefully over the jacket's lapels. And who would expect less than one or two thick gold chains hanging around his neck that would make Mr. T jealous—but I'm just being catty.

John and I sat on a love seat, upholstered in the same soft ivory-colored leather that matched the other furniture. Dollar signs floated all around the room above our heads.

After a pregnant pause that followed us sitting down, Roland Farley spoke.

"So, Mr. Jenkins, what will we be doing today?"

"I envisioned a number of things, Mr. Farley. By the way, I didn't know you did criminal defense."

That brought a startled look to his face. "I don't. I'm legal counsel to Mr. Scarano's corporation. What sort of criminal matter are you talking about?"

"We'll get to that shortly. First, I'd like to inform Mrs. Scarano that our investigation concerning her brother's death has been completed. The original finding of accidental death has been overturned."

"You can't be serious," Angela said. "My brother would never intentionally kill himself. If you think—"

I stopped her tirade by holding up a hand. "We're not saying it was a suicide. We've made an arrest and have a confession. Your brother was murdered."

Reflexes took over. She brought up a hand to cover her mouth. Her dark and usually nasty eyes showed more than her share of surprise.

"What? Who?" was Tony's contribution.

"It's a complicated story, but I think Mrs. Scarano has some idea about at least one of the contributing factors.

"What are you talking about?" Tony asked.

"As I said, it's a complicated story, but first I'd like to advise Mrs. Scarano of her rights..."

I went through the whole Miranda warning chapter and verse, like I might have played an audio tape or had been a detective action figure with a ring on his neck that when pulled set off a scratchy recording. Chatty Sam from Mattel came fully equipped with all the appropriate police gear.

"Since you have an attorney present, would you like to continue, or do you wish to stop here?"

She looked confused and turned to her mouthpiece. "Roland?"

"It's all right, Angela. It can't hurt to hear what he has to say."

I planned to do something I usually steer clear of...but these were desperate times, and I was prepared to try a desperate measure. I'd be playing a hunch, hoping to pull off a short con and get Angela talking.

"Okay. Let's begin with the good and official news. The insurance company can't claim that your brother took his own life." I paused a moment to let that sink in and to see if I'd get an interesting reaction. Nothing. Disappointing. I moved forward.

"As I mentioned, we've arrested someone. We have a confession and a boatload of evidence to corroborate things."

"So who is this guy? I'd like to know," Tony said.

"A former patient sent to Paul by the VA. More than that I can't say at the moment. But the story doesn't stop there. We'll get to that shortly.

"The next thing is extremely important. Please listen carefully. Ordinarily, an insurance company couldn't refuse to pay you the benefit under those circumstances alone, but here's the sticky part—"

"What sticky part?" Angela asked, not waiting for me to finish.

"We know that your brother knew Detective Leo Turner—the man who did the initial investigation. Remember him?"

She nodded.

"They had a prior, uh, what shall I call it? *A business relationship.* We also know that you wanted to clear out certain things from Paul's house before the police did any official looking around. I'm speaking about embarrassing things—photos, videos, compact discs containing less than tasteful images. Things just like I found in his post office box. I assume no one knew about that box since I found six months of accumulated mail there."

At that point, I was shooting in the dark, calling my guesses *gospel*. I hoped Angela and Tony would buy my act and credit me with knowing more than I did.

Angela tried to pull off an act of her own. "What are you talking about?"

John opened a brief case he'd brought along and dropped several advertisements for homosexual pornography onto the coffee table.

"This is only a sample," John said. "We've retained the rest in evidence. Along with your brother's laptop containing similar material. The man we arrested told us how Paul solicited him to pose for...pictures. We hope you understand."

The two Scaranos and Roland Foley looked closely at the *literature* lying on the glass-topped table.

"What kind of shit are you trying to pull?" Tony asked with more than a little heat in his voice.

"We're not pulling anything, Mr. Scarano," I said. "Nothing Paul had sent to him and was in his possession along with what I found in the PO Box constituted a violation of law—well, maybe a couple of the models in the photos we found on his computer were of a questionable age, but he's not here to answer any charges, is he?"

"Mr. Jenkins," Farley said, "We'd like to know where you're going with this."

"I'm sure you do. I was getting to the point when your clients asked questions. If I can proceed, I'll tell you what you want to know."

"Please do."

Huh, lawyers.

"Back to Leo Turner. We know that you wanted him to write off Paul's death as an accident because suicide would negate the insurance benefit. People are going to interrogate

Turner as we speak. They'll get his side of the story. I'm asking to hear yours, Mrs. Scarano."

"What do you mean my *side*? I don't have a side."

"You certainly do. Remember I said that ordinarily an insurance company would pay out the benefit if the insured was murdered? But, if the beneficiary was charged with conspiracy to defraud that insurance company, the half million dollars they might owe you could be denied, and if you really wanted it, it would be tied up in court for many, many years. Not to mention the cost to you for criminal defense and a civil litigator.

"So, while the other detectives are locating and interviewing Turner and offering him a deal for spilling his guts, I'll offer you the same. Whoever talks first—with the truth—gets the deal. The other gets charged."

She was about to speak and so was Tony, but I cut them off.

"Don't comment yet, please. I haven't finished. We fully understand you wanting to keep Paul's sexual fetishes from becoming public knowledge. That's not difficult to understand, is it? We really don't see you as a threat to the community and would prefer to give you a deal for *lots* of leniency if we can. Turner, on the other hand, is a proven bad apple. Mr. Farley, are you familiar with Turner's part in the Ryan Leary scandal that rocked the Sheriff's office back in July?"

He nodded. "Of course. It was all over the media."

"Then you know where we're coming from and can advise your clients accordingly. Turner is not in prison only because he testified against his former boss, Ryan Leary. I think he belongs behind bars, but he did well for himself by only being dismissed from the department—he's no longer a cop. We know him and believe he's capable of anything. We need you, Mrs. Scarano, to tell us the truth about what happened in Paul's house the day you found him. In return for a statement about Turner's activities, we're prepared to *somewhat* overlook what you might have done while you were *negotiating* with Turner. Would you like to do that?"

"Wait a minute," Tony said, getting hot again. "This smells fishy. I know what happened with Turner. Are you trying to pull the same thing?"

"What kind of *thing* is that, Mr. Scarano?" I asked.

Farley spoke up before Tony could answer. "Tony, be careful here. Why don't we have a word before you say any more?" To me, Farley said, "Excuse us a moment?"

"We've got all the time in the world."

He and Tony stepped out of the room.

"Mrs. Scarano," I said, "I'm not trying to apply any undue pressure on you, but I was serious when I said that the first one to speak up gets the deal. Remember, simply put, Turner is a proven informer and an all-around rat. He'll give you up in a heartbeat and tell a self-serving lie about it."

I took a rather obvious glance at my watch to put a little more of that unintentional and undue pressure on her.

"So you're saying if I confess to bribing that man to not investigate what looked like Paul's suicide, you'll just let me go?"

I shrugged, like it was something we did every day. "You'll have to write a statement. You'll get a good slap on the wrist, but you will not go to jail. If what I believe about Turner is, in fact, true he will go to jail—for what he did to you and for something much worse that he probably did to other innocent people. We're after him, not you, Mrs. Scarano, but we need the truth."

"Jesus, Mary and Joseph. I don't know what to do."

"That's why you have a lawyer here," John reminded her.

From the other room we heard Tony blow his top.

"Bullshit! I know what they want. Fuckin' cops. They're all the same. I'll throw those bastards outta my house."

Then Farley tried to smooth Tony out. "Calm down, Tony.

Calm down. I'll handle this. And for God's sake, don't say anything when we go back in there."

"Yeah, yeah, yeah. You just better make this come out right, Roly."

When that pair returned to the living room, Farley looked more embarrassed than Tony. But Tony's face was redder than the sports car in his garage. With any luck, he'd have a stroke.

"Gentlemen," I said, "What have you decided?"

Farley spoke, "I don't want to offend you gentlemen, so I have to word this delicately. How shall I begin? Let's see." He took a deep breath before continuing. "Mr. Scarano is fearful that, based on a personal experience, you are suggesting that you and his wife settle this, uh, matter outside the normal legal channels and uh—"

"Stop right there, Counselor," I said, trying to sound outraged. "I get your drift. He thinks that for some *monetary contribution* to our old detective's benefit fund we will let his wife skate, correct?"

"I, uh—"

"Save it. That's offensive. Who was it, John, who said, 'He who trusts no one does not trust himself'."

"Um, I forget."

"No matter. But I'm guessing that this *similar prior experience* involved Leo Turner, correct?"

Without wasting a second or skipping a beat, Tony blurted out, "You bet your ass it did. Five grand worth of experience. That bastard!"

Gotcha, I thought.

Farley attempted, a little too late, to mitigate his client's spontaneous admission.

"Tony, I advised you to say nothing."

"If that's so, Mr. Scarano, let's drop the hammer on Turner. But the clock is ticking, and it's your wife's fate that we're talking about. I think she should make the decision. Mrs. Scarano, what do you say?"

"Oh, for God's sake, Anthony, you just admitted paying off that bastard. Jesus, let's get this over with. Yes, I asked Turner to be...kind. It looked like Paul took his own life. He was a good Catholic for his entire life. Suicide is a sin. I didn't want that on his soul."

Sure, Angie, and that cool half million waiting in the wings never crossed your mind.

"Ready to tell us exactly what happened?" I asked.

"Yes. It seems like I have no choice."

"Alright. Let's get the story out, and then Mr. Farley can assist you with a statement. While I'm listening, Detective Gallagher will call another officer and tell him we have a deal, and Turner is out of luck. John, will you make the call?"

Obviously, Gallagher wasn't expecting that. "Uh yeah, sure. I'll call, uh. I'll go out and make the call. Excuse me."

John walked out of the room to kill time and make them believe he was calling some comrade grilling Leo Turner and was only seconds away from getting *his* confession. While John was away, Angela began her story.

She said that when Paul didn't show up for a Sunday dinner he had agreed to attend, Angela began calling. She got no answers to her calls on Sunday and at various times the next day to his home landline, his cell phone and to the VA offices. On Tuesday morning after no answers to her calls, she drove to his home and got no response knocking on the front and back doors. Having a key in her possession, she let herself in and found him slumped over the dining room table dead with a revolver lying partially in the pool of dried blood. To her, it looked like a suicide.

Knowing about Paul's fetish for pornography since they were teenagers, she scurried around the house scooping up any hard copies of videos and reading materials. She looked for a computer but found none. She confiscated his cell phone that she presumed might have photos stored on it or other embarrassing information. After doing as much as she could to protect Paul's memory and reputation, she called 9-1-1.

Shortly thereafter, the first officer arrived. He, in turn, called for a supervisor, and a road sergeant responded. The sergeant then called for a detective. Shortly after Detective Leo Turner arrived, Sergeant Hadley Runyan left, leaving the deputy Varnell Woodruff to assist Turner. After Angela spoke with Turner privately, Turner dismissed Woodruff. Then they waited for the police surgeon and mortuary people.

Angela described the subsequent conversation with Turner as follows: She told him how embarrassed she would be if people learned that her brother, a doctor and a somewhat public figure, had killed himself. She also feared that the church would not allow him to be buried in consecrated ground and perhaps he would even be posthumously excommunicated for committing the sin of taking his own life. She pleaded with Turner to report it as an accident. In what seemed to her like a shakedown, Turner bobbed and weaved about protocol and the risks he would be talking to do such a thing. Out of desperation—or perhaps from her past experiences as a mobster's wife—she asked the magical question all cops of low moral fiber long to hear: "Is there anything I can do to convince you to help me out here?"

Leo, being of the very lowest morals I could think of, picked up on that and saw dollar signs flash before his eyes. But, he wanted some money pronto. He would have to persuade a doctor to sign a death certificate and not question his assessment of an accidental death. Turner also probably assumed that a well-to-do doctor like D'Amato would have a sizable life insurance policy when he informed Angela he'd need $5,000 dollars to provide the help she needed.

With her back up against a wall, she agreed and called her husband, asking him to ferry the cash down to Paul's house immediately. With the deal in place, Turner looked through the house and found the brother's .45 automatic. He told Angela he would have to keep the .45 to prevent the responding police surgeon from getting confused—getting a seven to eight hundred dollar handgun *on the arm* might have had something to do with it as well. Turner could say Angela didn't want the gun and asked him to take the .45 out of the house. Keeping the gun for himself would be by no means ethical, but under those circumstances it was technically legal. With everything accomplished that he thought necessary to pull off the scam, Turner asked the dispatcher to send the on-call doctor out for a pronouncement. Once Tony arrived with the cash and the police surgeon left, Leo bid the Scaranos adieu and left them waiting for the funeral home people to remove the body.

"Is there anything else you'd like to add?" I asked.

"I can't remember anything else. That's the way it happened."

"Then I have a few questions. Any objections, Counselor?"

Farley shook his head.

"Did Turner take or leave the .38 revolver?"

"He left it," Tony said. "I wrapped the bloody thing in a towel. When I got home, I cleaned it up and have it here."

"I'll need that for the prosecution of the man who shot Paul. I'll also need the cell phone."

"I'll get the gun," Tony said. "It's in the garage." He stood up and walked out.

"I have the phone," Angela said. "Why do you need that?"

"As I mentioned, Paul and Leo Turner knew each other before this happened. I believe that ties in with another case. I'll need to secure a call history to see how many times and when Turner spoke to Paul."

"But why would it matter now how they were involved?"

"I believe and can substantiate with what I found on Paul's laptop, that Turner was selling Paul, uh...pictures, if you understand what I mean."

Returned from the garage and again seated on the cushy white leather, Tony heard what I just said and needed to interject something to the conversation.

"God forgive me, Angela, but that man was a pervert!"

"Anthony, he was my brother!"

"Yeah right, Angela. I know. I know."

John Gallagher had returned long before Angela finished her account of the day she found her dead brother. After Tony's last outburst, I asked John, "You made the call?"

He nodded.

"Everything squared away?"

"Uh, yeah. She took the deal first. She's good."

"Okay, Mr. Farley, will you help Mrs. Scarano put everything she just said into a statement? When you're finished, I'll notarize it."

CHAPTER FIFTEEN

"Sam, how in God's name are you going to tie all of this together?" Moira Menzies asked in the perpetually flabbergasted way she speaks to me.

I looked out the third-floor window of the DA's corner office toward the intersection of Washington Street and US 321. The brick-walled and landscaped entrance to Maryville College stood to the left and a busy Dunkin' Donut shop with a full parking lot and a line of vehicles wrapped around the building to the right. Drivers, impatiently waiting to pick up their orders at the drive-in window, sat there with motors idling.

Then I focused my attention on the frowning, fifty-something year old blonde with wavy hair sitting at the DA's desk, tapping the eraser end of an unsharpened pencil on the blotter.

"You've seen some segments of this already unfold, Moira. Mind if I recap things and tie them together for you? Remember, this is a theory, but so far, the dominoes have been falling into place, and I believe this plan will come together."

"Go ahead, we've got time. You probably get paid overtime, but I don't."

"Sit tight, woman. If this happens and we make an arrest or two, you'll be a shoo-in to get elected DA come November. And a word to the right guy from me won't hurt either."

"Judge Tipton, your godfather?"

Who else?"

"You're unbelievable."

"Hardly. Now listen up and follow how these seemingly unrelated things all meld together. I'll make this quick, and we can get the warrant.

"Paul D'Amato was killed by Francisco Gonzalez. You know that. It happened because D'Amato paid good-looking Cisco to pose for nude pictures. Margarita Gonzalez, Cisco's wife and D'Amato's cleaning woman, stumbled across these photos accidentally when she saw them on D'Amato's computer. She, in turn, confronted Cisco who flew off the handle. Cisco wanted to ensure no one else ever saw his indiscretion. He never wanted anyone to think he was a pato sucio."

"Wait. Hang on a minute. A dirty duck? I speak a little Spanish. What do you mean?"

"Sorry. That's not proper Spanish. It's a derogatory term that a Puerto Rican might use for a homosexual...which Cisco is not. But you know the old macho guy thing. He wouldn't want anyone to think... Anyway, Cisco demanded that D'Amato delete his photos or something like that. He and D'Amato argued and bang. Cisco shot D'Amato using the .38 that he brought with him, leaving the gun there but taking the laptop. Cisco confessed, and I arrested him—that you already know.

"Now, shortly after John and I started to reinvestigate the D'Amato death, something that Leo Turner wrote off as an accident, someone assassinated Margarita Gonzalez and her two children. You're lucky you didn't see that one. Everything suggested that the killer was looking for something. But what? At the time, we didn't know.

"Then Terri Donnellson from Prospect PD, who works for us part-time, spoke to a potential witness—a woman named Belinda Cancel who Margarita met through La Union Hispanica. They got friendly. After Margarita found the pictures of Cisco, Belinda went with her to D'Amato's home under the guise of cleaning the house and downloaded all the pornography from D'Amato's computer so Margarita could use it to get Cisco to agree to a divorce. Still with me?"

Moira rolled her eyes. "I guess so."

"Okay. Hang in there. I'm almost finished. We took the copy of the thumb drive that Belinda saved, but we didn't look at it immediately. After initially questioning Cisco, he admitted posing for the pictures for some pretty good money. That, of course, led us to arrest Cisco. But he said he didn't kill his ex and their kids, and I believed him.

"So, we're left with who killed Margarita and the children. The circumstances of the murder led me to believe that someone wanted something important, but what? Margarita owned next to nothing. Cisco stopped seeing his kids and paid no support. She collected welfare, bought what she needed in thrift shops and barely kept her head above water. So, the killer must have wanted Margarita's copy of the thumb drive. But at that point, she didn't have it.

"Then I found out she had extorted money from D'Amato in exchange for one copy of the thumb drive. But not being well versed in the art of blackmail, she led D'Amato to believe she possessed another thumb drive with all the photos. As I said, she actually didn't, but Belinda was sharp enough to make another copy in case Margarita needed it later.

"Obviously, prior to his death, D'Amato told someone else about the possibility of a second thumb drive. Then I remembered that Belinda told us that along with pictures of Cisco, D'Amato had saved similar photos of other men. Aha! I said.

Stupid me. I never looked beyond Cisco. When I looked at the entire computer file, who do you think I found?"

Moira took a long moment to shake her head in what I assumed was confusion.

"How do you keep all this straight in your head, Sam? A half-dozen best-selling writers couldn't make up this shit. You're telling me it's for real. How in Hell do I know who else you found on the thumb drive?"

"Hang on to your pantyhose, Moira. How about Ryan Leary and Leo Turner?"

"What? Back up. D'Amato had *nude photos* of Leary and Turner?"

"You betcha. Leary must have hired a photographer on some of his sex trips to Thailand. I won't elaborate on the pictures, but he did some *unique* things with young boys, girls and transvestites. Turner, on the other hand, decided to get kinda funky with a pretty hard-looking white woman.

"My guess is that Leary wanted these now close-to-being-public pictures to disappear before a member of the parole board might get to view them. Turner, already in hot water because of his association with Leary, also wanted them to disappear."

"So," Moira asked," how does this give you probable cause to believe Turner killed the Gonzalez woman?"

"Alone, it doesn't. It's a reach, but by back-dooring it, we might get the weapon used to kill Margarita and the children. Once we have the gun, obtained legally from investigating another crime—the bribe solicited from Angela Scarano—we can *accidentally* tie it to the murders."

"A reach huh? Sounds like you're trying to catch a fly ball high enough to sail over the center field fence."

"Not really. I've got a statement from D'Amato's sister that Turner solicited a bribe—five grand—to declare D'Amato's death an accident when it really looked like a suicide. She said he took D'Amato's .45 automatic. Margarita and the kids were killed with a .45.

"I want a warrant to search for the gun to prove his malfeasance and a conspiracy to defraud the insurance company when actually I want to compare the ballistics from D'Amato's gun to the bullets the ME retrieved at the Gonzalez autopsies. It's an end run, but if Leo still has the .45 and we get it legally, we see where it goes."

"I've heard some convoluted things, but this is a prize winner. You've given me a headache. Do you have the warrant application ready to go?"

"Gallagher is finishing it as we speak."

"Okay, let's get the stand-by judge down here and hope he's in a receptive mood."

CHAPTER SIXTEEN

We assembled the same six-man team who helped execute the arrest and search warrants on Cisco Gonzalez to collar Leo Turner. Specifically, they were Bo Stallins and Cliff Harvey from CID, John Gallagher and me, Deputy Barry Meyers and our final member, the deputy John and I had previously not known—Linwood Baron who asked us to call him Robber. I wondered how many young members of the department made the connection with his nickname.

Using three cars, one a marked police vehicle, we pulled up on both sides of Leo's house and quickly deployed ourselves around the perimeter. Stallins and I tried the front door. After Bo almost skinned his knuckles beating on the door with no response, we called the other cops to help us check the windows. All that accomplished was creating six pairs of dirty shoes. Apparently, Leo Turner was in the wind. But why? Did someone warn him we were coming?

Each of us scattered along the street and checked with any neighbors we could find to hear what they could say about Leo's whereabouts. The best we came up with was that neither he nor his car had been seen for two or three days. He asked no one to keep an eye on his place while he took a trip and didn't even say goodbye to those living next to him. That left us nowhere.

Our warrant was not granted with what cops and the courts call a *no knock* clause, because there were no foreseeable circumstances that while we knocked on the front door Leo could get rid of the evidence we were seeking. I mean, you can't flush a two and a half pound .45 automatic down the toilet. With good old police horse sense and modern technology, we could have found a handgun anywhere in the house if it was there. So, we couldn't break down the door and conduct our search in Leo's absence. The logical, but most costly solution was to post a twenty-four-hour surveillance on the house and hope he turned up sooner than later. Before we asked management to approve that, we headed back to the Justice Center to brainstorm other options.

Seated around Bo Stallins' desk, we began tossing out ideas.

"Has he got a girlfriend?" John asked.

Neither of the two uniforms knew nor did Cliff Harvey.

"Had him someone," Bo said. "Don't know her name, but she used to be a topless dancer up at that place on Alcoa Highway."

"The Mouse's Ear," I said. "Huh. Class place. Their sign called it a gentleman's club. What's the chance you'd find one genuine gentleman in that sleazy refuse heap?"

No one could provide an answer to my question.

"Maybe one of the DA's investigators knows something," Harvey suggested. "I remember him and Leary worked back and forth with that bunch for some time."

I grabbed a phone. "I'll ring Clete Dunn and see if he knows or can find out."

Cletus Dunn had been the senior District Attorney's investigator in Blount County for as long as I had been involved with Tennessee law enforcement.

A few minutes later, Bo's extension rang. I grabbed the receiver again and listened to what Clete could tell me.

"Okay, buddy. Thanks a bunch. We're still looking, so if you think of something helpful, give a shout." I hung up and reported to the group. "Clete doesn't know, and neither did any of the guys in the office. He'll check further, but who knows what that will get us?"

"How about his ex-partner?" John asked.

"Artie Bonnet?" I said. "Maybe. Those guys and Leary were pretty tight. We can ask, but what kind of leverage could we use on him if he tells us to piss up a rope? John and I aren't well liked by Leary's gang."

"I hear Artie's workin' for a retired IRS Intelligence agent who set up a PI's business specializin' in forensic accounting," Bo said. "Artie's no accountant, but he'd probably be good doin' the leg work. Artie was a pretty fair detective before tyin' up with Leary and Turner."

"Sounds like a nice job for a guy with some ugly skeletons in his closet," John said.

Bo continued, "I know somethin' about this ex-IRS guy. He's mighty straight, kinda like he's got a broom stuck where the sun don't shine. I'm surprised he'd hire a guy with Artie's past."

"Maybe we can make Artie think if he tells us to get lost, we might try to convince his boss that a guy who's a proven bad apple opens him up to a vicarious liability," I said.

"You didn't see Artie posing nude in any of Demento's picture files, did you?" John asked.

I shook my head. "No. From what I know, Artie went along for the ride and enjoyed Leary's power but wasn't that much like the other two sleaze balls."

"Maybe we could make Artie think we'll push the guilt by association thing with his boss," Bo suggested. "If you were a straight-laced ex-IRS guy with a serious business, would you want one of your investigators associated with a pair o' defrocked cops who just now got caught sellin' nekked pictures of theirselves to perverts?"

"We have to talk with Artie," I said. "Depending on how he treats us, we can lay it on thick or just appeal to his better judgment—or both. Let's go find Artie Bonnet and rattle his cage."

We waited until 6:00 p.m., figuring Artie would be home after a day's work or a Saturday at home doing all those domestic chores the average American does on the weekend. If we were lucky, he'd be having dinner and be a little off balance when we intruded on his evening.

He lived in the Louisville post office district, in a subdivision off Louisville Road, a main drag that ran from US 129 in Alcoa along the southern perimeter of McGhee Tyson Airport and into the tiny community of Louisville proper—not Looieville like the city in Kentucky.

The uniformed deputies stayed at the Justice Center, and four of us rode in one car with me driving. I took a left into a fairly new subdivision just west of the Green Meadows Golf Course and found the address.

The two-story brick home sat on what looked like a quarter acre lot. Lights glowed in several first-floor windows. A good sign someone was at home.

Getting the needed information from Artie Bonnet was crucial to moving our search forward, taking Leo Turner into custody, and then dusting off our set of thumbscrews, hoping we could get Leo to talk. If Bonnet decided to stonewall us, for old time's sake and protect his former partner, we were literally screwed. If Bonnet called Turner immediately after we left his home, the missing .45 might end up in one of the deeper spots of Fort Loudoun Lake.

Four grim-looking detectives converging on someone's home while his family tried to enjoy a scrumptious dinner of slaw dogs, baked beans and deep-fried pickles might be considered overkill. There was no margin for error. We needed to play this one right.

"All of us going in at once might tick Artie off big time," I said.

"I hear that," Bo said. "Don't want to start out on the wrong foot."

"It's your case, Bo. John and I can wait here for you guys and hope for the best."

In my opinion, the *best* would be Cliff Harvey not botching up another interview like he did with Belinda Cancel. I hoped Bo Stallins kept that in mind.

"Shoot," Bo said, "you was the one who talked him into giving up Leary and cooperatin' with the FBI. Maybe you and me should give him a go."

Just what I wanted to hear.

"Yeah, and if I get us thrown out on our ears, you can always blame me. Us contract employees are easy to fire."

"I hope the Sheriff only fires you," John said. "I can always use the extra money we get from her jobs."

I shook my head. "Don't you love it when your partner jumps in and backs you up?"

Bo took a deep breath and looked like he wanted to be doing anything but what he knew we needed to do. "Well, let's us go in and see how cooperative Artie's feelin' t'night."

"I'm right behind you, big man."

Actually, I led the way up the concrete path and knocked on the door. We waited a long moment before the outside light popped on. Seconds later, Artie Bonnet opened the door.

He was a slim man with narrow shoulders and stood a little less than six foot tall. His receding hairline and high forehead made his narrow face look even longer. Obviously, he was just home from work, his maroon tie, loosened at the collar, was tucked into his shirt between the third and fourth buttons of his pale blue shirt. I guess he wanted to keep it from dangling into his food. It took him a moment of frowning to process what he saw.

"What do you people want?"

I led off for our team. "I was hoping we could get a minute of your time. It's about something important."

"You've got a lot o' balls," he said, standing in the doorway with his hands braced defiantly on his hips.

"I know I'm not one of your favorite people, Artie, but Bo caught a case, and we need to find Leo Turner to get it sorted out."

"And you couldn't call? You just had ta show up here and ruin our evening?"

"I thought doing it face to face would be better."

"Yeah, right. I'm not Leo's keeper. And why should I help you?"

I sighed. "Because it's the right thing to do. And because we know you were able to find a good job with a good boss and might want to put past problems behind you."

"What the hell does that mean?"

I hoped that he read between the lines and inferred that if he didn't help us, we might drop a dime on his straight-laced boss and put the bad-mouth on him. Whether he took the hint or not, his snotty attitude was causing me to lose patience.

"It only means that a young woman and her two children— eleven and thirteen years old, a girl and a boy—were killed—no, make that assassinated—and we know that Leo can provide important information on the case. But, Leo's gone missing."

"Are you looking at Leo for these murders?"

A gust of wind blew our way, and a chill ran up my back. "If we could come in it would take less time, and the cold air wouldn't blow into your house. I promise we won't take up much of your evening."

He hesitated a little too long. I thought he might be ready to slam the door in our faces, but then, "Yeah, all right." He used his head to motion us inside.

"Let's go in here." He pointed to the living room. "Sit down." He looked at Stallins, perhaps for the first time. "Bo, how you doin'?"

Bo nodded. "Artie. You doin' aw right t'day?"

"I'll let you know when I get finished with you two. Let's get back to Leo."

"I don't know that Leo pulled the trigger," I said, "but did you know that Leo and Ryan were in the business of selling—and starring in—some really kinky pornography?"

With a genuine surprised look on his face, Bonnet pulled his head back a couple inches and opened his eyes wider than a frightened possum caught in the headlights of a speeding car. "What in Hell are you talking about?"

"Just what I said. In a totally—or almost totally—unrelated case that John Gallagher and I were working, we learned that Leo solicited a $5,000 bribe to call a murder an accident. We ended up finding a laptop with lots—and I mean *lots*—of photos of Leary and Turner having all kinds of weird sex. It's a complicated story, and I'd be happy to tell you everything when you have the time, but for now, the bottom line is, we need to find Leo."

He shook his head. "Ryan loved to tell us about his sex trips to Thailand. I always thought he would have sex with a monkey if he could catch one. But Leo? You sure it's him?"

"It's him. Leo and a woman who's got a spider tattooed on her neck."

"Oh, sweet Jesus. That one. I might be able to give you something to find her, but like I told you, it's not my job to watch Leo. I haven't seen him since...You know when. What do you want from me?"

"We understand he had a girlfriend, a dancer who worked at The Mouse's Ear. We're assuming she may be the one on film with Leo. Her name would be a good start, and any other leads you can provide." Then I thought it might be a good time to lay it on a little thicker. "We're having a hard time forgetting that young woman and her kids who didn't have enough money to buy used clothing. Their deaths looked like something out of a mob movie. Someone has to stick up for them. We hoped you would help."

Artie Bonnet leaned forward in his chair and ran his hand over the back of his neck. "Eleven and thirteen you say?"

"Yes, sir. Shot between the eyes with a .45 ACP. The mother was shot a couple times, probably to make her give up a secret, and then she took one in the head, too."

"Jesus have mercy."

"Uh huh."

"And Leo did this?"

I shrugged. "Possibly, but we don't know for sure. What is certain is he took five grand to phony up a murder as an accident and pinched an off-paper .45 automatic from the victim's house. The young woman worked as that victim's house cleaner. She and the kids were killed with a .45. Please believe me when I tell you all this mess is somehow connected, and we need to find him."

"Okay, okay." He paused for a long moment. "You know, I got no reason to help you. You screwed me. I lost my job. This new one pays only a little more than half what I used ta get. But,

Jesus, two innocent kids? Okay, look for Rita Jo Chadwill. I don't know specifics, but Leo said she lived in some trailer park in Prospect. Off Sevierville Road or somewheres."

"Rita Jo Chadwill," I repeated. He nodded. "Thank you," I said.

"Yeah, right. Now how about leavin' me alone?"

CHAPTER SEVENTEEN

The next day we did a little research on Rita Jo Chadwill, the one time and maybe current bimbo of Leo Turner, and learned that she lived in a single-wide at the Off Broadway Mobile Home Park in my old stomping grounds of Prospect, Tennessee. A cat named Bubba—a real feline, not some nuevo hipster who thought he was the reincarnation of Edd *Kookie* Byrnes—shared the digs with her. We thought that if anyone knew where to find Leo Turner, it might be Rita Jo.

We went back into action with our original six-man team. Barry Meyers and *Robber* Baron looked like they were having a good time working with us rather than out on the road answering mundane 9-1-1 calls. Bo Stallins and Cliff Harvey wanted to clear a major case, and John Gallagher and I were still collecting twenty dollars an hour plus expenses. I really needed to get back to a real life.

John and I were no strangers to the Off Broadway Mobile Home Park. A constant source of upheaval for the cops of Prospect PD, Officer Junior Huskey and I shot and killed a man there a few years earlier. It was a neighborhood gone so far downhill even the rats moved out.

As a courtesy, I called Stan Rose, my former nighttime road supervisor and now chief at Prospect PD and told him our intentions. Stanley, being a man of action, chose to add himself, Terri Donnellson and Prospect's number one gunslinger, PO Harley Flatt, to our task force hunting down Leo Turner.

We all met in the Prospect Municipal Building parking lot and formulated a plan. It was quick and simple. We would surround the house, and if Leo was present, take him into custody. The arrest warrant was good anywhere. If Rita Jo didn't know Leo's whereabouts, we went back to square one.

At 10:15 that morning, I was starving although Kate and I ate a fine breakfast about two hours before. The weather had broken, and the week-long freeze we had been experiencing lifted. The sun came up, the birds were singing, and the WNXX TV meteorologist told his audience to expect temperatures to hit fifty. So far, life looked good.

Now, with Cisco Gonzalez under our belts and the team well experienced in fugitive retrieval, my five comrades got ready to surround the trailer home of Rita Jo Chadwill. The three Prospect cops were excellent assistants and blended right in with our plans. Bo Stallins and I would approach the front door first, wearing bulletproof vests and blue jackets conspicuously marked with POLICE front and back, BCSO patches on both shoulders and cloth badges on our left breasts. John Gallagher and Stan Rose, all six-foot four inches of him in full uniform, would back us up. The rest of the team posted themselves around the house to insure no one tried to sneak out a window or back entrance and to keep any nosy residents far away from the action.

I knocked vigorously on the door.

"County Police!" I said. "Open the door."

That got no immediate response so I bashed on the door again with the side of my fist. "Police! We have an arrest warrant."

Finally, a female voice called out, "What the fuck you talkin' about?" The gravel voice sounded as if the owner smoked three packs of unfiltered cigarettes a day.

I shook my head in frustration, wondering what part of *open the door* don't you understand.

Using my well-cultivated *command voice*, I bellowed, "Open up, or we'll break the door down."

She yelled back, "Aw right. Hold yer horses. I'll open the gotdamn door."

Rita Jo Chadwill looked like a fine specimen of American womanhood having candy apple red hair with an almost metallic shine. She wore a slinky black, white and red floral printed robe and obviously nothing else. Unless I had become legally blind, she was Leo's porno co-star. I recognized her immediately from the tattooed spider crawling up the left side of her neck.

"Yeah?" she said. "What's this all about?"

"We're looking for Leo Turner."

"Leo who?"

Lying seemed to come as easy to her as falling off a log.

"Cut the crap, Rita." I pushed my way into the singlewide and took a quick look around. The place had all the ambiance of an 18th century outhouse. "Where's Leo?"

"I don't know no fuckin' Leo. So how about you get out, and don't let the door hit your ass on the way."

I turned and spoke to Bo Stallins, "Get the others. We're going to search this dump."

Stallins spoke into a handheld radio. In only a few seconds, John Gallagher, Terri Donnellson and Stan Rose pushed into the home.

"What the hell?" Rita Jo said.

"Sit down, and shut up," I said. "John, Terri, keep an eye on her."

Before we made a move to go further into the trailer, a mottled gray cat that must have weighed at least fifteen pounds moved cautiously into the living room and hissed.

"Call off that cat," Stan Rose said, with a cold sound to his voice. "Or I'll kill it."

"Bubba! Bubba, come here!" Rita cried. "Come here, Bubba!"

Obviously, Bubba hadn't been trained. The obstinate beast just stood its ground and hissed again. It had only one and a half ears, and one eye looked like it had sustained some serious damage recently.

"Open the door, and kick that thing out," I said. "Be careful it doesn't scratch you, or you'll get gangrene."

Bo Stallins accomplished that with a slight assist from his size twelve loafer.

I looked at Rita Jo sitting on a moth-eaten sofa. "Is Leo hiding in one of the back rooms?"

"Fuck you."

At 10:30 in the morning, she smelled like a distillery. She sounded arrogant and obnoxious, but surprisingly coherent. I assumed the woman could handle her booze like a panda could gobble up bamboo.

Closed doors suggested that there were only three additional rooms off the open living room and eat-in kitchen area, probably a bathroom and two bedrooms.

"How about I just start shooting through the walls?"

From the back bedroom, I heard a familiar voice. "What do you want?"

"Leo?" I called out.

"Yeah. Jenkins? That you?" came back equally as loud.

"It's me and half the 7th Cavalry."

"Fuck off, and leave me alone."

"Are you drunk or insane? I've got a warrant for your arrest."

"Never more sober in my life. A warrant for what?"

"Soliciting a bribe and a few other things."

"Where'd you get that information? From that queer doctor's sister?"

"If you're so interested, how about I come back there, and we talk about it?"

No response. I took a couple of steps toward a door that I saw opened inward. I wondered if the door would suddenly open, and I'd get a .45 automatic pointed at my nose. I took another two steps and felt about as secure as a goldfish in a toilet bowl.

"Leo? Open the door."

"Open it yourself."

"You gonna stick a gun in my face?"

Leo Turner was a reptile of the lowest order, and I assumed that he would rather contract malaria than talk to me.

"No. I'll listen to what you have to say."

"Good. I'm opening the door. You start shooting, and nine cops will pump you full of bullets."

"Don't sweat it. What do you have to say?"

I gingerly opened the door and peeked around the jamb and found Turner sitting on the bed with a 1911 .45 automatic in his lap. Leo had always been an odd duck, but today he looked like something out of a homeless shelter. His hair needed combing, his face hadn't met up with a razor in days and his clothes looked like he found them in a dumpster.

"Can we do this like gentlemen, Leo?"

"You still think I'm a gentleman?"

I'm no professional negotiator, but even I know not to get

sarcastic with a guy holding a cocked automatic with the safety lever in the off position.

"I'm more than willing to treat you that way. Why don't you put the gun down? Toss it onto the bed and away from you. You do that, and I'll lower my gun."

I felt John Gallagher's presence next to me with Bo Stallins directly behind him and next to Stan Rose.

"I guess you got me, huh?" Turner said.

"We know what happened with Paul D'Amato, and I know what you thought you had to do with the Gonzalez woman and her kids." I wanted him to think we had some real evidence.

"And you have the pictures?"

"Yes, we have the pictures."

He closed his eyes and shook his head. "Jesus! How did I end up here?"

"It happened. It's over. We can work something out. You know how the system works. Anything can be worked out."

"You got some line of shit, Sam. You think I believe that? The D'Amato thing is as important as pissin' in The Little River. But the killin's? Don't bullshit me. That's goin' ta go hard. And tell me what happens to an ex-cop doin' jail time. I don't think so."

"Leo, I'm telling you. Let's get you a good lawyer and make a deal."

"*Deal,* my ass. I killed a stupid woman and two innocent kids. She as good as told D'Amato she kept an extra copy of the pictures. Goddamnit, my mother is still alive. I wanted to save me the embarrassment if those pictures got out there. I wanted to save Ryan."

He elevated the gun, rubbing the muzzle end up and down his right cheek.

"Why are you still worrying about Ryan Leary? We all knew what he was about. Why not save yourself?"

"Ryan got me into this porno shit before you took him down. He used me to peddle his smut to that doctor and some other perverts he met on the Internet, in a chat room or some damn place. It was good money."

"The pictures of you and Rita didn't violate any laws. The stuff Leary put on film did. He used kids. Leary's head has always been out in left field."

"Left field? You don't know half of it. The things he talked about doing on his sex vacations would make anyone wonder. But he isn't going to be in jail forever. I keep in contact with him. He's promised to take care of me if I stuck with him and got the thumb drive back. He wants to get paroled as soon as possible. I help him, and he helps me. I don't exactly have much going for me, and my pension won't go as far as I need. He'd help me with money. Believe me, he's still got plenty squirreled away."

"Was the promise of money more important than the lives of those little kids?"

"I don't know how you found out it was me, but I took lots of care to clean up that scene. Still couldn't find the thumb drive though."

"She never had the extra copy, Leo. She just mouthed off to D'Amato. She was pissed at him and her husband who did the same as you and Leary. D'Amato made a mistake telling you about the copy."

"Then I killed those kids for nothin'?"

"It can't be undone, Leo."

He closed his eyes and jammed the business end of the gun under his chin pointing upward toward his brain.

"No, it can't, but I can do what I got to do."

I shook my head vigorously. "You don't have to do that. Nothing is non-negotiable. We can work something out. Put the gun down."

"And spend the rest of my life in prison with the scum I dealt with as a cop? Quit bullshittin' me. Your little speech is insultin'."

I watched his chest rising and falling in an exaggerated way. His breathing could only be described as labored and abnormal.

"I put the gun down, are you gonna let me go?" he asked. "And where would I go? What do you think?"

Some things can just make you lose your patience. This thing was taking way too long. "Where could you go? I don't know, Leo. I hear Kentucky is looking for a few new assholes."

He looked directly into my eyes. "Fuck you, Jenkins." And he pulled the trigger.

A Remington 185 grain .45 caliber jacketed hollow point bullet travels at 1140 feet per second and punches out more than 500-foot pounds of energy. The round Turner fired entered his head under the chin and travelled northbound taking off a chunk of skull and leaving a hole big enough to hide a tennis ball. He collapsed onto the bed. The gun fell from his hand to the floor, cocked and ready for another shot.

I looked back at Bo Stallins and said, "Damn."

Bo's face turned pale, and his jaw slacked open. "Oh, Lord have mercy," came out almost as a whisper.

As soon as the shot rang out, Rita Jo began screaming, "You sons-o'-bitches shot Leo! Bastards! Fuckin' bastards!"

I stuck my head around Bo and John Gallagher and said, "Terri, get her out of here, and stick a sock in her mouth."

Terri nodded and did the necessary.

Bo spoke to Gallagher who had stepped further into the room to look at the gun. "Why in hell'd he do that?"

Gallagher shrugged and offered an opinion, "Look at it this way, Bo, you won't have to spend a lot of time in court now."

Stan Rose stood close to me. "You okay, Boss?"

"Me? Yeah, I'm good. It's your town and your crime scene now, Stanley."

He nodded. "I'll get this squared away, make the phone calls. You take it easy. Relax. I gotcha covered."

"Thanks."

I looked at John Gallagher. "Gonna be a bitch to write up."

"Not really," he said. "I turned on my phone when it started. I got everything on video. I figured if that stupid Samples kid could do it, so could I."

———

John and I left the trailer home to Stan Rose, Bo Stallins, the Prospect cops and all the support personnel who would soon be on the scene. Terri Donnellson had placed Rita Jo Chadwill in the backseat of a marked Prospect police car. John and I walked over.

Terri asked, "You guys okay?"

I nodded.

John said, "Yeah. No problems here."

Rita Jo looked straight ahead over the headrest of the front seat and paid me no mind until I spoke.

"Your friend is dead."

She looked at me with clear cold eyes. Her expression came close to the warmth of dry ice. "You killed him?"

"He killed himself."

She shrugged and looked as sentimental as a wrecking ball. "Fuck you. Was you who killed him."

What does one say to that?

Terri put a hand on my shoulder. "Anything I can do for you, Boss?"

"No, thanks, kid. I'm good. Stanley is taking over now. Lock her in the car and give him a hand. John and I are going to take a break."

———

Before we got into our unmarked car John asked, "No big deal, was it?"

"Not to me. You said it best. Bo won't be spending his valuable time in court over this. The world did not lose one of its finer people today."

No sooner did I answer John than Cliff Harvey walked up. He was about to light up a cigarette when he chuckled and said, "I guess that went well."

I really didn't need any shit from him. "You're saying that tongue in cheek?"

He paused a moment, holding a cigarette in one hand and a Bic in the other. "Yeah, I guess so. You didn't talk him down. You win some. You lose some."

"Depends on your point of view. If Turner had pointed his gun at John or me...or even you, I would have killed him. He saved me or someone else the trouble. And he had the grace not to commit suicide by cop. He confessed to killing Margarita Gonzalez and her children. And for what? Now your case is closed. My opinion? He deserved to die. Doing it himself, he saved the state the time and drama of a lethal injection."

He looked at me like I had two heads. "He was a cop."

I shook my head and laughed. "He might have collected a check from the Sheriff's Office for quite a few years, but he didn't deserve to walk the same halls with the good cops in this county. I put his death into the *tough shit* file of Life. End of story."

"Well, like you said, that's one man's opinion."

"Uh huh, it sure is. By the way, we talked to someone who

mentioned your name plus a few expletives. She didn't sound very happy to have met you."

Harvey finally decided to light up and blew a stream of smoke toward the heavens. "Who was that?"

"The woman who gave us the info to clear the Gonzalez murders. You could have gotten that same thing a few days before us. She told us how you two...didn't exactly click. We heard her story. You were there. If you did something wrong, maybe you can learn something from that. I'm just saying."

"Yeah, and you're not my boss. Far as I'm concerned, that Spic bitch has problems with cops. End of *my* story."

"But not exactly mine. Don't even think about some kind of half-assed retaliation against that woman. If I hear about any, you won't like the outcome."

"You threatening me?"

"You get two for the price of one, Sport—a threat and a promise. Don't push your luck with this."

He shook his head in disgust, turned and walked away.

John got the stupid look on his face he uses when he wants to harass me. "That went well, huh, Boss?"

"Screw him, John. In fact, that's exactly what I may do, figuratively, of course. Call your wife, and I'll call mine. Then I'm going to tell Stanley we're going to get something to eat. We can do our statements later. Work for you?"

"Hey, I'm always hungry."

CHAPTER EIGHTEEN

John and I finished our day early and went home. As usual, Kate asked how my day had gone. When I finished explaining, she frowned.

"Good Lord. I'm not a qualified gunslinger like you, but I know something about a GI .45—like the one you've got in the safe in the basement—they make *BIG* holes. He shot himself under the chin? That's about as extreme as you can get."

"You bet. Stupid bastard. I'll never get my head around why he killed those three people. For Leary? So no one would see him and his tattooed bimbo making home porn pictures? Jeez!"

"Relax Sweetie. I'll make you a drinkie-poo. It's still early. We've got plenty of time. Should I make something for dinner, or do you want to go out to eat?"

"Going out sounds good. You pick the place. I want to call Bettye first. Give me a few minutes."

I was glad it was Sunday, and I didn't have to listen to any static from Cynthia Wilkins. When her daughter answered the phone, I got right down to business.

"Hi, Missye, this is Sam Jenkins. I need to speak to your mom. It's important, very important."

A moment later: "Sam, what's wrong?" Bettye asked.

"I assume your daughter told you that I'm not my usual happy-go-lucky self."

"Something like that."

"Well, has anyone from CID or Prospect PD called you yet?"

"I've taken several calls. Bo Stallins told me the whole story, and Stanley called with news about what they were doin'. Even Terri Donnellson called to tell me you and John are all right. Now you tell me."

I gave her my side of the story and ended with a question.

"Don't you have someone working for you called the complainant/victim liaison officer?"

"Yes." She named her.

"How very modern of you. Okay, here's something I want you to have her do. Contact a woman named Belinda Cancel at La Union Hispanica in Maryville. Tell her what happened with Cisco Gonzalez and that we found the man who killed Margarita and her kids. Then ask about her two recent interactions with personnel from the Sheriff's office. Call me after you hear what she has to say."

"That's it?"

"Yeah, that's it. No, that's not everything. Maybe you should start looking for a likely candidate to fill an upcoming spot in your detective division."

———

The next day after John and I explained everything to Janetta, I called Terri Donnellson to fill in any gaps left unanswered on her side of the fence and thank her for her participation in clearing one of the biggest legal messes I'd seen in a very long time. I even called Chet Lightner at the VA office to give him an insider's view of what happened to his doctor and clients. Then I called Ramón Goldbloom to tell him about what happened to the killer of Margarita and her kids and thank him for his help. Then I heard from Bettye.

"Darlin' that was one angry woman you wanted Brianna to call."

"Brianna? Who's that?"

"Sergeant Brianna Grant, my complainant/victim liaison officer. I told you about her."

"So you did. What can I tell you? The older I get, the quicker I forget names. What did Brianna learn?"

"She started talking to Ms. Cancel on the phone then thought it better to see her in person. Lord have mercy, but did that woman chew off her ear."

"Come on, Blondie. Don't keep me hanging. What does Sergeant Brianna know?"

"She heard that you were the best thing since corn dogs and Mountain Dew, but she didn't hear much good about Cliff Harvey."

"Huh."

"All you got to say is *huh?*"

"Don't try to brow beat me, Miss Bettye, I suggested you speak to Belinda Cancel because she had something important to tell you."

"She certainly did. So, former po-leece chief and world's greatest detective, what do you suggest I do? Should I send Cliff Harvey back to patrol? Maybe assign him as a jail guard?"

"Madame Sheriff, the principles of good police management might suggest that, before giving an employee who screwed up the royal sack, to give him...or her a chance to modify their unacceptable behavior and change their attitude.

A guy named O.W. Wilson wrote all that many years before you were born. It still works today. I'd suggest a serious talk with Mr. Harvey by you or his immediate supervisor. Give him a chance to clean up his act—and maybe quit smoking, the bastard—then keep an eye on him. If he straightens up and flies right, you're a winner. If not—police work is not baseball. You don't get three strikes. Find a new detective."

"Did you speak to Harvey about this?"

"Right after Turner killed himself."

"And what did he say?"

"Short and sweet. I'm not his boss and mind my own business. And that's after John and I handed him and his partner a triple homicide clearance on a silver platter. If that's the way he wanted to be, I figured it was time to call in the big gun."

"You're a hard man, Sam Jenkins."

"I'm a realist, kiddo. I don't like Cliff Harvey, but my opinion of him doesn't matter. I don't know if he got promoted to detective through merit or if he had a rabbi pulling strings for him. But he screwed up big time, and he won't admit it. He shows no remorse. I say give him an opportunity, and if he doesn't straighten out, send him packing. He's got no union protection or contractual tenure as a detective. You should resolve any conflicts in favor of your department."

"I hear you, darlin', and thank you for that insight."

"You betcha."

———

When John Gallagher and I left the Off-Broadway Mobile Home Park around 11:30. We ate lunch at Howell's Pub in beautiful downtown Prospect—barbeque sandwiches half the size of soccer balls, homemade coleslaw and baked beans. John guzzled down a pair of diet Cokes while I sipped two pints of Bass Ale from the tap.

At five o'clock when Kate and I were ready to head out to dinner, I vetoed her idea of a big Italian meal at the Villa Napoli and opted for something lighter at Lemon Grass in Maryville—a couple of sushi rolls and any variation of Thai curry as an entrée would be great. And as anyone knows, a bottle of Riesling goes well with Asian food.

Our waiter had been working at the restaurant for as long as we'd been going there—twenty years or so. He dropped off our sushi and wine, smiled professionally and disappeared, temporarily.

As I spread a cloth napkin on my lap, Kate spoke up.

"This sounded like the most complicated and almost impenetrable case I've ever heard you talk about. The TV stations showed up in Prospect to report on the suicide quickly. I suppose the newspapers will have a big spread tomorrow."

"I'll buy The Daily Times. I'm interested in seeing what they say...and who they talk about."

"Are you finally finished with all this? Any court appearances coming up?"

"Don't think so. Our muscle-bound buddy The Cisco Kid took a plea to keep his career as a porn star a secret, not to mention his confession being caught on video. Leo Turner saved everyone lots of trouble by eating the gun. His co-star, Rita Jo, probably won't be charged with anything. The warrant for Leo was too recent for her to know about it, so there goes any charges of harboring a fugitive. Angela Scarano is getting a sweetheart deal because she ratted out Leo Turner. But she's the one that really bothers me. I know what's going to happen. She'll show up with two lawyers, one of whom Roland Farley picked as co-counsel because he found someone who plays golf with the sitting judge. They've already got something of a deal in place where she'll plead down to misdemeanor bribery and only get three years probation, but with a sympathetic judge and because she's almost sixty years old and a first offender, she'll be granted an adjournment in contemplation of dismissal. Then, because the lawyer and the judge are good buddies, that will only last for the minimum of six months. As long as she doesn't get arrested for something else during that time, the charge will be dropped, and the whole mess will be expunged, and it's like it never happened."

"When you think about it, for a $5,000 dollar bribe and some inconvenience, that half million dollar payoff works out pretty good for her."

"Well, maybe I can do something about that."

Kate frowned. "Like what?"

"What did I just mention only moments ago?"

She showed me one of her mischievous smiles. "You love how this sushi chef makes an asparagus roll?"

She always makes me smile. "Besides that. Remember that I wanted to get tomorrow's edition of The Daily Times? Suppose someone—and I'm not saying who—clipped the article about this business which will probably mention Angela Scarano's part in a conspiracy to falsely classify Paul D'Amato's death as accidental and sent it to that obnoxious insurance investigator? Angela actually thought Paul committed suicide. She said that to me. He didn't, but the legal impossibility of that being true doesn't mitigate her culpability. At the very least, she'd be guilty of attempted conspiracy to defraud. With that knowledge, Lone Star Mutual might just sic their lawyers on her and attempt to get a ruling of no payout because of her attempted criminal conduct. Remember, in a civil suit, the plaintiff only has to prove a preponderance of the evidence—fifty-one percent—and a prior criminal conviction is not necessary. I can envision old Velma Barnett receiving a plain envelope with no return address and a postmark from somewhere like Knoxville containing that article—sent anonymously, of course. She'd experience an orgasm."

"Has anyone ever called you vindictive?"

"Yes, just recently. As long as Lone Star acts quickly, before the court expunges Angela's arrest, they can subpoena all the records and use them down in Texas. Just another example of how we used to hammer the boys and girls of organized crime when arrests were not possible—make them feel pain in their bankbooks."

Kate shook her head. "Calling you vindictive would be a compliment. You're absolutely diabolical."

"Thank you. I try to use my extraordinary powers for the greater good."

"My superhero."

"That's me, Baby."

"How about a question, Sambo?"

"This sounds dangerous. What if I said *no*?"

"I'd ask it anyway."

"What else is new?"

"You've been working at least ten hours a day—generally more—ever since you and John got involved with this last thing. Then you two got pulled into someone else's case. I know Bettye loves you and wants your help, but the county commission will only allow her to pay you guys in peanuts. Why do you do it?"

I stalled by unwrapping my chopsticks and drizzling a little soy sauce into my tiny dipping bowl.

"Hmm, I don't exactly know. Maybe because I'm in business with John and don't really want to get involved in peeping into motel rooms on those sleazy divorce cases I tell him not to take. But he says he needs the money. So I hold up my end when a real case comes our way."

Kate mixed soy sauce with a little dab of spicy wasabi paste prior to dipping a circle of shrimp roll into her bowl. "But *you* don't need the money. With your pensions and the cost of living down here, you're loaded, Sweetie."

"So? That only makes me a good catch for some lonely woman, but I'm already hooked on you. These cases don't come up all that often. I'm yours in between gigs."

"Does John really need you? Is he that busy?"

I shrugged. "He won't put Pinkertons out of business."

"You refuse to work some of the cases he accepts. You're not working there five days a week. Give him your half of the business. Be like one of those old lawyers who never show up at work but keep their names on the letterhead as *counsel*."

"Like Howard Baker who's been dead for years?"

She rolled her eyes. "Something like that." She popped another piece of sushi into her mouth.

"Hmm. You know that guy we met, the retired detective sergeant who lived across the road from Doctor Demento? He offered to help out if we needed someone with investigative experience. I told John to use him and to remember Terri Donnellson. Horne seemed like an okay guy. Milwaukee had to be a pretty busy place. He must know what he's doing, and Terri is good at the job. John would be all right."

"That sounds like a start. You wouldn't have to disappear totally."

"Yeah. I must admit this last business was tough. That scene with the dead mother and two kids was a bitch to look at, like a scene from a bad Oliver Stone movie."

"I've never been able to understand how you did it for all these years."

"I think it's called disassociation."

"You're a smart guy, Sammy. Don't you think that you've seen enough things that contribute to your post traumatic stress for one lifetime?"

Still working on our sushi, the waiter brought our meals. Kate had ordered Massaman shrimp, and I picked the Penang chicken. We shifted things around on the table to accommodate the new plates, and the waiter topped off our wine glasses. When he left, we continued our conversation.

"What were you saying?" I asked.

"You know damn well what I said last."

Caught with my pants down. "Yeah, you're probably right. I'm not getting any younger, and I sure don't handle stress like I did at forty."

"Very true." She shifted the plate holding her curry and rice to her front.

"With extra time off," I said," we could travel more. But you would have to slack off on a lot of your volunteer work. I don't want to hang around the house by myself. What would I do? Write my memoirs?"

"That might be interesting, but we can make this work, Sweetie."

"Okay. Unless the Son of Sam resurfaces in Blount County, I'll take a break—go on hiatus, so to speak."

"Sounds good."

———

Home again at 6:30, we watched the national news and then a few episodes of *New Tricks*, a British cop show about three retired, middle-aged Scotland Yard detectives who came back to work on cold cases. Hmm, I said to myself, I wonder why I like that show.

At ten o'clock, we agreed to hit the hay, but first I tended to a domestic necessity.

"The clock needed winding," I told Kate, "and so do I. I'm pooped."

Kate stepped well within my personal space, put her arms around my neck and spoke in a voice somewhere between an impersonation of Mae West and John Wayne. "I hope yer not too pooped, big fella, 'cause I think I can wind ya up. Only I won't use a key, I'll just open up a few buttons."

"Holy smokes, doll face! Sounds like something Lauren Bacall might say."

"Ya got that right, Bogie."

The End

———

If you enjoyed *Death of a Doctor* and would like a free copy of the award winning *A New Prospect*, the first novel in the Sam Jenkins mystery series, simply go to www.melange-books.com/authors/wayne-zurl/

Don't miss out on your next favorite book!
Join the Melange Books mailing list at
www.melange-books.com/mail.html

———

THANK YOU FOR READING

———

Did you enjoy this book?

We invite you to leave a review at your favorite book site, such as Goodreads, Amazon, Barnes & Noble, etc.

DID YOU KNOW THAT LEAVING A REVIEW...

- Helps other readers find books they may enjoy.
- Gives you a chance to let your voice be heard.
- Gives authors recognition for their hard work.
- Doesn't have to be long. A sentence or two about why you liked the book will do.

ABOUT THE AUTHOR

Wayne Zurl grew up on Long Island and retired after twenty years with the Suffolk County Police Department, one of the largest municipal law enforcement agencies in New York and the nation. For thirteen of those years, he served as a section commander supervising investigators. He is a graduate of SUNY, Empire State College and served on active duty in the US Army during the Vietnam War and later in the reserves. Zurl left New York to live in the foothills of the Great Smoky Mountains of Tennessee with his wife, Barbara.

Wayne has had nine Sam Jenkins mystery novels traditionally published. Twenty-eight of his Sam Jenkins novella or novelette mysteries are currently available in five anthologies, putting all of these stories in print or in all the usual eBook formats.

He has won Eric Hoffer and Indie Book Awards and was named a finalist for a Montaigne Medal and First Horizon Book

Award. He is a regular member of the International Thriller Writer's Organization.

For more information on Wayne's Sam Jenkins mystery series see www.waynezurlbooks.net. You can read excerpts, reviews and endorsements, interviews, coming events, and see photos of the area where the stories take place.

––––––––––

www.waynezurlbooks.net

facebook.com/WayneZurl

x.com/waynezurl

goodreads.com/waynezurl

amazon.com/stores/Wayne-Zurl/author/B0045W1MC4

ALSO BY WAYNE ZURL

A New Prospect

A Leprechaun's Lament

Heroes and Lovers

Pigeon River Blues

A Touch of Morning Calm

A Can of Worms

Honor Among Thieves

A Bleak Prospect

Sins of Eden

Festival of Felonies

From New York to the Smokies: A Collection of Sam Jenkins Mysteries

Murder in Knoxville and Other Sam Jenkins Mysteries

The Great Smoky Mountain Bank Job and Other Sam Jenkins Mysteries

Graceland on Wheels and More Sam Jenkins Mysteries

Death of a Doctor

www.ingramcontent.com/pod-product-compliance
Lightning Source LLC
Chambersburg PA
CBHW050458260626
47157CB00004B/1106